THE SOLE SURVIVOR

AND

THE KYNSARD AFFAIR

by

ROY VICKERS

D0920457

DOVER PUBLICATIONS, INC.
NEW YORK

This Dover edition, first published in 1983, is an unabridged republication of the novels as originally published in one volume by Victor Gollancz Ltd, London, 1952.

Manufactured in the United States of America
Dover Publications, Inc., 180 Varick Street, New York, N.Y. 10014

Library of Congress Cataloging in Publication Data

Vickers, Roy.
  The sole survivor; and, The Kynsard affair.

  Reprint. Originally published: London: Gollancz, 1952.
  I. Title. II. Title: The Kynsard affair.
PR6043.I183S6   1983   823'.914   82-17733
ISBN 0-486-24433-4

CONTENTS

THE SOLE SURVIVOR

THE SOLE SURVIVOR

Mr. Justice Sheilbron was chosen to hold the inquiry into the wreck of the *Marigonda* and the subsequent circumstances resulting in almost total loss of life. He was not at all pleased. A retired Chancery judge, virtually unknown to the general public, he disliked cases in which the human element tended to predominate, and he genuinely detested publicity. It looked as if there would be a good deal of publicity in this inquiry.

There was, for instance, a desert island in it. Good heavens! He had taken it for granted that desert islands had ceased to exist about the time he left his prep school. And then there was that preposterous suggestion about a wild man inhabiting the island. Not even a Robinson Crusoe, but a Ben Gunn, slap out of *Treasure Island*. Well, as no one claimed to have seen the creature he could probably be kept out of the evidence as being hearsay.

On top of it all, was a Sole Survivor—a character which, for some obscure reason, always fascinated the popular newspapers. This sole survivor was an educated man, fortunately—a history don. All the same, his affidavit was somewhat highfalutin—in parts very highfalutin! Accusing himself of moral responsibility for the death of one of the party! A man who accused himself of anything in an affidavit was an ass.

This sole survivor obviously had plenty of intelligence but no common sense. As a university lecturer he probably hated being made a fool of in the newspapers as much as did the judge himself. When the rescue party was known to be imminent it was intelligent to dress himself in the clothes he had saved from the wreck, but it revealed an ignorance of publicity values. After nine months on a desert island a man is expected to look like a scarecrow. As it was, whole columns had been devoted to this man's grey lounge suit, his creased trousers, his "spotless" silk shirt, his something-or-other hat,

7

his shaved chin and—incredibly!—his rolled umbrella. The fact that the umbrella was rolled was itself worth a cross-heading.

Mr. Justice Sheilbron tried to imagine himself passing nine months on a desert island, without success. His car stopped at Chaucer Hall—a building which contained a number of halls of varying sizes, mostly used for banquets and board meetings. An official bowed him to "his" room, off one of the middle-sized banqueting halls. Here, his advisory panel—a shipowner, a naval captain and an insurance-company director—greeted him reverentially. Someone took his coat and hat.

"There's no ceremony, of course! If you're ready, gentlemen . . ."

He had the sensation of slinking into court—if you could call it a court! There was certainly a dais and a long table with an extra large chair at the centre for himself. A small public gallery, crowded, of course. Plenty of long tables. One for counsel—a job to know them without their wigs—he felt a little lost himself without his robes. Another table for solicitors and marine insurance men. The press table—decent fellows in private life; not their fault if the public preferred trivialities to essentials. Rows of witnesses, including three naval ratings in uniform; some expert witnesses. He tried to pick out the Sole Survivor but could not.

He had settled himself and was about to open when the Attorney-General bustled in. Sheilbron was surprised. He had not suspected that this was to be a full-dress affair. They ought to have picked on a Common Law judge—one of the younger men.

The clerk was reading the terms of reference of the Commission. Loose terms, loose procedure, loose behaviour in general, thought the ex-Chancery judge. His eye fell on a table close to the dais containing exhibits. That board with panels of colour and numerals was presumably the dartsboard—he had never seen one before. A large aerial photograph of the island; five small cardboard boxes with red labels *Care: Plaster Cast*; several boxes the size of boot-boxes; manuscript books, documents; photograph albums. The clerk had finished.

"Call the first witness," ordered the chairman, as the judge had now become.

"Flight-Lieutenant Shendry."

Up bobbed the Attorney-General, Sir Brian Tukeley.

"I ask, sir, that the chief witness, Mr. Clovering, should leave the court while the evidence of the rescue-party is being given."

That meant he had something up his sleeve, reflected Sheilbron. Just what the newspapers liked!

"Very well, Sir Brian." He looked over to the witnesses' benches. "Is Mr. Clovering in court?"

"Yes, I am here, sir." Clovering extricated himself from the others. Sheilbron regarded him with some interest. He saw a rather small man in a grey lounge suit made by a good tailor. A broad brow, intelligent eyes, middle thirties. Sole survivor!

"Mr. Clovering, I must ask you to leave the court until we send for you. You can wait in my room, if you like—you will be more comfortable there. Usher, show Mr. Clovering to my room."

"Thank you, sir." Clovering spoke as one who is accustomed to receiving such courtesies but is nevertheless appreciative. The desert island, thought Sheilbron, had not affected the man's stance. He looked a clear-headed, reliable man who would kill that fantastic story about the wild man. Sheilbron's thoughts shifted, as often, to his own obituary which *The Times* would eventually print: *As a Chancery judge he was rarely in the public eye. That his name should happen to be associated with the notorious "wild man" inquiry . . .*

The airman was relating how, in the course of a fleet exercise, he had flown over the island and seen a man on it, though it was marked as abandoned. In command of a flying-boat he had returned to rescue Clovering and later had flown a working-party back to the island. There followed the members of the working-party, which included expert witnesses. There was no cross-examination. They all seemed to have a high opinion of Clovering and acknowledged his helpfulness. Their evidence was completed within an hour.

The chairman addressed the tribunal.

"Before we call the chief witness—Mr. Clovering—we have to consider the troublesome point of his affidavit. You have all received copies and you know that the affidavit is itself a colloquial—I might almost say 'chatty'—report of all that happened on the island, written by him on the island. Mr. Clovering insisted—in my opinion very wisely—that no word should be cut from his report. That affidavit must be put formally before the court. Unless the Attorney-General objects, therefore, I propose myself to read the first and then the last sentence and take the affidavit as having been read by the clerk in the ordinary way."

The Attorney-General made no objection. The chairman began to read: "*I, William Edward Clovering . . .*" The chairman mumbled the formal preamble, but raised his voice for Clovering's own text.

"*Approximately a week has passed since I caused the death of Gramshaw . . .*" During the pause which the chairman considered necessary to indicate the reading of the full text, he reflected that this was a theatrical and totally unnecessary statement. He then read the last paragraph.

"*Tomorrow I shall shave and dress myself decently and—I hope—hand this document to the officer in charge of a rescue party. I intend to do all in my power to assist his investigations.*"

Approximately a week has passed since I caused the death of Gramshaw. I was very upset for a couple of days, lying in the hut and taking no food. Yesterday I felt better. I slept well last night. This morning I am as normal as a man can be who is alone on a desert island with no real certainty of being rescued before he starves.

A couple of hours ago I became afraid. Quite suddenly. I mean afraid that I may be accused of murdering Gramshaw. And, of course, the others. Fear finds odd symbols. Out of a calm sea a large wave crashed on the beach—at least, it made an unusually loud noise—and started the fear. Note, please, that I am not afraid of the wave, like a neurotic, but afraid of what it chances to symbolise. To me it symbolises interruption. It symbolises a naval captain or a coroner or a judge, interrupting me.

"I am giving you every latitude, Mr. Clovering, but you must try to confine yourself to answering the questions. The manners of your companions are as irrelevant as are the rambling anecdotes about a silk nightdress, carbon copying paper and whatnot."

They say that kind of thing, and in the next breath ask you a question calculated to reveal your state of mind—to discover whether you were acting "feloniously and of malice aforethought".

The danger of myself corrupting my own evidence will begin the moment the rescue-party lands, if it ever does land. I imagine a boat's crew, under a petty officer. I shall probably be rather odd to look at. There will be an exchange of hullos and cheeriness. Then the Robinson Crusoe joke. Then they'll ask if there's anybody else on the island.

"Well—er—there is no one alive, but there are six dead bodies. You see—er——"

Questions will be hurled at me before I've shown them the bodies—two of them sea-sodden, suggesting an attempt to conceal. There will be an amateur cross-examination on the spot. Later, they will repeat my answers, without the context.

Then the captain's inquiry as a preliminary to the civil inquiry.

By the time all this happens, if it ever does happen, I may be near starvation—delirious, melancholic. I shall overlay one incident with another and contradict myself.

I have a typewriter and reams of paper, brought from the wreck. I was in charge of rescue operations—a crude signalling system and messages in bottles. The bottles all drifted back. I've kept them. I am using my pen, because my handwriting will prove my sanity at the time of writing. I shall make copies afterwards on the machine.

I intend to write down every material detail, including incidents which, taken by themselves, would tend to incriminate me. I shall fit the incidents into the pattern of our life here. Tear the pattern, and you convict me. But you will not be able to tear the pattern, because you will not be able to interrupt me. I am frightened of the seamen's cross-examination but not frightened of that of the Attorney-General. When I have written my account I shall feel safe. Already some of the fear has gone.

I cannot give a coherent account of how we were wrecked, nor of the riot that broke out before our party got away in the boat. Attached to this is a more or less knowledgeable report by Gramshaw (*Appendix A*). I have never taken enough interest in ships even to pick up passengers' jargon.

The *Marigonda*, cargo and fifty passengers from the Cape to London, had been at sea for some days when the bad weather started. I went to my cabin and stayed there. On the third day of bad weather, I felt the ship strike something. I was not interested. For me there is some reality in the old joke that when you have reached a certain stage of sea sickness you are afraid the ship will *not* sink.

After the bump, nothing much seemed to happen. There were alarms and boat drills, which I did not attend. A Greek steward came to tell me that the ship was being abandoned. Before he had finished dressing me he was called away. I managed to crawl back to bed in my clothes. These details are essential because they explain how I came to possess the only firearm on the island.

It was Gramshaw who found me. He was a big, genial bully, an ex-international footballer—or it may have been cricketer. In an irritating but kindly manner he had adopted me before we were out of harbour, intending to convert me to some kind of sport. That I am a history don of 35 did not discourage him.

"Come on!' He lifted me out of bed and forced me into my overcoat. "The Lascars have run amok and everybody else is mad. No damned discipline anywhere! I'll look after you, Clobbers, old boy. Hang on and don't talk."

Perhaps I caricature him a little, though I am trying only to report him. The difficulty is that he was himself a caricature of the English hearty, but did not know it, because he never read anything and never went to a theatre. He treated the shipwreck as if it were a football match in which the referee had given some foolish decision.

He was carrying me pick-a-back through the empty saloon when a woman screamed his name and he dumped me on a bench near the staircase (I shall avoid nautical terms in case I misuse them). Presently a passenger staggered in. His face was bleeding. He was talking volubly, possibly to himself. He unhitched a revolver in an armpit holster.

"I want you to keep this for me, Clovering, and give it back afterwards. I wouldn't ask you, if it could possibly do you any harm with the authorities. There are five live rounds in it, and one empty shell."

He unbuttoned my coat and slung it under my left arm, saying he would come back. He did not come back. His name was Brassett. He was a commercial traveller, employed—he told us, many times—by one of the free-lance soap firms. That revolver, which I shall hand to the rescue-party, will be traceable to Brassett.

Gramshaw later agreed that it was about a couple of hours before he came back for me. He carried me to a boat. I was grossly ungrateful for his efforts, which, we both believed, were saving my life.

Gramshaw had put himself in command of the boat. It took a very long time to launch it. I have no recollection of it actually touching the water. It was growing light when I became fully conscious that I was in the open air, that I felt inexplicably healthy, although the boat was tossing about. It was a lifeboat capable of holding about thirty, but it seemed nearly empty. A sail was groaning and occasionally flapping. Gramshaw shouted and the sail was lowered. There was commotion in the boat. After a while I counted four men at the oars and one man asleep, opposite me. Gramshaw was steering.

"Clobbers, old boy," shouted Gramshaw, "d'you think you could relieve Titch!" It was an order, not a question. "Here, drink this, and don't talk. You'll feel fit as a fiddle in a few minutes."

The incredible thing is that I did feel more or less normal in a few minutes. In these ghastly surroundings, quite a number of Gramshaw's nonsense speeches have turned out to be justified.

Titch was a small Welshman, a stoker—a malicious, quarrelsome little man, with a police record. (For the full names and details of these men, see *Appendix B*.)

As I took his place I changed my line of vision.

"Why, there's the ship!" I exclaimed.

"There's the blaggin' ship. And there's the blaggin' island. And this is the blaggin' sea. Get crackin', mate!" This from the man behind me, Jim. There remained Pom, asleep, Steeve and Ginger. To anticipate, these men were of the labouring class, employed on the rough work of the ship, except Ginger, who was a skilled agricultural hand, commanding a high wage. He had been a passenger, though I had never noticed him. I was soon to recognise the social advantages of Gramshaw.

Jim's reference to an island had seemed meaningless. As the angle of our direction changed, I saw it, could even see the Nissen hut, with its chimney. Seen in profile at a distance of a couple of miles, the shape of the island suggested a high-heeled satin slipper. We seemed to be rowing away from it.

"Why don't we make for the island?" I shouted.

"We're lookin' round for somethink a bit better class!" jeered Jim. From Ginger came a laugh which set the teeth on edge. He was even bigger than Gramshaw, but he laughed in a falsetto giggle. But he alone had the civility to answer my question. His speech was a deep rustic burr.

"The boat couldn' land yet awhiles. The seas 'ud smash 'un like a eggshell."

To my ignorance, it seemed unimportant that the boat should be smashed, provided we could land.

"Looks to me like an old fuel dump, Clobbers old boy," said Gramshaw. "Abandoned years ago. The captain didn't mention it. There's a hell of a strong current trying to pull us on to the beach. We've got to keep circling until the swell dies down. It's only swell. There's very little wind, now."

Presently Titch piped up, his high-pitched voice and Welsh accent emphasising every syllable.

"Clobbers is not pulling his weight. Perhaps it is because he is still a sick man!"

14

"Give 'im a chance, Titch!" This was Jim. "He ain't never done no work before. He's a gent, ain'tcher, Clobbers, mate?"

These men lived and died believing my name to be Clobbers, thanks to Gramshaw. They held the opinion, common in their class, that nothing counted as work except muscular exertion.

"You're doing fine, Clobbers old boy!" shouted Gramshaw. "Keep your head up and your back straight, and your weight will do the work."

I know the principles of rowing. I had a short period of "tubbing" as an undergraduate, but the sport did not appeal to me. The revolver under my left arm prevented me from doing myself justice.

"Oh, for God's sake, but it is painful to see it!" Titch, the malicious Welshman, elbowed me out of the way and reclaimed the oar of which I had but recently relieved him. Thus I became the butt of the party.

A few minutes later the sail was hoisted again and the rowing stopped. The technique of sailing against the wind was beyond Gramshaw and everyone else in the boat.

Towards the end of the day the sea became calm enough for us to land. We had only to rest on our oars and let the current carry us to a short sandy beach, close to the hut. Gramshaw was no seaman: we were badly swamped as we struck the beach. We lay on the wet sand until the tide had receded enough for us to start unloading the rations and the various extras which Gramshaw had made them put in the boat. He was very good at that kind of thing.

Gramshaw asked me to report on the hut and to find the best way up to it. It stood on a flat ledge some twenty feet above the beach. The ledge widened into a plateau, the breadth of the island. The track, circuitous and narrow, had been hacked out of the rock, which was of a kind I had not seen before, being greenish and smooth, not unlike chalk.

I walked round the hut. On the land side was a large lean-to shed, containing empty oil-drums and other junk.

The hut itself was some thirty feet in length. The windows were intact but coated with sand and fungus. When I tried the door, the latch came away in my hand. I pushed the door—it fell inwards. I stepped over it somewhat heavily: my feet went through the floorboards to the rock some six inches below. Many of the boards were cracked and uncertain. Yet the hut had the appearance of having been abandoned days rather than years ago.

Abandoned in a hurry. On the table, which was screwed to the floor, was a writing-block, an ink-bottle with the sediment of ink, and a pen: the nib disintegrated into powder when I touched it. In the drawer was a dirty pack of cards, a cribbage board and dominoes. A dartsboard hung on the wall, among wartime pinups. In the tray of the stove were cinders.

Under the table was a ditty-box—the box issued to naval ratings for storing their personal belongings—of which the lock had rusted. Inside were tobacco tins containing nails, screws and the like, a hacksaw rusted to uselessness and a machinist's hammer.

The hammer was double-headed. It had been coated with oil. That hammer was the one object in a state of perfect preservation.

At dawn the sea was nearly dead calm. Gramshaw took me out of earshot of the others and explained apologetically how he had lost touch with the captain's boat in the dark. Some of the boats had started too soon and must have lost themselves. The captain hoped to lead the others to the mainland, believed to be a couple of hundred miles away.

"It seems that I've been elected sort of informal skipper on the bridge. So if that's okay by you, Clobbers old boy, I want you to be camp commandant while we're boarding the wreck for supplies. I see there's a grand lot of flotsam: drag all you can above the tideway, and when you see us start back make a fire for tea—you'll find a packet o' matches in the ration box—treat 'em like gold. We won't attempt more than tea today—and go easy with the water—we've only a couple of gallons. We'll talk about cooking later. And if you've time, explore the place for water."

Gramshaw was happy. He had tumbled into a Boy Scout's heaven. It was as if his ebullient boyishness had contrived the wreck and conjured up the island. There is the hard fact that he had stowed in the boat a number of things, including three large fire-axes, which would have been useless in an open boat—yet at the time of loading he had not known that the island existed.

On the other hand, I must admit that he perceived before I did that the island was a death-trap—if only in the sense that the party as a party could not survive. But his fears were not awakened until the evening.

Except for about an hour, I worked throughout the tropical heat of the day, whereas on the wreck they took a siesta of four hours. Flotsam was beginning to appear on the beach, notably three rafts and a crate of eiderdowns. I had to hack the rafts into sections before I could drag them above the tideway. This relieved my depression. I did not like being the butt of the party; but the resentment did not go much below the surface. I knew I was not guilty of sponging on the energy of the others. I acquired increasing handiness every hour.

The island, which I had first seen as a high-heeled slipper, I now perceived to have the shape of a scalene triangle. The longest side—which I will assume to run north and south—was roughly half a mile long, the east side about a third of a mile. These sides—though there were many fissures giving on to outcrops of rock—were mainly precipitous, the highest point, about eighty feet above the sea, being at the northern apex; the lowest, about fifteen feet, at the southern end. The third and shortest—the south-eastern side, on which was the hut—provided a twenty-foot cliff edge to the plateau, which I had seen as the toecap of the slipper. On the opposite side of the plateau were crumbling cement beds, laid for the storage tanks; there were traces, too, of other hutments. The ships had loaded from the west side, which gave directly on to deep water.

The plateau can be pictured separately as an equilateral triangle, having a base of three hundred yards, the breadth of the island at this point. Within the triangle was the plateau, with a single boulder ten feet high, looking like a mushroom, but nicknamed The Knob. North of the imaginary base you would ascend, threading your way between boulders and craters; some of the latter were filled with sand, some with water, an undrinkable mixture of rain and spray.

At the base-line, too, the sandy beach was broken by long tongues of rock stretching into the sea, like breakwaters at a seaside resort.

It was—it is—a horrible island. The dry rock—a dingy grey-green tinged with yellow—has a faint smell which is not of the sea. It is rather like the smell of acetylene gas. At night the rock glows grey-green but it is not radiant. It is clearly visible at a distance of ten yards. In pitch darkness you could see the silhouette of your companion's feet, though you could not see his face.

My timing was fairly accurate. I had a good fire going and was ready to make tea for them when they returned, but they did not want it. The men were not drunk, but they had been nipping. I could tell from Gramshaw's face that he had tried to keep them from drinking and had lost some stature by his failure. But they obeyed him readily enough in unloading the boat, which took more than two hours. The first item was a case of whisky carried on his shoulder by Jim; his other hand held my suitcase, which was itself almost a cabin trunk.

"Catch 'old, Clobbers!" He was a large, thickset, professionally cheerful cockney. "Thought you'd like to 'ave your dress clo'es in time for supper." This remark, which seemed to me pointless, was received with prolonged laughter.

There were cases of canned beef, of biscuits, tinned milk and the like, a number of vessels for catching rain-water, about a hundred table knives and forks, a lot of rope, another fire-axe and a small fire-hatchet—brought specially for me, as a kind of personal present, to lighten my task of cutting kindling for the fire. Other thoughtful items were a typewriter, with paper and carbons, manuscript books and a good stock of stationery—all this the result of Gramshaw's personal labour.

For the rest, there was a stock of tobacco, two battery radio sets and one gramophone (but no records). There was a litter

18

of gewgaws, looted for the sake of looting, including a cavalry saddle, a tennis racket and a green silk nightdress. Also, there were three cases of whisky, two of rum and two of gin—making more than eighty bottles of potential trouble.

"No damned discipline, Clobbers old boy!" Gramshaw confided to me that night. "They'll obey an order when they see it's for their own good, but they can't see farther than their noses. Fact is, it's rather got me down!"

At that moment I felt that I liked him and even admired him a little. Absurd though it sounds in view of the fact that I caused his death, I never lost that feeling.

"They've no sense of time, Clobbers old boy. We're safe now for a month or so—longer if we can cut those table knives into serviceable fish-hooks. So they think there's no need to worry—sure to be rescued before the rations give out!" The bitterness dropped out of his voice as he added quietly:

"We're *not* sure to be rescued."

That was another surprise—Gramshaw staring an unpleasant fact in the face without smothering it in optimistic platitudes.

"Have we any chance at all?" I asked.

"Mustn't let the mind dwell on it, Clobbers old boy!" Gramshaw was in constant fear of his mind "dwelling" on something or other. "We were a good bit off our course when we stuck on that sandbank. The ship's radio collapsed some thirty-six hours previously. If we aren't rescued in a few days we can forget it for six months. Even then—all we know is that this line runs a half-yearly service and that the sister ship may be within fifty miles of us in six months."

"And we have rations for a month or so, you said?"

"There's plenty of stuff on the wreck." His thoughts were on the chance of eventual rescue. "Fifty miles! Chucks it all into the lap of the gods! Even if the others make the coast of Africa, they may be weeks trekking through scrub before they reach civilisation. And then they'll report that we were drowned. And another thing I'll tell you, Clobbers old boy! That wreck may heel over at any minute."

The wreck did heel over two days later. But there had been no second expedition for provisions. The men were sleeping off the whisky. When Gramshaw did succeed in getting them up, the boat was high and dry and they refused to attempt to drag it over the sand.

The wreck remained visible, looking like a whale. The men found some kind of pleasure in gaping at it. They strung eiderdowns into a canopy under which they passed the heat of the day, not yet realising that, at its worst, the hut was cooler than the open air.

In the hut, Gramshaw and I were agreeing that we must list the stores and equipment. I was in a hurry to know the worst, but Gramshaw kept manufacturing delay. The ditty-box which I had examined the day we landed was still under the table. Gramshaw opened it and rummaged.

"Not a regular issue, Clobbers old boy. An amateur carpenter who scrounged what he could. All the tools are carpenter's except this hammer. Machinist's hammer."

The hammer, double-headed, was of the kind sometimes supplied in the toolkit of a car. One head was like that of a carpenter's hammer, the other had four sharp edges tapering to a small flat surface.

"What they call a 'double preen'," explained Gramshaw, fingering it. "Very useful!"

"What for?"

"Oh, I dunno!" He turned the hammer on his wrist, struck at imaginary objects. A boy with a toy.

"Hadn't we better start work, Gramshaw?"

"Rightho, Clobbers old boy! No good putting off the evil day. The sooner we start, the sooner we'll finish." He dropped the hammer into the ditty-box. "We'll have to assume that that ship will come within hailing distance. Six months' survival is our target. We'll find out how much food we have in hand. Got to tot it all up in terms of a food-day. And then divide it by seven. *Phew!* I wish it weren't so damned hot!"

He was openly funking the job; again I found myself liking him. My own panic lay along a different line.

Stocktaking occupied less than an hour. Gramshaw's "food-days" kept us guessing for three times as long, although the arithmetical part of it was painfully easy.

"Neither of us knows the minimum on which life can be sustained," I said. "It's impossible to do it scientifically. We must stick blindly to your target figure of six months."

Gramshaw looked haggard, then rallied himself by purporting to encourage me.

"Don't let it get you down, Clobbers old boy. You've forgotten fish. We can make hooks out of those table knives, and we've more cord than we can use. The sea round here may be teeming. Of course, fish every day will get monotonous, but . . ." The platitudes petered out. I was afraid he would break down and cry. "I'm going to put that ditty-box in the stores-shed. Those tools will be useful and we don't want them messed about."

He picked up the ditty-box and went out.

The heat certainly seemed substantially worse than on the three previous days since the storm had subsided. The holster under my arm seemed to have trebled in weight, and there was the added strain of avoiding discovery. Why avoid discovery? Why not hand it to Gramshaw? He was in effect, and probably in law, captain of the ship and its survivors on the island.

I cannot now defend my concealment of that revolver. I ought to have handed it to Gramshaw. Apart from subtle points of legality, I was behaving dishonourably towards the man who had shown me friendship. I myself do not know why I clung to that weapon at this time. I will therefore offer the explanation that is least favourable to myself.

I kept that revolver in order to make sure that I would receive my share of the rations. I would kill anyone who deliberately reduced my chance of getting off that accursed island and resuming my normal life.

When Gramshaw came back from the stores-shed he stood waiting near the door while I checked my final figures. I looked up to find him gazing at me with an expression of deep misery.

"I've checked it twice—and here it is . . ." I read aloud the items of the "food-day". To soften the blow, I added: "That's ample to sustain life."

"For six months!" ejaculated Gramshaw. "But we've no

certainty that it will be only six months. We're hoping. Pretending!"

"We've already agreed about that," I snapped. I had fair-copied the final list of items. "There's the ticket. That will sustain seven men for six months."

"*Don't!* You make it sound like one of those blurry little sums they give you at school." His nerve broke in an idiotic laugh. "Sustain seven men for six months. Or three and a half men for one year. Or one and three quarter men for two years."

He flung himself on his bedding.

"Or one man for three and a half years!"

To me Gramshaw had revealed his fear and his misery. To the men he revealed neither. That evening he was, in his own jargon, splendid.

He began by telling them all he knew of our position, waited for questions, which were not asked.

"Well, boys, now you know the set-up as well as I do. We have to face the fact that we may be here for six months—we won't look beyond that. We all want to get home, but as we can't, we may as well make the best of our position and the best of each other. And so we come to the question of food.

"Let me say first that we mustn't reckon on any food drifting on to the beach from the wreck. And I'm not counting the fish which are still in the sea. The more we haul out of the sea and into the pot, the more we can increase our meat ration.

"Clobbers and I have listed the stores. There's the list over there and you can check it with the stuff, if you want some exercise. The ration works out like this."

Here was the brick wall—Gramshaw took it in a flying leap.

"There's two ounces of bully beef per man per day, three biscuits, half a cup of tea every other day, half a cup of milk every other day. There's plenty of tea and plenty of milk, but as we have to condense our drinking-water from sea-water, that's the ration. Fuel for cooking and for condensing the water is our weakest spot. Talk about that presently. You're bound to feel thirsty during the heat—it's at its worst between ten and four. You'll find that the desire to drink will be much less if you bathe in the sea twice a day and don't dry yourself.

"In addition, there are some trimmings: canned vegetables, chocolate, sweet biscuits, but not enough for a regular ration. We'll keep that sort of thing for special occasions. Also medical supplies—bandages, antiseptics and a few drugs. We've less than fifty candles, so we'll ration at one candle for one hour per day—which will leave us a small margin for emergencies."

Gramshaw went on to outline camp duties. Certain kinds of seaweed could be sun-dried for fuel: it could be laid on the roof of the hut, where it would serve an extra purpose in reducing the heat from the corrugated iron. The lives of all, he told us, depended on the labour of each. The platitudes rolled over the men, flattening them into silence.

"To sum up—not counting the extras and not counting the fish—the rations we've worked out mean that the seven of us can wait for that rescue ship for a hundred and eighty days—if we have to."

I had expected uproar, but none came, only a dumb sullenness. Gramshaw started to talk about fish, and their attention wandered. When he had finished they drifted to the beach to have another look at the wreck.

The tide was coming in, bringing more flotsam, invaluable for fuel if for nothing else. They would break open a case, in the hope, always vain, that it would contain something to eat or to play with, then leave case and contents in the tideway. Gramshaw and I had to drag it all in. There were bales and packing-cases containing a variety of goods, some of which were indirectly useful. We had already acquired eiderdowns and table napkins; we were now enriched by three bales of blue serge, four packing-cases of wallpaper and three of bicycle parts; also one case of sand-shoes—rubber soled, with white canvas uppers, commonly known as plimsolls.

"There's going to be trouble over the rations, Clobbers old boy. We've no means of locking anything up. After a day or two they'll demand more."

"And spoil our chance of getting off the island!"

Gramshaw did not deny it. He said nothing for a minute or more.

"Seven of us!" He was muttering as if I were not present. "As it is, we shall have to catch a lot of fish, or we shan't make it."

By dusk the mood of the men had changed to fatuous optimism, helped by the whisky. I dished out the ration of bully and biscuit. It was getting dark in the hut. Jim produced three candles and lit them.

"One candle for one hour for one day!" said Gramshaw, and blew out two.

"That's okay, Mr. Gramshaw, but not tonight, for cripes sake!" said Jim. "We start all that tomorrer. Tonight's special-like. We gotter drink the 'ealth o' the poor old *Marigonda*!"

Ginger, the big gorilla-like man, slowly relit the two candles. Gramshaw's face gave nothing away.

"Please yourselves, boys. I only handed out the orders because you asked me to. I've told you how we're fixed. It's up to you!"

"That's all right, Mr. Gramshaw," said Steeve. "You won't have no complaint about your orders being obeyed, I'll promise yer. Beginnin' tomorrer. Tonight's special-like."

"That's right, sir," echoed Jim. "Begin tomorrer."

"We shan't be here six munt's—nor nothink like it!" said Pom. "Shouldn't be surprised if a ship turned up tomorrer to take us orf 'ome."

They were not quarrelsome, only sloppily optimistic. Soon they were singing. They had so little sense of time that they were pleased because the heavy labour of loading and unloading the lifeboat was at an end. No doubt, every night would be "special-like" for as long as the liquor lasted. Before the last bottle had been opened, the ration system would have broken down.

I was not only cook but also orderly. While I was clearing up, Titch, the malicious Welshman, crept up behind me and slipped the green silk nightdress over my head.

"'Ullo, there's Ma!" guffawed Jim. "Ma Clobbers!" said

somebody else, and the obvious jokes passed. The nightdress had imprisoned my arms and it split as soon as I moved, freeing my left arm. I could have pulled it over my head, but I did not want to perform acrobatics with my left arm, because of the holster. So I tore the nightdress down the middle, then rolled it into a ball and, with what good humour I could muster, lobbed it at Titch's head.

Titch did not dodge. He let the thing hit him and flop to his knees. Then he picked it up as if it were verminous, opened the stove, from which the ashes had not yet been removed, and dropped it inside. The others watched him in silence.

"My act was light-hearted, without malice whatever." The Welsh sing-song was charged with venom. "It has made Clobbers angry. Perhaps he has good reason for his anger."

The silence persisted. Gramshaw told me afterwards that, by their code, I ought to have challenged him to a fight. The idea did not occur to me, because I was not in the least angry. I took their jokes—my forced association with them—as part of the general tribulation resulting from shipwreck.

The next morning Titch was missing.

The rationing system was now in force. Drinking raw spirits overnight had at least saved water. The condensing plant, cobbled by Gramshaw out of an open Army kettle, a strip of corrugated iron and some sailcloth, was able to provide the half cup of tea, which tasted of the sailcloth. When Titch's tea grew cold, it became obvious that something had happened to him.

"Clobbers sleeps nearest the door—must have heard 'un go out," said Ginger, his slow speech and heavy, yokel accent seeming to add significance to his words.

"I heard more than one of you go out," I answered, "but I didn't check your coming and going. Why should I?"

Gramshaw's qualities of leadership came into action.

"There's no need for panic, boys. He probably missed his direction in the dark—may have sprained his ankle; I daresay we shall find him behind a boulder. We'll tackle this job with a spot o' system."

He formed us up in line, with twelve paces between us. They liked that kind of thing and responded to it. It was of limited value because, as soon as we left the plateau and came upon the boulders, the line was inevitably broken. The method provided no certainty of finding a dead or unconscious man—had there been one to find.

During the night, Titch's body was washed up on the beach. Gramshaw, who was always up and about before anyone else, found it. I was stoking the fire for the condenser when he whistled to me from the winding track.

"It's Titch!" Gramshaw's mouth was trembling. "At least, I'm pretty sure it's Titch."

The body was lying face upwards and there could be no doubt of identity. I turned it over.

"He must have turned completely round in the dark and walked over the ledge the other side into the deep water," babbled Gramshaw.

"He wasn't drowned, Gramshaw. There's a hole in the back of his head—half a square inch, I should think. Look!"

"The truth is—I don't mind admitting it, Clobbers old boy—my stomach isn't as steady as yours. I—I suppose it's my duty to look."

When Gramshaw supposed something to be his duty he always did it.

"Ghastly! The poor chap must have hit a sharp point of rock as he fell."

But the rock was not sharp. Though different in colour, it was, in substance as well as appearance, more like chalk than rock. Also, it would have to be a freak kind of sharpness. The wound was almost a perfect square.

"I'll have to go and break it to the others!" said Gramshaw.

He had been standing seawards of the body. As he moved, a yellowish glow from the rising sun illumined the wound. My eye was caught by a tiny point of opalescent green in the hair at the edge of the wound.

"Half a minute, Gramshaw! I'm not so sure about that rock."

"What've you found?"

"A spot of mechanical oil on the edge of the wound."

"It must have come from the beach. . . ." He looked round. "If it hadn't, it would have been washed away."

"Put a spot of oil in your own hair and try and wash it off with sea-water. You won't succeed."

There was a long silence, before he asked:

"What's in your mind, Clobbers old boy?"

I took my time over answering. That machinist's hammer was in my mind. The almost perfect square was about the right size. And the hammer had been coated with oil.

I shrank from saying so for the sole reason that I did not wish to lead Gramshaw's thoughts. There might be other explanations which he could discover if his thoughts were left unbiased. It might even be possible that there was a sharp bit of rock, or metal driven into the rock by the naval party, and still oil-stained.

"It's in my mind that he may have been struck with a weapon."

Gramshaw's jaw twitched and hung loose.

"I had that idea for half a second—that wound looks too tidy for an accident."

As he had got as far as that, I expected him to think of the hammer. But he did not mention it. The twitching of his mouth stopped.

"That settles it, Clobbers old boy! I shall have to hold an inquiry. Make it as formal as we can—you'll have to record it on the typewriter. Carbon copies. Everything in triplicate. The trouble is, I'm damned if I know how to set about it!"

Nor do I. But one point was crystal clear to me, which Gramshaw had missed.

"You'll have to hold an inquiry," I echoed. "And you'll have to make sure that the inquiry does *not* find who killed Titch."

He looked at me with sudden suspicion. Suspicion of my sanity, I supposed.

"If you do find the murderer, Gramshaw, you must do your utmost to pretend you have failed. I'll do everything I can to help make the pretence realistic."

"Clobbers old boy, you are talking in a devilish odd way!"

"For God's sake, wake up!" I snapped at him. "Your legal standing, if you have any, is captain of the ship, which equals local magistrate—not High Court judge. You can't hold a trial and sentence a man to death. If you find the murderer, your duty is to put him in irons. And we haven't got any irons—no means of keeping anybody in close arrest. If you incite the others to kill him, the whole lot of us will be charged with murder, even if we prove that he murdered Titch."

Gramshaw blew out his cheeks.

"*Phew!* We're in a tight spot, by the look of it!"

"We'll be in a tighter spot if we let one of those toughs know that we intend to hand him over for trial as soon as we're rescued—if we *are* rescued!"

"You're right!" In spite of his chubbiness, his face looked haggard. "This is too much for me, Clobbers old boy. Why, there's no way of doing the right thing!"

"Then let's do the sensible thing. Find the murderer if we can. Then keep it a secret. Go on exactly as we were. Encourage 'em in that sentimental gush they hand out when they're drunk. 'All pals together', and all that! It'll sound funnier than ever!"

He accepted my offer to tell the others. I didn't break it gently to them, knowing there was no need.

"Titch's body on the beach. Gramshaw is there!"

When they had scampered off, I slipped round the hut to the lean-to and opened the ditty-box. The hammer, as I had expected, was inside. The murderer would have replaced it as soon as possible.

I picked it up and examined the head, in the vague belief that I might find bloodstains.

I found no bloodstains, but I did find that the head was very much oilier than it had been when I handled it in the hut. I glanced ət the litter of empty oil-tins. There was always some oil left in empty oil-tins.

This merely added to my conviction that the hammer had been the weapon. The ditty-box had been under the table in the hut for the better part of our first two days. Anyone could have marked down the hammer. And anyone could have taken it from the lean-to, unobserved.

On the beach, I joined Gramshaw, who was by himself. The others were huddled round the corpse. All four turned in the same instant and looked at us. Steeve approached, the other three following him.

"Mr. Gramshaw, 'ow would you say as Titch got that hole in the back of his 'ead?" asked Steeve. The others were standing behind him, three abreast, as if supporting their spokesman. Gramshaw's leadership hung in the balance.

"Well, Steeve, we're going to start a proper inquiry presently. And Clobbers will write a report to hand to the authorities when we're rescued."

"He didn't get that from no blurry fish!" said one.

"The only guess we can make at present," said Gramshaw, "is that he missed his way in the dark—he was a bit drunk, you know—and stepped over the ledge on the other side. In falling, he may have struck his head on a sharp bit of rock."

"I've been along with Titch for nigh on two years," said Pom. "He was always steady on his feet and he'd always walk home all right, no matter 'ow drunk he was."

"Reckon if he went over the ledge, somebody shoved 'im," said Steeve.

"An' I lay it wor Clobbers as shoved 'un." This from the taciturn, bucolic Ginger. He was not excited, only reflective. It was as if he were contributing a last word before the topic was abandoned.

"You can't stop there, Ginger!" cried Gramshaw. "You'll have to tell us why you think that."

"I seen Clobbers when Titch put that skirt on 'un. Fair murderous, he looked!"

"Put a sock in it, Ginger!" Jim unexpectedly came to my rescue. His help was, in some ways, more valuable than Gramshaw's.

"Have you anything else to say, Ginger?" asked Gramshaw ominously. I realised, with surprise, that he could be very formidable.

"I 'aven't nothing to say, barrin' as someone killed Titch."
He still had the air of expecting his words to pass unchallenged.
"And I lay it wor Clobbers."

"Look here, boys!" Gramshaw was making a statesmanlike
effort to preserve the peace. "We don't know yet that Titch
didn't die by an accident. If he was killed, we're all going to
do our best to find who killed him. And every one of us must
give all the information he can. But guessing isn't information.
Ginger may have meant well, but he has pointed to one man
without any proof at all, except that that one *might* have done
it. Anyone of us might have been that man—including me,
of course. We shall all go mad if each of us is going to be
picked out on grounds as slender as that. We've all got to
keep our mouths shut unless we have something solid to offer.
What do you say to that?"

"That's right, Mr. Gramshaw," said Jim. Pom and Steeve
murmured assent. We all looked at Ginger.

"Aye, it's right enough!" he grunted. "But I lay it wor
Clobbers."

Gramshaw had to deal with four tough men with the
minds of children. He was nearly as big as Ginger and his
nerve reactions were much quicker.

He hit Ginger squarely between the eyes and knocked him
down. I put my hand under my shirt. If Ginger produced a
knife I would fire at his stomach.

Ginger rolled over and, with his over-long arms, levered
himself to his feet. He made a bull-like rush at Gramshaw,
who side-stepped and landed a light blow on the other's nose.

I am not wholly ignorant of boxing. It was obvious to me
that Gramshaw was a boxer and that, although the sand
spoilt footwork, he had Ginger at his mercy. He was not
feeling merciful. Ginger could conceive of only one kind of
blow—the heaviest he could deliver—a theory based on the
assumption that one's opponent will not move out of range.
Gramshaw planted five short jabs with his left before swinging
with his right.

Again Ginger went down, but not out. He rose, his face
streaming with blood, and rushed in. Gramshaw's foot caught
on a piece of flotsam; he guarded Ginger's blow with his right,

but it knocked him down. He was up in a second, but Ginger stepped back and grinned at him with swelling lips.

"I knowed it worn't Clobbers afore you started fightin' me," he said. "Now I knocked you down, I tell you I knowed it worn't Clobbers."

"Then why did you accuse him?" Gramshaw spoke gently, as if to a child. He repeated: "Why did you say you'd bet Clobbers killed Titch?"

"I was scared. A man don't take shame for allowin' he's scared o' some things. I'm glad I hain't done Clobbers no harm."

"All right, Ginger. We can shake hands," said Gramshaw.

"Now I knocked you down, I tell you I knowed it worn't Clobbers," repeated Ginger, shaking hands. "It worn't none of us!" He grinned at each of us in turn, rivulets of blood running down his face. "There's been no gulls on this island since we bin 'ere, an' they worn't 'ere afore we come. No nests—no droppin's. I've watched 'em fly round and out ter sea again."

No one made any comment. Ginger slouched off to clean up his face.

We covered the body with damp serge, part of the flotsam. Pom lashed the serge, adding a sufficiency of rock splinters, which Jim hacked off with a fire-axe. Gramshaw and Steeve made a pretence of helping, while I frankly looked on. We drifted back to the hut.

On the plateau, Gramshaw detached himself. Without intending to do so, I watched his movements. He walked slowly, almost stealthily, round the hut to the lean-to shed. I at once felt sure that he had reached the same conclusion I had reached half an hour previously and that he too wished to see if the hammer were still in the ditty-box.

I hung about near the door of the hut. When he appeared, I grinned at him, expecting him to mention the hammer, if only in a whisper. I was more than a little offended when he said nothing. We stood together for a minute or more in silence.

"Better double the ration for breakfast, Clobbers old boy. The rowing will be hard work."

"Righto! I suppose it's necessary." I added: "But it spoils my figures. Titch's ration means that the whole party can survive another month."

"I think that's a beastly way of looking at it!" Gramshaw was flushed with embarrassment.

"It's a storeman's way of looking at it," I retorted. "Titch's death gives us all a slightly better chance of survival. Why humbug ourselves?"

After breakfast we rowed out about two miles to the south-west. Owing to some confusion as to the nature of my profession—I hold a travelling Fellowship in ancient history—I was asked to extemporise a burial service.

When we returned and had beached the boat, there was still more than an hour before the heat would become severe. Gramshaw immediately opened his inquiry. Sitting on a packing-case at the head end of the table, with writing materials to his hand, he contrived to look competent. But he had a hopeless task. There was nothing to be done but to ask each of us to account for his movements.

This part of the inquiry petered out and was tacitly abandoned. Gramshaw got up and walked purposefully from the hut. We followed him while he paced out the distance from the hut to the latrine.

"Sixty-three yards!" he announced, as if he were making an award. "Will you all wait here, please?"

He paced the distance from the latrine to the north-western limit of the plateau. A Boy Scout trick, I thought, that could have no value in the investigation. He turned at the cliff edge, military fashion, and began to pace his way back, presumably to check. About half-way he stopped, turned from his line.

"Everybody here!" he shouted, and beckoned.

When we arrived, he pointed to a substance on the rock.

"Do you all agree that this is blood?"

It was a formal and rather silly question. In spite of the sun of yesterday, there was no possibility of its being anything else.

"Same as I thought!" cried Pom. "Someone done 'im in."

In the first few seconds I was inclined to blame Gramshaw for forcing the issue, since we had agreed that we would have to evade it. Later, I reflected that he couldn't help himself. Someone else might have discovered the blood, which amounted to irrefutable evidence of murder.

"The wound is on the back of the head and could not have been self-inflicted!" intoned Gramshaw. "One of us standing here killed Titch!"

The last was said with an impressiveness which produced in me a feeling of fear. Someone, I felt, would point at me before I could draw another breath. I suspect that everybody else felt the same. A long silence was broken by a grating, falsetto giggle.

"There's no living thing on this yere island," said Ginger. "No flies. No insecks!"

"Titch never missed 'is way," Pom reminded us. "How did he get as far as this—that's what I wanna know?"

"He could have been stunned at the latrine—then dragged," said Gramshaw. "The death blow was struck here. Then the body was dragged to the ledge and tipped over."

"S'right!" ejaculated Pom. "Titch 'ad steel on heel and toe of 'is boots. Look a' that!"

There was a clear scratch on the rock. It was broken by undulations of the surface, but there was little difficulty in tracing it to the cliff head.

"That's 'ow the job was done, right enough!" contributed Jim.

"There's no liddle fish an' no sea insecks in the pools left by the tide," giggled Ginger.

"Dry up, Ginger! You fair gimme the creeps!" growled Steeve.

In a bunch we walked back to the hut. We had nearly reached it when Jim startled everybody by shouting.

"Hi! Mr. Gramshaw! It don't have to mean one of us scuppered Titch!" He was almost bellowing, though Gramshaw was within three feet of him.

"That's what Ginger seems to believe," said Gramshaw patiently.

"I ain't talkin' spooks, nor none o' that foolery!" Jim was emphatic. "I mean maybe we ain't the first lot to be washed up on this blaggin' rock. What say there was one all by his-self—or the last of a boatload like us? He might 'a' bin dodging about among them rocks laughin' at us while we was lookin' for Titch yesterday. Maybe he was one of the naval blokes takin' care to be left behind, dodgin' a court martial. Found a way of feedin' 'isself, but gone mad—a man gets like an animal if he's left alone long enough."

"You've got something there, Jim!" I cried before Gramshaw could make objections. "Anyone could dodge a search-party among those boulders and craters."

Gramshaw looked hard at me and seemed to pick up the idea. Steeve and Pom were already agreeing with Jim.

"He wouldn't 'a' had time to lose his wits," said Ginger. "They'd 'a' served 'im like they served Titch."

As soon as I could, I detached Gramshaw from the others. "That's a stroke of luck for us!" I said. "Jim has solved the problem of the inquiry."

"But it's all bosh, Clobbers old boy! You couldn't live on this island without supplies—you couldn't live more than a week or so in the summer without a condenser."

"Of course it's bosh! But that doesn't matter in the least, provided they go on believing it. We'll find the bogy-man guilty."

"While we stop looking for the real murderer?" Gramshaw was on his high horse of moral rectitude.

"We agreed that we must not find the murderer," I reminded him. "That lout has accidentally shown us how to set about *not* finding him."

"I didn't agree not to find the murderer—I agreed that we might be driven to pretending we had not found him."

I felt angry and did my best not to show it.

"All right, then. Use this wild-man nonsense as a screen while you get on with the detective work." I added grudgingly: "I will, of course, give you all the help I can."

"That's a good compromise, Clobbers. I hate playing skipper on the bridge, but this community is my moral responsibility. I feel that we must find the man if we can. What we're to do with him when found is a separate problem. Thanks for saying you'll help, when you don't really agree with me."

The scoutmaster was awarding me a badge for loyalty. This overgrown boy was my only ally in handling a dangerously delicate situation. I had realised, with acute discomfort, that I had been thrust into the position of leader, that he would be dependent upon me in every emergency that was not connected with the handling of material objects.

That evening, while I was alone in the stores-shed cutting the meat ration for supper, I had a ridiculous experience. I had been bending over the meat for some minutes. I straightened my aching back and the next instant let out a gasping cry. Standing within a few inches of me was Ginger. The others, hearing my cry, came rushing to the shed and I had the humiliation of explaining.

Ginger wanted a pair of pliers to remove a loose nail from his boot. He lingered after the others had gone.

"I ain't scared no more, like I was this morning," he said in belated apology for having accused me. "I'm glad I ain't done you no harm."

"That's all right, Ginger! We're all a bit nervy. Look what a show I made just now!"

"Aye, we're all scared o' summat," he agreed, and took himself off.

Boots on the rock. I had not heard him approach. Though I listened, I could not hear him when he left. In his movements the man was as quiet as a cat.

In the hour before dusk, which was the best in the day, Gramshaw made another oration, which included an ingenious plan. He was often ingenious. If he had been more intelligent or more of a fool he would have been easier to handle.

"Well, boys, we've given poor Titch as decent burial as we can. The question is what we're to do next in this affair. I've had a talk with Clobbers and we both think that Jim's suggestion is a valuable one. We have held an inquiry and we've found nothing pointing to one of us as the murderer. True, we haven't found any traces of a wild man on the island, but that doesn't prove that there isn't one. So we are going to act as if we were certain that there is one.

"It's no good searching for him over again. He dodged us once and he can dodge us again indefinitely. He's killed one of us for no reason. He'll try again—at least, we have to assume he will. Now, he has shown us that, wild or not, he's cunning. Too cunning to break into this hut while we're asleep because he'd be bound to wake us, and that'd be the end of him. He'll stalk us until he finds one of us alone."

"That's right!" approved Jim, and the others, except Ginger, echoed.

"Thank heavens there's a simple answer to that one!" Gramshaw had reached the cheerful, encouraging pitch of voice. "He's *never* going to find one of us alone. At night, no one will go out of this hut alone in any circumstances whatever. That's an order, boys. In daylight, we shall all be in sight of each other all the time. And this is how we'll do it.

"Except Clobbers, who's on duty more or less all round the clock, with stoking the fire and rations and the rest of the camp chores, we shall do a four-hour working day, in two even shifts. It's about all we can manage on the rations. And the work, until further notice, will be collecting the seaweed and drying it. Jim and Steeve will work together on the beach rocks. Ginger and Pom will work the rocks on the north-west side, using the fissure where the boulders begin. I shall be on sentry-go between the two working parties. For the whole way I shall be able to see Clobbers, except when he's in the hut or the lean-to, and even then I can see the clear space round the hut. In half an hour I shall relieve Jim, who will take sentry-go; then Jim will relieve Pom for sentry-go. In this way, each one of us will have done the same amount of work on the seaweed and work as look-out by the end of the day." He paused, discovered that he had nothing more to say, and added: "Any questions?"

The last was unnecessary—a mere flourish. It led to an incident, trivial in itself, which had an unfortunate effect on the general morale.

"I'll ask *yew* to tell *me*, Mr. Gramshaw——" Ginger was groping for words. "You said Titch was thrown into deep water t'other side of this yere island. How come he wor found on the beach this side?"

"There are currents in the sea, Ginger," answered Gramshaw. "One current took the body out. We have no means of knowing exactly what happened, but eventually the body must have been caught in another current—perhaps in several, one of which washed it up this side of the island."

"Or maybe it wor meant that his bones should come back to this yere island, an' come back they will, so often as you put 'em in the sea."

He looked from one face to another.

"There ain't no man on this yere island barrin' us."

"Listen, Ginger!" Gramshaw was justifiably angered by the man's insistent mysticism. "You're entitled to your own opinion, but you must keep it to yourself. You'll give us all the creeps soon, if you go on babbling about your *damned spooks!*"

As he spoke, Gramshaw thumped the table. There came a cracking sound and the packing-case on which he was sitting subsided. He grabbed at the table, missed and slithered to the floor.

There ought to have been a laugh, but there was only a silence. Men as ignorant as these were the victims of every superstitious fancy. There could be no doubt that they believed "the spooks" had punished an insult.

While Gramshaw picked himself up, Jim examined the packing-case.

"It's all right, Mr. Gramshaw—I can fix this for you in a couple o' shakes. Wants re-nailin'—that's all!" He turned to me. "We got a hammer an' a few nails, ain't we, Clobbers?"

"In the ditty-box in the stores-shed," I answered.

"Thanks, Jim," said Gramshaw; then raised his voice, "Wait! You'll be out of sight. You go with him, Pom."

I was glad Gramshaw had not picked on me. Titch had been killed with that hammer. Jim was almost certainly innocent, or he would not have had the nerve to ask for the hammer.

That left Pom, Steeve and Ginger to be watched for their reactions while Jim was displaying the hammer on the packing-case.

"Clobbers, the blaggin' hammer ain't in the blaggin' ditty-box. What abaht it, mate? Skipper's waitin' for 'is seat."

At that moment I saw only that my efficiency as store-keeper was in question.

"That hammer was in that ditty-box at dawn this morning. I saw it there a few seconds after I'd told you about Titch. Who has had it since?"

I looked at Gramshaw, expecting him to add his testimony that he also had seen the hammer in the ditty-box, some half an hour later than had I.

As he said nothing, I concluded that he had not, after all, gone to the shed to check on the hammer.

A moment later I drew the obvious inference. The murderer, along with the innocent, had inspected the body when it lay on the beach. He had noted that the wound was clearly marked and that someone would be likely to connect it with the hammer. He had therefore regained possession at the first opportunity—to bury it in the sand or throw it into the deep water.

Jim was still grumbling.

"Here, Jim, you can manage with this." I offered him my fire-hatchet.

"No blaggin' choice, seein' as you've lost the 'ammer." Jim was in an ungracious mood. The hammer-end of a hatchet is not designed for carpentry, being some three inches long by half an inch wide. Jim's imprecations suddenly ceased.

"*Hi*, Mr. Gramshaw! Did j'ever notice that 'ammer wot Clobbers has lost? Got two knockin' heads—one of 'em a funny sort o' shape. Not far off the shape o' that hole in pore ole Titch's 'ead."

"That's right!" mumbled Steeve.

Gramshaw looked thoughtful.

"It didn't occur to me at the time, Jim."

"Wot I mean is, the wild man might 'a' pinched it when Clobbers wasn't about!"

"There's no knowing." Gramshaw damped the discussion. "The hammer may turn up—things are bound to get mislaid sometimes."

Gramshaw was keeping a log, in a large cloth-bound manuscript book brought from the wreck for this purpose. I have never seen a ship's log. I imagine Gramshaw's to be more detailed and colloquial. It served also as a daily report —as well as a record of the exact time at which routine trivialities occurred.

Today's log, which I read in the evening, contained a summary of the inquiry. The wound was described, but without reference to the hammer. The log noted the time at which Jim had propounded the wild-man theory, the time at which Ginger had been reprimanded for spreading despondency with his spook talk—even the time at which the packing-case on which Gramshaw had been sitting had collapsed.

But there was no mention of the fact that the hammer was missing from the stores-shed.

At dusk, lounging on the beach in the first cool period, I had a word alone with Gramshaw.

"What about that machinist's hammer?" I asked. "I thought of it when we were looking at that wound. I didn't mention it because I didn't want to bias your judgment. Evidently it occurred to Jim and Steeve, too."

"I don't see that it helps us much," he answered. "I'm all against an excess of probing. The truth is, Clobbers old boy, I've come round to your way of thinking. We want *pro*tection, not *de*tection."

The next morning Gramshaw's plan was put into action and found to be effective, with a few minor adjustments. It was a clever plan, because it gave protection against the real murderer. At any given moment every man, with the partial exception of myself, was in sight of at least one other—paired off with him. As detection would be inevitable if a second murder were committed, it was reasonable to suppose that it would not be committed. It was all done without offending anybody, under the cloak of the postulated wild man, of animal mentality, deemed to be hiding among the boulders.

But the wild-man theory sustained a jolt two days later, and Ginger's spook-theory was given an undeserved boost.

During the heat, Gramshaw had gone out of the hut alone. He was not breaking his own rule. Steeve was sitting at the table turning over the dog-eared, incomplete pack of cards in some kind of solitary game of his own. I had cleared the windows of fungus, so Steeve was able to keep an eye on him.

According to Steeve, Gramshaw stretched himself and strolled towards the edge of the plateau, looking out to sea. He was wearing a stained and battered Homburg. He raised both hands in additional protection of his eyes. Then he dropped flat and peered over the ledge.

He ran the few yards back to the hut. He stood panting and haggard, gripping the lintel, and stared at us.

"Titch's body! Without the shroud we made."

There came a falsetto cackle from Ginger, no sound from anyone else. Gramshaw walked out of the hut. I followed him. We took some more serge, went down to the beach and covered the body. We could not do anything energetic during the heat.

"Ginger prophesied this," I remarked. "They'll all think he was right about the spooks."

"It doesn't matter any more what they think." He spoke in a loud whisper. "It doesn't matter what you and I think."

It was the whispering effect that made me look at him. There were tears on his cheeks.

"Gramshaw! You don't believe the spook stuff? The spiritualists themselves would laugh at the suggestion that a disembodied spirit can bash in a man's head and then fish him out of the sea to prove that you ought to believe in spooks!"

"It's nothing to do with disembodied spirits." My tone had stung him into bracing himself. "But what about a spirit that has never been embodied? The spirit of the island, if you like! Ginger's right in saying that there's no life on the island—not even insect life. This island—it's anti-life!"

Perhaps I looked shocked at being offered this kind of thing.

"I'm as sane as you are, Clobbers. I know that a geologist wouldn't be worried by this queer kind of rock. A chemist could tell us why it has that peculiar stink—which is probably due to some element which keeps the birds and the insects away. And a navigator could work out why the currents have played this grisly monkey-trick on us. Add the lot up, and you get something that is more than the sum of its components, as a termitary is more than the sum of the individual ants. Why d'you think me an ass if I lump all the horrors together and call 'em the spirit of the island? And I tell you again it's an anti-life spirit. It resents our presence and will try to destroy us."

The scoutmaster's version of Ginger's spooks! The unnerving part of it was that I found myself acknowledging that it was essentially true, even though he used romantic words about it. It was a reasonable thesis that conditions on the island had awakened murder mania in the brain of one of our party.

We now entered upon the second phase of our existence on the island. The first phase had been one of ill discipline and quarrelsomeness. The second was one which I can only call the mystic phase. It lasted almost until the end and it came into existence very suddenly—was actually in being when we returned to the hut.

The first sign of it was an unprecedented silence. No one asked what we had been doing, nor mentioned the return of the body. Steeve continued to turn over the cards. Jim was lying prone, as if asleep. Pom was squatting on his bedding mending his trousers. Ginger, sitting on the floor with his shoulders against the corrugated iron, was carving something with a massive pocket knife. I was aware of a new calm. We had become a unit. There could be no more pep-talks from Gramshaw.

Our new-found unity would not have been apparent to the eye. Except Gramshaw, we all had nearly a fortnight's growth on our faces. Our clothes, not yet ragged, were ill adapted to our situation. Ginger came out best. With the first threat of shipwreck he had changed into his working clothes of corduroy. My tweeds, intact but nearly buttonless, were held together by an army belt of webbing from which my hatchet dangled during working hours.

Gramshaw turned us into a pack of down-and-outs. Without a trace of physical vanity, he nevertheless spent the better part of an hour a day tittivating himself, believing that as leader he could strengthen morale by looking spry. He shaved daily in hot sea-water, using a cut-throat razor. He wore white flannel shirts, khaki shorts and plimsolls. Like the rest of us, he wore no socks: the sea's gift of plimsolls made them unnecessary, though Ginger clung to his boots. Gramshaw's plimsolls alone were always clean—the hue of the rock. He cleaned them with powdered rock out of which he made a paste, applied with a toothbrush.

When the heat passed, we carried the body of Titch to the biggest crater and buried it in the sand, marking the spot with a board from a crate. There is the oddity that Gramshaw had given no order and there had been no discussion. The whole operation was carried out by tacit consent.

Gramshaw's entries in the log often included comment. Today he had added: *There is general realisation that our hold on life on this island is very precarious.* It seemed to me a senseless remark. Our hold on life was menaced only by the normal risk of accident and disease plus uncertainty whether the ration would last until we were rescued. I did not count the chance of a second murder, because I thought Gramshaw's plan made it impossible.

I had myself made one or two suggestions which he had accepted. There were two danger points in the original plan —danger for the lookout man between the two working parties, and danger for me. Danger, that is, from the imaginary wild man living among the boulders. Actually, neither I nor the lookout man was in any danger, because the one of our party who was the murderer could not leave his work without his partner and the lookout man knowing that he had done so.

The supposed danger to the lookout man arose during his walk from one working point to the other. His path, from a point above the workers on the beach to the fissure on the opposite side of the island, ran about a hundred and twenty yards from the hut and about a dozen yards from the limit of the plateau—that is, very close to where the boulders begin. So the imaginary wild man must be deemed to have had a sporting chance of sneaking up from cover.

I therefore suggested that, on his way, the lookout should give me a shout and receive an answering shout from me. As the lookout was a half-hour spell, I would exchange shouts at fifteen and at forty-five minutes past the hour. We had four good-quality watches between us, to say nothing of an ornamental alarm-clock, so the time-keeping was fairly accurate.

On the second day after the burial, Gramshaw interrupted the routine to set us altogether on an engineering job which involved unpacking the crates of bicycle parts. It was to do with the boat, which was on his mind. There was no present use to be made of it, but it had to be preserved for emergencies.

He had found that the second of the tongues of rock on the north-eastern end of our beach had a natural ramp leading to a ledge close to the cliff-head. At high tide that evening we brought the boat to the edge of the ramp. The others had cobbled the bicycle parts into acting as a block and tackle, wheels providing pulleys and the cogged gears linked together acting as rollers. With the mechanics of it I did not concern myself—to me it seemed something of a conjuring trick when we all pulled on the rope and the boat began to crawl up the ramp. In an hour it had been raised to the ledge and lashed to a belt of rope encircling a boulder.

Gramshaw's plan worked smoothly until the sixth day after the second burial of Titch. The evening spell began at five-thirty. I had received my routine shout from the lookout—Gramshaw himself—at five forty-five, the second shout at six-fifteen from Jim. That meant that Jim, working with Steeve on the beach, had been relieved by Gramshaw.

The next shout, due at six forty-five, should come from Steeve, relieved by Jim.

I was working in the hut, removing the floorboards. They were unreliable as flooring but valuable as fuel, and the rock beneath was flat enough for us to sleep on, until the rains came. It was laborious work—knocking out the nails with the hammer end of a fire-hatchet—and I was making such heavy weather of it that I timed myself. Between five-thirty and six I removed only six boards, an average of five minutes per board. Between six and six-thirty I moved ten boards, bringing my average down to three minutes. At six thirty-six I had done two more, but decided to have a breather of three minutes, equal to one board removed.

That is how I know that the lookout's call actually came at six forty, instead of six forty-five.

It was not Steve's voice, as it ought to have been. It was Gramshaw's. He did not call "Hallo" as we always did, he called "Clobbers!"

When one lives in a void—in a prison-camp or on a desert island—a simple routine soon takes on a quality of inevitability. I was excited and alarmed by this triple breach of routine. I ran out of the hut.

Gramshaw, a hundred yards distant, gave the military signal to double. As I bustled along, Steeve's head and shoulders appeared over the cliff-top as he climbed up from the beach. He reached Gramshaw before I did. They both turned their backs on me, staring downwards.

On the rock, in a puddle of blood, was Jim. He was dead. There was a hole at the back of his head; if not a perfect square, it was certainly rectangular. But this time there was no smear of oil on the hair.

It has become a cliché that nowadays it is impossible for an innocent man to be hanged. Yes and no! An acquittal is often preceded by a protracted retirement of the jury. Why the long discussion if the innocent man has been in no peril? Moreover, most biographies of eminent counsel contain anecdotes of the hairbreadth escape of an innocent client.

I am reducing my own peril to a minimum by making sure that nothing in my disfavour can be brought out in cross-examination. Everything in my disfavour is set down here and emphasised. That is why I find it necessary to record not only events but also my own perspective at the time, even when it has been stultified by later events. "If you thought this, why did you not do that?" I do not intend to be set stammering and floundering by that sort of question, which might be asked—I refuse to deceive myself on this point— in the hearing of a jury.

I imagine that I must have stared at that wound for quite a long time. There is some truth in the phrase "startled out of his wits". I was not thinking. I was mentally gaping at the postulate that Gramshaw's plan—inadequate as it might be against an imaginary wild man—would be certain to detect the murderer in the event of a second murder. The plan had, apparently, failed.

"Didn't you see nothink, Clobbers?" demanded Steeve.

I turned away from the corpse. Gramshaw was waiting for me to answer Steeve's question.

"I was inside the hut, working on the floorboards."

"For how long, Clobbers old boy?"

"For the whole of this shift. I came out just before the three quarter and one quarter, to hail the lookout. I wasn't expecting Steeve's call for another five minutes."

We stood in embarrassed silence, as if we did not know what we were expected to do next.

"Now Clobbers is here, Steeve, you might tell the others —and tell 'em to come up."

I could not fathom Gramshaw's mood. I assumed he was as bewildered as I was myself. When Steeve was out of earshot I asked:

"Where do we go from *here*, Gramshaw?"

"It's our lack of imagination, Clobbers old boy, that's killed Jim. I blame myself, not you. But you did encourage me to laugh at what you called the bogy-man. And this has happened!"

Before I could make any comment, he went on:

"Your being in the hut, apart from the others, left the lookout man—and you, too, in a lesser degree—at the mercy of the wild man. You must have seen that, as I did. But, of course, we neither of us believed in the existence of the wild man—then.''

''I still don't believe in the wild man, Gramshaw.''

''But you *must*—now!''

''I'd as soon believe in Ginger's spooks.''

Gramshaw smiled, a sickly but patient smile.

''Follow me closely, Clobbers old boy. Jim was on lookout six to six-thirty. I was on the beach with Steeve. Jim was due to relieve Steeve. Jim was late. I gave him five minutes' grace, which is a lot on our routine. Then I climbed on to the plateau. I couldn't see anything—not even the body. There's an undulation here to about three feet depth—you didn't see the body from the hut. I decided to explore, and then—in less than a minute I was shouting for you. You didn't hear my first shout, because you were hammering.''

As he said this I had a feeling that he was wrong in point of detail, but I could not then locate the point. He went on: ''So I shouted for Steeve, and when he answered I shouted again for you—and you came out of the hut.''

I nodded, expecting him to continue. But he was waiting for me.

''Where does the wild man come into it, Gramshaw?''

''Try ticking us off on your fingers, Clobbers old boy. There are six of us. I'm on the beach with Steeve. I know Steeve didn't kill Jim and he knows I didn't. That's two. Ginger and Pom are still in the fissure. One of 'em couldn't have come up—come over here and killed Jim, without the other knowing. That's four. Jim himself—five. Six—yourself, in the hut!''

''Good lord, Gramshaw!'' My wits had returned. ''If a wild bogy-man didn't kill Jim, I did!''

Behind my sense of shock was a sense of absurdity. I could not believe in the bogy-man. And I knew I had not killed Jim.

''Either you killed him, or someone not of our party killed him,'' Gramshaw was saying. ''That's why I'm quite certain that there *is* a wild man on the island, Clobbers old boy!''

I might have accepted that as the apotheosis of loyalty to a friend. But I was not thinking noble-mindedly. I was wondering, in fact, why Gramshaw had been so damned reticent about that hammer.

"What sort of weapon d'you think made that wound?" I asked. "Exactly the same wound as Titch's."

"Haven't a notion!" He refused to interest himself in the question. "That'd be a job for a trained detective."

"What sort of weapon could a wild man make—an imbecile, animal-like man—out of this chalky sort of rock? And what could he make it with? His bare hands?"

"I don't suppose he made it. He must have had it with him when he was wrecked."

"Or he might have stolen it from us?"

"He might have. Here come the others."

Again I felt intuitively that I must not force Gramshaw into a corner about that hammer. It was not a deep feeling, but a faintly warning note—the kind of feeling one has with strangers, that it would be wiser to dodge certain topics, without knowing why. I was morally certain that he knew something about that hammer which I did not know. Something which made the bogy-man theory less absurd to him than to me. He leaned on me for mental and moral support in all his difficulties and I resented his keeping something up his sleeve, even if it was only the exact time at which the hammer had disappeared.

Ginger and Pom looked at the body, which was lying face downwards, then joined us, Steeve following them. Gramshaw related all we knew of the circumstances.

"It's the same wound as Titch's!" I contributed.

"An' it wor made by the same hand," said Ginger. "We can't see it in the dark and we can't see it in the light, nayther."

"Chuck it, Ginger!" Pom measured with his eye the distance to the nearest boulder. "Must've slipped from be'ind that one. A good twenty yards. Mus've crept up be'ind Jim, quiet as a cat."

All had seen the wound. All had heard Jim nagging me about the missing hammer—he had kept coming back to the subject every few hours. Again and again that hammer had been thrust into the consciousness of everybody. If they believed in the wild man, why didn't they surmise that he had stolen it from the stores-shed?

"It's no good trying to bury him at sea, boys," said Gramshaw.

"Jim'd come back same as Titch!" giggled Ginger.

There and then we carried the body up to the big crater and buried it in the sand near that of Titch. This time, there was no demand for a burial service.

We drifted back to the hut, one by one, myself substantially in the rear, no one noticing that I was unprotected from the bogy-man! Gramshaw's words began to echo disturbingly in my thoughts. *Either you killed him or he was killed by someone not of our party. That's why I believe there is a wild man.*

I did not believe in the wild man. Therefore I must believe that I killed Jim, without knowing I had done so—which, in fact, I did not believe. But there was some danger that I might come to believe it. This must be tackled systematically.

Let it be granted that I am schizophrenic without knowing it. There must be a lapse of time for which I cannot account. Locate the lapse. I answered Jim's call at six fifteen and Gramshaw's at six forty, both in my normal personality. I have what I will call the illusion that, after answering Jim, I began on the second row of floorboards and that I had removed eighteen when Gramshaw shouted.

According to Ginger and Pom, Jim was alive and talking to them at six twenty-five, when he announced that he was going to relieve Steeve. Allow a couple of minutes for him to stroll to the spot where he was killed and one minute between Gramshaw coming in sight of the spot and shouting to me. Gramshaw did not see me. Therefore we can allow another minute during which I scuttled back to the hut.

At this point in my reconstruction I reached the hut. I counted eighteen floorboards, then returned to my calculations.

Jim must have been killed before six thirty or he would have relieved Steeve. He must have been killed at approximately six twenty-seven. Assume I miscalculated the time on the floorboards by a few minutes—which would be a very big miscalculation. In "a few minutes", centring on six twenty-seven, I have a schizophrenic attack, kill Jim, hide the hammer, completely recover from the attack and resume work on the floorboards.

An assumption a great deal more silly than the assumption of the wild man.

This, of course, does not prove that I did not kill Jim. I do not offer it as such. I offer it in answer to the question "Did you not at any time suspect yourself of homicidal mania?" The answer is, "Yes—for a very bad quarter of an hour."

In the hut nobody was chattering and nobody was sitting down. I had been preoccupied with my own calculations. Gramshaw had tuned in to the general feeling.

"I'm not giving any orders," he exclaimed, "but it's all together or not at all! What about another search for the wild man?"

Steeve and Pom instantly agreed. Ginger giggled.

"I'll join if everybody else wants to," I said with secret reluctance. I was physically tired and there were still chores for me to do.

"What about you, Ginger?"

"I don't mind lookin' for 'un. But it worn't no wild man that killed Jim—nor Titch nayther."

There was a short respite while Gramshaw gave instructions as to what each of us was to do if he came upon the wild man single-handed, and then the senseless search began. We could not keep line among the boulders. We were constantly converging on each other or getting too far apart. Once I blundered upon Gramshaw—saw him some seconds before he saw me. His expression was one of violence. He was holding an open knife behind his back. There was no doubt in my mind that he believed in the wild man.

It was dusk when we got back to the hut. While I was serving the rations, Ginger suggested that they should be doubled.

"Double the supper ration, Clobbers old boy. It's certainly been a heavy day."

"And double tomorrer, Mr. Gramshaw, barrin' supper."

49

"No," said Gramshaw. "We must build a reserve for when we have specially hard work."

"They rations," giggled Ginger, " 'ull last longer than us who'm meant to eat 'em."

I do not offer Ginger as one possessed of "second sight", nor of any other mystic powers, if such exist. He believed in his own superstition—considered on that basis his prophecies were intelligent deductions. And some of them came off.

"I told you to keep your trap shut on that stuff!" snapped Gramshaw. "We are faced with a purely practical danger. We're being sniped—as soldiers are sniped in the bush and the jungle. The one who's in most danger is Clobbers. He mustn't be left alone in this hut any more."

The next day, without consulting me, Gramshaw altered the routine. The wild man, he said, would never tackle two of us. The lookout man had been a mistake. I must join in the early-morning shift on the seaweed. There would be no second shift. In the evening we would all remain in the vicinity of the hut, sharing my chores and preparing the fishing lines. If the latter continued to fail we would all go in the boat and try deep water.

My first shift was with Ginger on the beach. He showed me how to cut the seaweed and lift it without waste. He had a tolerant patience which made him a good teacher. I learnt quickly enough to satisfy him, though I was giving him only part of my attention.

I did not kill Jim. Nor did any bogy-man. The other four had been paired off. No one of them had said to his partner: "I'm going to leave you for a few minutes in order to murder Jim; don't tell the others."

Never mind who killed Jim. By what means did one man contrive to leave his partner without the partner knowing at the time, or afterwards?

There was the theoretical possibility of conspiracy. Gramshaw and Steeve. Or Pom and Ginger. Conspiracy made the whole thing a physically simple matter. In point of common sense it was untenable. One could hardly postulate two homicidal maniacs. One might as well stick to the bogy-man.

Suddenly I realised that, while I had been stating the case to myself, I had been unconscious of the presence of Ginger. The killer could have sneaked up behind him and killed him without my noticing.

Ginger was some twelve feet away. He had given me a salient of rock to myself. I was in his line of vision. I edged backwards, working at the seaweed. Then I dropped down on the sand below the salient so that he could not see me.

I took out my watch. No fewer than eleven minutes passed before he appeared round the salient.

"I'm not as strong as you, Ginger!" I apologised. "My arms have gone numb."

"Maybe that's along o' you havin' a gun under your shirt." Again that nerve-tearing giggle. "That gun's a foolishness, Clobbers—there ain't nuthin' f'r you to shoot as 'ud feel the bullet!"

The man was ten times as observant as the town men. Fortunately his obsession made him assume that I packed the gun as a protection against spooks. The same obsession robbed those eleven minutes of value as evidence. Ginger did not believe that the killer was visible to the human eye and therefore saw no sense in Gramshaw's precautions. If I were to fall down dead at his feet with a gaping wound at the back of my head he would be unsurprised—would accept it as confirmation of his theory.

For the rest of the day I followed that train of thought along different lines. In the hut, a man was deemed to be in sight if he were in sight of the windows. Before the heat came, Pom volunteered to dump the garbage that could not be used for fuel. I was nursing the fire; the others were in the hut. Pom carried it to the north-west side and dumped it in deep water. I myself did not realise until he returned that he had necessarily been out of sight for about four minutes.

During the heat, Steeve fiddled incessantly with the cards, now and again throwing improvised darts at the darts-board. Pom would sleep or try to coax dance music from one of the radio sets. Ginger was always making something, even if it was only the fish-hooks which never caught a fish. Gramshaw would post his log. I typed messages to be enclosed in bottles, entering the number of the bottle and the date and the state of the tide when it was launched, and the date of its return. I was amused by the mathematical freak of the odd numbers turning up on the beach nearly always a tide ahead of the even numbers. I concealed this fact from Ginger.

For the evening shift we tackled the floorboards en masse. They were all much quicker at it than I had been, though everyone worked very slowly, owing to their half-starved condition.

It was during the five-minute rests that a man would amble out of sight for a couple of minutes or more.

When the floorboards had all been removed, we saw that the rock sloped perceptibly in the direction of the door. Our floor would drain itself when the rains came.

The next job was concerned with fishing—which pleased nobody. Gramshaw's original theory was that, even with bad luck, we would catch small fish suitable for bait. But there had been no small fish, and there was, in effect, no food waste from our meagre rations.

"You'm be throwin' good food after bad, Mr. Gramshaw," said Ginger. "There baint no fish hereabouts, for there baint nothin' to come inshore to feed on."

"We're using pieces of rag, Ginger," answered Gramshaw, "smeared in my bully ration for tonight. Cut off my ration, will you, Clobbers old boy?"

It was dramatic and effective. At the first opportunity I congratulated him.

"You'll share my bully ration tonight, Gramshaw, and if you refuse I shall give the lot to Ginger."

I must emphasise that this was not a gesture. Like everybody else I was perpetually hungry—the ration gave us just enough strength to go on being hungry. He was the kind of man whom, in normal circumstances, I would go far to avoid. Nevertheless, after a few days on the island, I had begun to reciprocate his genuine friendship. His childish belief in the bogy-man had touched my emotional being, because it had been created by his faith in me—by the refusal of his imagination to envisage the possibility of my being a murderer.

The fishing lines were of string and of thin rope. There were upwards of a score, each carrying some half-dozen hooks of different sizes made out of the table knives. We laid five on the beach at low tide, then straggled across the island to lay the rest in deep water.

In the north-west, precipitous side there were a number of fissures. The biggest was the one we were working for seaweed. It began with a narrow, steeply sloping gully and fanned out into salients of rock very rich in seaweed. At a guess there would be another month's work for us in clearing it.

While we were laying the lines, I kept glancing at my watch, noting the number of minutes any one person would be out of sight of the others, concealed by an outcrop of rock. Before we had finished I had established the principle that men, working even desultorily, cannot keep continually conscious of the exact whereabouts of each other.

We returned to the hut with two hours of daylight in hand. I read Gramshaw's log, wondering what he had said about the death of Jim.

6.30: Jim failed to report. 6.35: I climbed to the ledge to look for him. 6.37 (approx): I found his body, wound identical (refer description 4th inst.). 6.38: Could hear Cl. hammering, in removing floorboards of hut 120 yards away; shouted to Cl., who did not hear me; ran back and called Steeve, then back to body. 6.40: Called Cl., who answered and came from hut.

Again came the feeling that the record was wrong at some point. Suddenly I remembered that between six thirty-six and Gramshaw's shout at six forty I had been taking a breather. Therefore he could not have heard me hammering at six thirty-eight.

At that moment I did not regard this as important. Gramshaw was a few minutes out in his reckoning, that was all.

In bed that night I worked it out. Jim had left Steeve and Pom at six twenty-five. It would not have taken him more than three minutes at the outside to cover the whole distance to the others. Why should Jim linger, for about ten minutes, on or near the spot where he was killed? For one thing, Gramshaw would have cursed him for not keeping time. For another, all the men were very scrupulous about relieving each other.

Jim had almost certainly walked straight from point to point and would have arrived not later than six twenty-seven if he had not been killed on the way.

Was Steeve conscious of Gramshaw's exact whereabouts on the beach at, say, six thirty-six? If he had been unaware of Gramshaw for as little as three minutes, Gramshaw could have killed Jim and returned to the beach by six thirty.

By the same reasoning, if Gramshaw had been unaware of Steeve for the same three minutes, Steeve could have killed Jim.

So far—ignoring the bogy-man nonsense—the evidence would weigh about equally against the three of us—in the eyes of a fourth person—with slight odds in my favour, as the other two were nearer. I alone knew that if one of the three of us killed Jim, the killer must be Gramshaw or Steeve.

The devil of it was that I could not put the most indirect questions to Gramshaw. The bogy-man theory made it impossible to question anybody.

Besides, it was the kind of question which could not produce a reliable answer. A man could hardly say that he had been "aware that he was unaware" of another man's proximity.

The next morning I caught myself out being "aware of unawareness". I was working in the fissure with Steeve and Pom—Ginger and Gramshaw taking the beach. I was on the left wing, Steeve in the middle and Pom the other side of Steeve. Had I been alone with Steeve I would have watched him consciously the whole time, taking good care that he did not get behind me.

Pom and I were both working on outcrops fifty yards apart, approached by separate chimneys from the plateau. Every time I looked up I could not avoid seeing him, and vice versa. I was already sufficiently practised to be able to cut the seaweed without thinking about it. My conscious thought was devoted to trying to find a flaw in my own theory of how Jim had been killed. While I was trying out possibilities of error I felt a vague nagging at myself—such as I might have felt if I were missing out some process in cutting the seaweed. Then, with a laugh at myself, I realised that, possibly for some twenty minutes, I had been unaware of the exact whereabouts of *Steeve*.

I looked round. He was working on the other side of my outcrop within a few feet of me.

"How much have we done, Clobbers, mate?" he asked.

I glanced at my watch.

"There's another ten full minutes to go," I answered. "It's twelve seconds yet to the twenty past. Good lord—look round, Steeve!"

On the cliff-top, some thirty feet above us, stood Ginger.

Ginger cupped his hands, though it was unnecessary, and bellowed down at us.

"Maister Gramshaw sprained his ankle. We must carry 'un home."

"You go back to 'im, Ginger!" shouted Steeve. "You oughtn't to've left him, yer grassfed son of a cattle louse! Come on, Clobbers. Never mind the blaggin' seaweed."

"There's no great hurry—a sprained ankle isn't much."

"We dunno who might get at 'im—Ginger leavin' him alone like that! I'm off." Over his shoulder he called, "*Hi*, Pom, we're knockin' off!"

I followed at a reasonable speed. I could not hurry up that chimney. I could only get up at all, unaided, by using my hatchet as an alpenstock. I was, I suppose, about three minutes behind Steeve and was therefore surprised to see that he had not descended to the beach.

"The skipper ain't 'ere," he shouted.

When I drew level, we both looked over the ledge.

"Where's the skipper?" repeated Steeve.

"We'd better look among the rocks."

Between the tongues of rock, jutting into the sea, was smooth sand. We shouted as we scrambled over the rocks and ran over the sand. We reached the sand on the far side of the fifth and last tongue.

"What's the ga-ime, Clobbers, mate?"

"We've missed him somehow—we'll go back on our tracks."

"Hey, Clobbers! If a sprained ankle is like what you said, he won't be unconscious. He'd 'a' heard us shoutin'." Before I could answer he added: "It's that son of a cattle-louse leavin' 'im. Shan't see the skipper again!"

We did see him again. I saw him first, at the second tongue of rock. He was lying in the shadow of the ledge on which our lifeboat had been dry-docked.

"Gramshaw!" I shouted. A hand moved, then the other, and he sat up as we hurried to him.

"You gave us a shock, man!" I exclaimed. "Didn't you hear us shouting the first time?"

"So sorry! I heard you and tried to get up—trod on the wrong foot and went down again—must have fainted."

"We thought he'd got you, Mr. Gramshaw, after Ginger had left you alone," said Steeve.

"Not this time, Steeve," grinned Gramshaw. "You fellers haven't enough work, so here's a casualty for you. Skidded on a bit of seaweed. Ginger brought me here. I thought I could hop up to the ramp, but I can't."

"Rough luck, Gramshaw! Hurts like the devil, doesn't it?"

"Only when I stand on it. I expect it'll crock me for at least a couple of days."

"We'll get you up between us!" I said, though I had not the least idea how we would do it. "Where's Ginger? We thought he had run on ahead of us."

"We'll never get 'im up there," said Steeve. "Carry 'im along the sand to the other track, crossed hands. Come on, Clobbers, mate! Let's get crackin' before Pom comes. He and Ginger can take second spell. If we start now, we'll get a breather."

"Are those two together?" asked Gramshaw.

"Pom was up on that bit o' rock. He'd got to go down, then up again. Slippery job, too!"

"Ginger may be with him," I contributed. "But we thought he had hurried back to you."

"We'll wait till they come," said Gramshaw, looking at his

watch. I did the same. For forty seconds Steeve chattered, and then was silent. We were all three silent for six minutes.

"What the hell!" cried Steeve. He climbed on to the plateau and looked ahead of him, then southwards.

"Cor, 'ere they are! Ginger, anyway. Carrying some stuff."

Presently Ginger appeared on the ledge, a floorboard under his arm and coils of rope over his shoulder.

"Good work, Ginger!" applauded Gramshaw. "Is Pom with you?"

"I hain't seen Pom. I thought 'un was with Clobbers an' Steeve."

I looked at Gramshaw. His mouth was twitching.

"We'll get you back first," I said in an undertone, so that the two on the ledge could not hear. Gramshaw nodded.

"Pom must 'a sprained 'is blaggin' ankle too!" ejaculated Steeve.

It took us ten minutes to lift Gramshaw some twenty feet up the cliff without hurting him, my own share in the work being honourable in intention only.

"Clobbers! You 'eard me shout to Pom after Ginger 'ad told us?"

"Yes."

"Did you 'ear Pom shout back?"

There was a clamant urgency in Steeve's voice. On the premise that Steeve had killed Jim—and Pom, if Pom should turn out to be dead—not to mention Titch—I now had to believe that Steeve was a good actor with excellent voice control. Which took a lot of swallowing.

"Clobbers, I'm askin' yer."

"Shut up, Steeve, I'm thinking!" I was reconstructing the moment following Ginger's announcement from the cliff-head. "No—I did not hear Pom answer."

"Cor! That's awright, then! He hadn't got no watch and he don't know yet that we've knocked off. He couldn't've seen us climbing up from where he was."

"That settles that, then!" chirped Gramshaw. "I'm in your hands, boys."

When we perched him astride the floorboard, the board cracked in the middle.

"That's beaten us!" exclaimed Gramshaw, and glanced at his watch. It was the kind of triviality he always logged in detail.

"Don't you worry, maister!" Ginger took charge. Telling me to hold one end of a rope and Steeve the middle, he made a sort of cat's-cradle. He took my hatchet and, with a single stroke, produced from the broken floorboard two firm sticks, so that Steeve and I could carry at one end of the cradle and he at the other. The whole job took him less than a couple of minutes. Ginger's slowness was an illusion.

At the hut, I helped Gramshaw to hop to his bedding.

"Clobbers old boy, could you see Pom when Steeve shouted?"

"Yes—no—yes—wait a minute!"

Ginger and Steeve were outside the hut. Ginger was hacking out a rough crutch from a floorboard. I was trying to give Gramshaw an accurate answer.

"Every time I looked up from my work I saw Pom—three-quarter face, so he could also see me. Seeing him became mechanical. I don't remember individual occasions on which I saw him. I don't remember seeing him—that is, I don't remember looking consciously in his direction—after Ginger turned up."

"Nor immediately before?"

"Nor immediately before!"

"I say, Clobbers old boy! You know how fearfully important it is for us to guard each other?"

"I do, but it's impossible to keep one's attention fixed for a whole hour when you're spread out. I've checked on myself and others, including you. The funny part is that I did pull myself up for not keeping a tab on Steeve—found that I was 'aware that I was unaware' of his exact position. That was before Ginger appeared."

"After you'd pulled yourself up like that—did you see Pom again?"

"I must have. But it didn't register in the consciousness. Sit back and I'll take your shoe off."

As I began to unlace the plimsoll, I noticed that he was wearing socks. I removed the shoe as carefully as I could.

"I'll pull the sock off, if you can stand it. You'll have to have that ankle bathed and bandaged."

"That's out of date. Nowadays, the medicos advise you to leave it absolutely alone and let nature do the work. I say, Clobbers old boy——"

"Well?"

"Pom! I feel in my bones it has *happened*. It's three-quarters of an hour since you and Steeve left him."

I nodded, then called to Steeve.

"Let's go and tell Pom he's working overtime."

As we set out together I determined to keep conscious of Steeve the whole time, particularly to take care that he should never be behind me. I kept dropping behind him on the chance of spotting the outline of a hammer.

We did not find Pom.

From the cliff-head we could have seen anyone on the spurs who was not deliberately hiding from us.

"He's gone, Clobbers. What say we go down and make sure! You take this end, and I'll take the other."

We were to make separate descents and would lose sight of each other. He was much more agile in slipping about on the rocks. He might slip behind me.

"Rotten, Steeve! The wild man might pounce on either of us singly. We'll stick together. And we'll begin at Pom's end. You go down first."

"You scared o' the wild man, Clobbers?"

"Yes. So are you, if you have any sense."

I led him to the point where Pom had been working. We found nothing. Back towards the cliff-face, then across a sloping shelf, a couple of feet above the deep water, to the next spur.

"*This is it!* Cor!"

In a dip in the shelf was a pool of blood.

"Got 'im here an' tipped 'im into the ditch!" gasped Steeve.

From the shelf where we were standing, which gave on to the second spur, I could see nearly the whole of the third

59

spur, on which Steeve had been working. Pom, obviously, had been enticed to the shelf. It was not on his way to the chimney by which he would ascend to the cliff-head.

"The skipper will want a full report for the log," I said. "We'll go to where you were working and where I was working."

Steeve led on. At the end of the shelf we had to do a bit of clambering.

"I was down there, look!" He pointed. "I could've seen anyone on that shelf, plain as anythink."

"That's what I can't make out!" I said carefully. "Were you there the whole time?"

"Barrin' about the last five minutes when I started on the near side of where you was. You could see that shelf, couldn't yer?"

"I don't remember. Let's find out."

We climbed to the point where I had been working.

"No, the shelf is hidden by that shoulder of number 3. But I could see Pom himself all the time. I must have seen him if he had walked back across the top of the spur to get to the shelf."

"Nothink in that, Clobbers, mate. He didn't hear me call. Maybe a wave splashed—you do get 'em sometimes even in a calm like this. He stayed where 'e was and was scuppered after we'd gone."

It might have been so. For convenience I told Steeve he was right.

Ginger was outside the hut, carpentering, when we got back. He did not ask for news.

"We'll be seein' 'un on the beach—come tide after next!" he remarked.

I ran into the hut to dodge that nerve-racking giggle. Gramshaw was sitting at the table, his leg on a packing-case, writing his log. He made no comment at all on my report but resumed his writing as if I had not spoken.

During the heat, he hopped to his bedding and lay down. I read the log.

I had already decided that my own evidence as to Pom's whereabouts was unreliable after six fifteen. On the assumption that Steeve was the murderer, the whole of his evidence was unreliable. On the more probable assumption of his innocence, his evidence would be substantially true but inaccurate. When he said five minutes, the period might be two minutes or ten.

The log noted that while Ginger cut the seaweed, Gramshaw had been binding and carrying it to the point where it would be hauled to the plateau, some thirty yards from where they were working.

6.5: I slipped and twisted my ankle; could not continue working. Ginger tried to help me to foot of ascent; attempt abandoned. 6.10: Sent Ginger to prepare means of hauling me up cliff and thence to hut and to call other three, working in fissure. 6.30: Cl. and Steeve arrived on beach. Not seeing me, they shouted. I tried to show myself but fell; hurt ankle afresh; apparently fainted. 6.38: Cl. and Steeve found me. I failed to notice Pom's absence. 6.45: Ginger arrived with extra rope and floorboard.

I too went to my bedding, to rest my back, which was aching badly. For the next couple of hours I was so absorbed in my calculations that I was barely aware of the heat. In the end I achieved not a conclusion but an approach—a means of thinking about the problem, a standpoint.

The three murders—Titch, Jim and (assumed) Pom—were the work of one man, not one in conspiracy with another.

The use of the same weapon in the same way did not justify my previous suspicion that the murders were obsessional. The murderer's brain might be as normal as any murderer's brain can be.

Prove that a man *cannot* have committed any one of the murders and he is thereby proved innocent of any other murder, no matter how strong the *prima facie* case against him may be in respect of any one murder. Take my own case, for example, as seen by an outsider. In those circumstances, as detailed in the log, it had been just physically possible for me to kill Jim, but it had not been physically possible for me to kill Pom. To do so, I would have had to pass Steeve and do the deed—on the shelf—in circumstances in which Steeve would have seen the act if he had happened to look up from his work.

61

Titch: There was no *prima facie* case against anyone.

Jim: At the time of the discovery of the murder, a strong case against Gramshaw, Steeve and myself, severally; a not so strong case against Pom and Ginger because, with the climb and the walk there and back, the murderer would have been out of sight of his companion for a total of ten minutes or more.

The death of Pom eliminated Pom and myself from suspicion in the matter of Jim.

The death of Pom also eliminated Gramshaw. It was obviously impossible for that murder to have been committed by a man hopping long distances on one leg. I was quite certain that I had observed Pom later than six five, when Gramshaw sprained his ankle.

Therefore Pom had been killed by Steeve or by Ginger.

Given that Steeve could have thought of some trick for inducing Pom to leave his work and go to the shelf, the rest would have been easy. But there was no evidence at all that Steeve had, in fact, done so. As in the case of Jim, it would have been enormously easier for Steeve to commit the murder than for Ginger. This was noteworthy, but in itself proved nothing. Only the uneducated mind believes that the simpler of two explanations must be the true one.

When the heat lifted we did no work but the hut chores. Not until the following evening, when the body of Pom had been washed ashore and buried in the crater, did Gramshaw hold his inquiry.

Steeve and I told our respective tales, Steeve emphasising that he could see me during the whole of the spell whenever he cared to look, but could not see Pom. In the same way, the shelf had been in his line of vision.

"Then Pom must have been alive when you and Clobbers left the fissure?" asked Gramshaw.

"O' course he was alive, Mr. Gramshaw!" Steeve could conceive of no mental state between total certainty and total ignorance. "He didn't hear me shout, and he didn't see us go. The wild man slipped down the crack after Clobbers and I'd gone."

"But you didn't leave together?"

"Well, Clobbers was about three minutes behind me, bein'
slower on the rocks, but that don't make no difference, Mr.
Gramshaw."

"Even so, Pom wouldn't have walked on to that shelf—
which was out of his way—if he had seen the wild man. He
must have been taken by surprise. And there's no hiding-place
at that point. Why do you think he went to that shelf?"

"Search me, guv'nor!" This was the state of total ignorance.
"Only that's 'ow it 'appened, betcher life!"

The absurdity of supposing that Pom had allowed a wild
man, whom he knew to be a murderer, to entice him to a
convenient spot, did not embarrass Steeve. I could see from
Gramshaw's face that he perceived the absurdity. I wondered
again whether he really believed in the bogy-man.

I said nothing on the point. This inquiry ran us into the
original danger of being successful and having to face the
insoluble problem of how to deal with the detected murderer.

This danger loomed up large when Ginger's turn came.
Gramshaw dealt with him perfunctorily. But I knew that it
would make trouble for us with the authorities if we were to
pass those entries in the log without explanation.

"We've got the times wrong somewhere, Gramshaw," I
said. "Ginger may be able to put us right. In the log, you've
entered that your accident occurred at six five and that you
sent Ginger to fetch us at six ten."

Gramshaw opened the log-book, checked and agreed.

"When Ginger called to us from the cliff, it was six twenty-
five. It can't take more than a minute or so to walk from one
side to the other. What happened, Ginger?"

"Nowt happened," answered Ginger, and would have left
it at that but for Gramshaw.

"Why did it take you so long, Ginger?" he asked.

"It didn't take me no longer 'n it would ha' taken Clobbers,
once I started. I did lose a bit o' time down at the hut, though
I couldn' see there were no special hurry."

"Then you went to the hut before you went to the cliff-
head?" I asked.

"Aye, and after I'd been there too! I wor tryin' to make a
seat for Mr. Gramshaw out o' that spare sailcloth, only it

ripped when I put strain on 'un, on account o' oil bein' spilt. Soon as it ripped, somethin' came into my mind." The falsetto giggle now had a ring of genuine amusement. "It wor your talk about that wild man that came into my mind. An' this watchin' each other for what we'll never see. I reckoned Maister Gramshaw hisself might be gettin' scared, layin' on the beach alone, so I gave up and went to call you and Steeve. Then I went back to get that floorboard and the ropes, which you had left in a fair tangle, else I'd a' bin back to Mr. Gramshaw afore you."

If that was true, my own case against Steeve was complete. But how on earth was I to discover whether it were true or not? I could arrange facts in a logical pattern as well as any detective, but I was wholly without the latter's specialised ability to ferret out new facts.

"I don't think we need alter the log, Clobbers old boy," said Gramshaw. "The essential times are all recorded. If you'll write the report on the facts we've together assembled I think we shall have done all the authorities require of us. Unless anybody else has something to say?"

He did not expect an answer but one came, from Ginger.

"I've nobut this to say, Mr. Gramshaw. We wor seven when we come to this yere island. We'm four now. To my way o' reck'nin', allowing I may be wrong, that should oughter be double rations for all every day, barrin' one in seven."

"No!" said Gramshaw firmly. "We've had a setback in not catching any fish. Until we can find a means of catching them, our lives depend on our reserve of food."

Ginger glowered at Gramshaw like an angry child.

"They'm laughin' at us, starvin' ourselves when there's plenty. Maybe they'd leave us alone if we showed some sense."

That night Gramshaw took a tot of rum. There were still five unopened cases of spirits. Since the death of Titch there had been very little drinking—which was the more remarkable because Gramshaw had not rationed the spirits. Anyone was free to help himself. This strange abstinence would have imperilled my bottle-launching chore but for the fact that the bottles always came back. Out of a total of seventeen, of which eight had contained fruit, I had lost only three.

Ginger's eye fastened on the bottle of rum. Steeve and I had a tot each to keep Gramshaw company. Ginger eventually finished the bottle. He was a very orderly drunk. This, illogically, increased my suspicion of him. Enough of my normal self had survived for me to be ashamed. Was I falling into the uneducated fallacy of assuming that any slightly unusual characteristic must be the hallmark of the murderer?

Oddly enough, I felt no physical fear, though I have no pretensions whatever to physical bravery. I believed that, thanks to the revolver which never left me, I need only take care that no man had a chance to creep up behind me. But I was the prey of a kind of moral fear contained in the knowledge that we were living cheek by jowl with a multiple murderer and could do nothing about it except watch our backs.

The dried seaweed made a good slow fuel, provided it was carefully picked out. It was useless for cooking or making tea, but it would keep the sea-water steaming into the condenser for twenty-four hours, when subsidised with half a pound of packing-case or floorboard splinters. Ginger had made a beam-balance and cut wooden weights, taking a packaged pound of raisins for standard. When the drying seaweed slithered off the roof, it was Ginger who devised a thatch, thereby making the hut perceptibly cooler. To Ginger we owed a number of crudely fashioned but helpful gadgets.

"We'll let up on the cutting for a few days," said Gramshaw the following morning, "and bring the stuff closer in."

"We've cut enough seaweed to last for a year," I told him at the first opportunity.

"I know. But we have to make work, Clobbers old boy, or we shall go melancholy mad. My foot will be all right in a couple of days. Then we can start deep-sea fishing."

"In our present state," I pointed out, "I doubt whether we're strong enough to row against the currents."

"What're we going to *do*?" moaned Gramshaw. "We can't sleep for more than about a third of the time at the most. The radio is running down, too."

I tried to think of something while we were bringing in the seaweed. There were large dumps of it above the two collecting points. We dragged light loads held together by serge, taking turn about, one of us staying near the hut, pairing with Gramshaw. The pairs were Ginger and Steeve, Ginger and I, Steeve and I. On these trips to the dump on the fissure and back with the load, it was not necessary to guard my back. We were not spaced out, as we were when cutting the seaweed. We were within six feet of each other the whole time. The murderer could not have returned alone, with a story of how the wild man had struck and disappeared.

Without planning, we had stumbled upon the only effective means of protection. In future we would be all four together or in two pairs, each man, in effect, answerable for his partner's life.

Before the killer could operate, he would have to find a means of upsetting this grouping.

In the meantime there was the small but important duty to keep ourselves occupied. During siesta I thought up a job which could be made to seem necessary. When the heat passed I made an oration, like one of Gramshaw's.

"We're off the sea-lanes. And we're off the air-lines. But what about aircraft carriers? They like exercising in out-of-the-way waters, so that no one can observe them. No false hopes, mind!—it's very unlikely to happen. But I have the feeling that we ought to go half-way towards meeting any luck that might turn up unexpectedly. By the laws of chance we're about due for a bit o' luck. We ought to set up a plant so that we could send up a smoke signal. What does the skipper think?"

"Fine, Clobbers old boy!" Whether Gramshaw really had any hope of a military aircraft happening along just when we wanted it, I never knew. "We'll start at once. Good lord, why didn't I think of it myself? I ought to have."

"That's all right, skipper!" chortled Steeve. "There ain't been no aircraft about since we bin on the island."

Ginger emitted his abominable falsetto laugh. Steeve turned on him.

"Your spooks 'ad any practice with aircraft, mate?"

Ginger thought it over.

"It won't do us no 'arm with them if they see we do be tryin' to get off their island."

"We must go into committee over this!" Gramshaw got up and hopped to the table. "We want a pile of small splinters that will fire quickly. There's a hell of a lot of that serge. That'd make the best smoke. We have to find a means of breaking the column of smoke. Three short, three long, three short. That's the SOS."

The next day, Gramshaw was able to walk, with a limp. Even the limp, I noticed, was intermittent. When he became enthusiastic in directing operations, he would walk normally.

This, I thought, was a tactical mistake. While he was unable to work, there was more work for the others—which was what we wanted. He had, in fact, recovered too quickly.

He decided to invest one whole packing-case in splinters for the fire. It made a respectable pile of splinters. While we were working on the problem of the smoke, Steeve contributed a suggestion.

"Suppose 'e flies over after dark? We'll want fire then, not smoke."

In time they knocked together a contraption by which the serge could be flung clear of the splinters in a single movement. The whole plant was set twenty feet from the hut. In a tobacco tin was our one remaining box of matches, so that there should be no delay in starting the blaze.

I was surprised that Gramshaw was so enthusiastic. He was intelligent enough to know that the chance of the alarm being used was utterly negligible. I had observed earlier that he possessed the power of planting an idea in his own head and forcing himself to believe in it. Ginger worked with a will. Steeve was as keen as Gramshaw. Even after the work was finished he chattered endlessly about it and constantly suggested improvements.

There followed a period of eleven days, different from the other periods. The mystic phase had passed into an astonishing unity. We behaved like a family. We did little work and did it all together: very rarely did we pair, and then only for a few minutes. Even I had the feeling that rescue was imminent though I knew there was no justification. For the gramophone that had no records I drew a rough design which enabled Steeve and Ginger to turn the revolving table into the crude semblance of a roulette board. We played for forfeits, mainly the carrying up of sea-water. The loser would be watched by all three while he paid.

For me the sequence of events which ended this phase is symbolised by a vivid dream. The psychologists say that a man who tells his dreams tells the truth about himself to those who can read it. So be it! I dreamed that I was in full academic dress, cap, gown and robes, standing beside an admiral in gold braid who addressed me confidentially: "They're all asleep, Clobbers old boy, and we can't wait. I'll send over an aircraft."

"*Aircraft!*"

That, beyond all doubt, was Gramshaw's voice. The outlines of Ginger's boots scuttled past the foot of my bedding.

"Wot did I tell yer!" yelled Steeve. "We're goin' 'ome!"

Then Gramshaw's voice from outside the hut:

"*Clob*-bers! Where are the matches?"

I ran out of the hut, put my hand on the tobacco tin. I could hear no engine.

"Are you sure, Gramshaw?"

"Light up!" he bellowed, and I obeyed.

"I 'eard 'im after Mr. Gramshaw shouted!" claimed Steeve, convincing only himself. "Miles over there beyond the wreck, it sounded like."

"If we can't hear him, he's too far off to see the fire," I suggested.

"Not necessarily!" snapped Gramshaw. He was excited and ill-tempered. "Besides, if it's a fleet exercise there may be others. And they'll fly in a circle and come back to the carrier. Get another packing-case, Clobbers."

There were three packing-cases on the other side of the shed. It would be madness to sacrifice them for anything short of a moral certainty. With much misgiving I brought one.

68

"We can't afford to keep a blaze going indefinitely," I grumbled.

"Quite right, Clobbers old boy!" He had better control of himself now. "I'm going up The Knob to listen. Break up the case, but don't put it on until I flash my torch—one long and three short. Repeat!"

"One long and three short. But we've plenty of dry seaweed —I'll use it until you flash."

Gramshaw approved and hurried off.

"Did you hear an engine, Ginger?" I asked.

"Somethin' did wake me up afore Mr. Gramshaw shouted out." His admission was guarded. "Kind of a roar like, on'y quiet. I'm not sayin' it wor an airyplane."

I went to the shed for my hatchet. Steeve was alone when I returned to the now fading fire.

"If that plane come off a ship, it'll fly back to the ship! Means it'll come back over 'ere. Stands to reason!"

"I hope you're right, Steeve." I began to break up the packing-case.

"Can't hear nothin', with you makin' that bleedin' row!"

He moved off, but not towards the hut, as I was careful to observe.

The blaze was dying down. As I noticed this, I felt for the first time a spasm of physical fear. After a second or so the panic faded into a dull dread.

"Gramshaw on The Knob is not more than seventy yards away," I reminded myself. "He can see me as clearly as if I were standing in a lighted room. If anyone were to creep up behind me he would bellow a warning and I would have time to shoot."

I put my hand on the butt of the revolver, then laughed at myself. The killer would know that Gramshaw could see him and therefore would not make the attempt.

That was very reasonable, but the dull dread remained. The fire now was hardly blazing at all, though there was a good red glow. The nearest seaweed was on the roof of the hut. The glow would not reach as far as that. I must get that seaweed—there was nearly an hour to endure before dawn.

I had left my torch in my bedding and I needed light. Against orders which I had accepted, knowing that my act was dishonourable and even treacherous, I threw half a dozen large splinters of packing-case on to the fire. As the dry wood crackled into flame, I ran to the hut, pulled down an armful of seaweed with the hatchet; then back to recover the hatchet and bring a second armful. I must make that last until dawn.

It was tricky work. The seaweed was black and brittle and would crackle and flame at first: then it would settle into a dull glow. I was fairly expert in this fuel. I knew how to ventilate it so that it would continue to produce fitful flame. I managed to keep a light strong enough to illumine to a radius of six or eight feet.

I kept moving round the fire, irregularly, never completing a circle. I confess that I was in the grip of a superstitious fantasy—that if I could live until dawn I would eventually be rescued and return to normal life.

At regular intervals I glanced in the direction of The Knob, against the remote possibility of Gramshaw signalling the approach of an aircraft. Twice I wheeled round with the gun in my hand, but as soon as my back was to the light I saw that there was no one within ten feet of me. After this I did not face the fire directly, stood sideways while I tended the fuel.

I was wondering uneasily whether the fuel would last, when I became aware that dawn had already broken. I moved away from the fire to help my eyes with the half light.

Gramshaw was on top of The Knob, flapping his arms to warm himself. I waved and he waved back, then slithered down The Knob.

"Aha! Nothing to report so far, Clobbers old boy. Keeps you up on your toes knowing that you may hear it any minute." He had obviously enjoyed himself, and wanted more. "I think we ought to post a listening guard for at least another six hours. I'll do the first hour myself. What about a spot of tea?"

"Righto, I'll get it ready."

"Where are the others?"

"I don't know. I've been glued to this fire. In the hut asleep, I expect."

Gramshaw laughed immoderately.

"You've libelled your comrades, Clobbers old boy. There's Steeve, anyhow!"

He pointed to the northwest side. A hundred yards away was a clear outline of Steeve squatting—looking, even in the half-light, as if he were deep in thought.

"He looks like Rodin's 'Thinker', but actually he is incapable of thought. I bet he's asleep. He'll wake up with pneumonia." I shouted: "Tea up, Steeve!"

There was no answer. Gramshaw shouted, without effect.

"Quite right, Clobbers. He *is* asleep."

As he spoke, we looked at each other. The next moment we were both running full speed across the plateau.

Gramshaw got there first.

"God!" he moaned. He nearly overbalanced, trying to avoid stepping in the blood. "Oh God, I can't stick it!"

I gave him a few seconds to pull himself together, then rubbed his nose in the truth.

"You can stick it at least as well as I can, Gramshaw, if you'll drop this childish nonsense about a bogy-man. Ginger killed Steeve. And Jim. And Pom. And Titch."

Gramshaw strode half a dozen paces from the body, turned his back on it. He shook himself violently, suggesting a dog shaking off water.

"We've got to talk this out, now we've started. I've got to say just what's in my mind at this moment, Clobbers old boy. Ginger accused you of killing Titch on the ground that it had been possible for you to do so. You now accuse Ginger on the same ground."

"Ginger had no proof. I have."

Gramshaw shook his head.

"We're civilised men—or try to be. We can't accuse a fellow man on the principle of 'if he didn't, who did?' "

"If he didn't who did?" I echoed. "Did I? You were on The Knob waiting to signal me. Facing in my direction. You know I didn't budge from that fire except for less than a minute when I collected the seaweed."

"Y-yes. But that's incomplete. I mean, if it comes to bedrock, you don't know that I was on The Knob the whole time, because you couldn't see me."

"I don't know whether you spent more than a few minutes on that Knob. But I do know that you did not kill Steeve, because I know that you couldn't possibly have killed Pom. I know he was cutting seaweed at least ten minutes after you had sprained your ankle."

"What the devil has Pom to do with it?"

"And from Steeve's evidence at your inquiry, you know with equal certainty that I could not possibly have killed Pom."

"Why d'you keep dragging in Pom?"

Gramshaw was an emotional man who was very little more capable than Steeve of detached thinking.

"There's only one killer on the island, Gramshaw. Prove any one man innocent of any one murder and you prove him innocent of the lot—even if you find that hammer stowed under his shirt."

"That hammer! You're letting it get on your nerves."

"That wound—" I pointed to the body of Steeve— "almost the same as the three others—was made by the machinist's hammer which you and I found in the ditty-box the first day here. And I think you know it."

"I certainly do not know it!" snapped Gramshaw. "A similar wound could have been made by any metal object of about the same measurement."

"How many metal objects of about the same measurement are there on the island?"

"I can't say off-hand. We agreed that we can't afford to play at detectives."

"We don't need to any more."

In silence we walked back to the hut.

"Ginger's not here!" exclaimed Gramshaw.

"I'll make that tea."

"Not yet!" He took me by the arm, urged me into the hut. We both sat at the table. "I shall have to get used to this. Ginger! Ginger a homicidal maniac!"

"Not at all! He's as sane as we are. If he has a mania, it's food. He wants the rations all to himself."

"Doesn't that mean he's mad?"

"No, only ignorant of common usage. He thinks that the rescue-party will ask no questions. He can have no conception of the technique of cross-examination."

I went out, revived our beacon fire and made tea for two. When I brought it in, Gramshaw was in an advanced state of nerviness.

"Clobbers—Clobbers old boy! If he were to kill one of us two, he'd know the other would *know*——"

"I'm glad you realise that. The moment you and I both go to sleep, we're finished." I added: "Unless we encourage him to get drunk—and both go for him at once? We'd state the full facts and throw ourselves on the mercy of the court. Plead justifiable homicide."

"Can't do it, Clobbers. Can't kill a chap in cold blood. Unreasonable, I know, but it's the way I was brought up. I've never been educated out of it. *You* can do anything you think sensible—I have to sort of feel it's right."

"If I stick a knife in his back on my own, I shall certainly get no mercy from the court," I said. "The only way of our living another twenty-four hours is to keep awake. I'll keep on guard until dawn tomorrow. Then you take over. It'll be difficult in the dark. Even with his boots on, he's as quiet as a cat."

Gramshaw nodded agreement.

"We can think up the details later. Not safe to lie down on the bed. You might nod off. The best thing——" he broke off. "Here he comes," whispered Gramshaw.

Boots on the soft rock. Footsteps, still some twenty paces from the hut—making as much noise as I would make, in boots. Yet Ginger, I repeated to myself, could walk as quietly as a cat when he chose.

"Hullo, Ginger!" Gramshaw's voice was in complete control. "Where've you been?"

"I bin in the dip, near where they oil-tanks used to be. It's the best place for hearin'—like a big ear, it be. And I hain't heard no airyplane. Shouldn't wonder if there hain't bin no airyplane, start to finish."

I was more than a little inclined to agree with Ginger on that point, but I did not intend to admit it.

"Have you seen Steeve, Ginger?" I asked.

"I sure-ly have!" We both winced at the falsetto giggle. "I could do with some o' that tea an' a bite to eat afore we bury 'un."

Gramshaw had apparently forgotten his plan to post a listening guard for aircraft. Ginger was helpful with ropes and floorboards in the matter of carrying the body to the burial ground.

At supper that evening I served the usual rations. Ginger regarded his portion with disgust. We both waited for him to recite his formula. We were not disappointed.

"We wor seven when we came on this-yere island——"

"Ginger!" barked Gramshaw. "You can go to the shed and you can bring back with you all the food you like."

Ginger emitted a grunt of satisfaction. He was about to rise from his packing-case.

"Why bain't Clobbers to go, Mr. Gramshaw? He'm in charge o' victuals."

"He doesn't want any more food, nor do I. You take what you want for yourself."

Ginger, unperturbed, left the hut. Gramshaw leant towards me and lowered his voice.

"The three fire axes! Collect them quietly and dump them in the corner by the head of the bed. Better put your hatchet there too! Make it your job to see that they're there—by my bed—every night."

Ginger returned with a half-pound tin of beef, four biscuits, a tin of peaches and a bottle of rum. We sat with him while he ate it all except the peaches, half of which he left in the can. He drank less than half a cup of rum—to my disappointment— then retired to his bedding.

I myself, instead of drinking tea, had opened one of the tins of coffee essence. I trebled the quantity advised on the label, in the hope that it would help to keep me alert. I am a poor sleeper as a rule—and this applied equally on the island. But tonight I felt that heaviness in the feet which, with me at any rate, betokens deep sleep. When Gramshaw lit the candle for the statutory hour I began to tick off the minutes.

Since Titch's death, when Gramshaw and I changed places, there had been no rearrangement of our beds. The area that had been occupied by Titch was left vacant. Pom had slept next to Titch. We had all slept in line, with our heads against the north-west wall. Thus Gramshaw was now sleeping close to the door. At the opposite end lay Ginger. Between Gramshaw and myself were the spaces that had been occupied by Titch and Pom; on the other side of me were two more spaces, then Ginger.

When Gramshaw blew out the candle, I sat up, with my shoulders resting on the corrugated iron of the wall. This soon began to hurt. I upended the pillow of lashed eiderdown, making a cushion of it. I unbuttoned the holster of my revolver, placed the torch where my left hand could instantly find it. I was comfortable, but for the heaviness in my feet.

During my period of training in the Army I had done night-guards. Moving about in the open air with a rifle for one hour, followed by two hours' rest. This was a very different matter—to sit in the dark, without more movement than a sleeper normally makes—for some six hours without a break.

Could one go to sleep without knowing it? I had heard tales of motorists falling asleep while driving, so presumably one could. How would I know when I was becoming drowsy? I began by forcing myself into an extreme of alertness, to discover that alertness requires incident to feed on or it soon languishes. I tried to create incident.

Every object in the hut which touched the luminescent rock was visible in black outline to a height of about half an inch—looking like a blot of ink on grey-green paper. I began to count and identify all I could see without moving. The flattened ends of the legs of the table, the packing-cases on which we sat, oddments of clothing and equipment. The blade of one of the fire-axes next to Gramshaw's bed seemed to pick up some of the luminescence of the rock.

Next, I tried training myself to judge time in the dark. I would look at my watch every five minutes. I kept this up for an hour and a half without making perceptible progress in accuracy, and then decided that I was over-driving myself. Ginger, after all, was snoring.

Paradoxically, I was without the stimulus of physical fear. I felt only a sense of moral obscenity. If Ginger had had the appearance of a brute it would have been easy to regard him unemotionally as a dangerous animal. Actually, he looked more civilised than any of us—his beard looked natural. A film company might have employed him as an extra—as "a son of the soil". He had no unpleasant characteristic except his gluttony—even so, he had never stolen any food. That I had to lie awake to protect Gramshaw from being killed by Ginger was, in the most intense sense of the word, disgusting.

The fact that I was also protecting myself did not loom large. I believed that Ginger would try to kill Gramshaw first, because he knew that I carried a gun. Get the easy one out of the way first. He could not deliver that hammer blow without making enough noise to wake me—were I to fall asleep. A light sleeper would be beyond his imagination. That I could derive a certain comfort from this line of thought will indicate the extent to which my own moral perspective had been distorted by what Gramshaw called "the spirit of the island". But the fact that I was conscious of my own moral shabbiness——

I was startled by a sudden silence. It was several seconds before I understood it. Ginger had stopped snoring. I looked at my watch. Four minutes to three. With a shock I realised that I could not remember what the time had been when I last looked at it. Ginger muttered and turned over, but the snoring was not resumed.

Had I dozed? There was no means of telling. I removed the pillow and helped the corrugated iron to hurt my shoulders. I moved the layers of serge that were a mattress and sat on the rock.

When dawn came, I wondered how many more of such nights I could survive.

"It's the devil keeping awake in the dark," I told Gramshaw. Ginger, who had never accepted the bogy-man theory, had wandered off by himself.

"I meant to tell you, Clobbers old boy. The golden rule is to sit up. Never lie down, or you may get drowsy."

Poor old Gramshaw! I realise now that it was this sort of juvenile cocksureness which made one regard him with grudging affection. There was enough sterling manhood in him to inspire friendship, but it was his damned stupidities—his golden rules and his pumped-up enthusiasms—that inspired one to gentleness.

Those golden little rules, of course, have some value if you believe in them. Gramshaw made a much better job of his guard than I did. He believed he could manage it and he did manage it, whereas I spent most of my night off guard urging myself to get all the sleep I could. I must sleep well on alternate nights, I told myself, or I would never leave the island. When I did sleep, I dreamed that I had fallen asleep on guard, and kept starting up out of this nightmare.

I began the day brooding on my failure to sleep properly. I worked out precautions. From a dark-blue jersey which I found in the pile of flotsam I unravelled a long thread of wool and put it in my pocket.

The day passed with unexpected calm. In the morning the three of us made a leisurely job of carrying in more of the piled-up seaweed. I was not conscious of tension. Gramshaw was humming or chattering as if he had no secret dread. The truth is that one cannot live continuously in a state of terror when it has no external manifestation. The fear would well up for a few minutes, then subside to a point just below the consciousness.

For the second spell of work, after the heat, we started again on those wretched fish-hooks.

"Mr. Gramshaw, you'm need to go a mile or more out in deep water t'other side afore you catches any fish."

"I'm afraid you're right, Ginger!" Gramshaw kept up his indulgent, rather patronising tone to Ginger. "But I doubt whether we could do much rowing on our rations."

"We'm don't need no rowin', Mr. Gramshaw. Titch went out an' come back without no rowin', an' so did Pom an' all o' Clobbers' bottles as wasn' smashed. We'm only to sit still for a couple o' tides."

It was the kind of extraordinarily sensible remark that Ginger would make from time to time—the result of close and intelligent observation. I seconded it with enthusiasm. I would far rather spend the night in the boat than sitting with my back against the corrugated iron, wondering whether I would betray my trust.

But Gramshaw vetoed it.

"We may have to risk it in a month's time. But we don't know that the currents would carry a boat in the same way. We might never get back."

Ginger giggled and the subject dropped.

When Gramshaw blew the candle out, I twisted one end of my wool securely round one of the bolt-heads that held the corrugated iron of the walls. I had marked it down as ideally situated. It was near the centre of the wall opposite the one against which we slept and it was about two feet from the floor of rock—a bit higher than Ginger's knees. I passed the thread under the table to the opposite wall within a few inches of my bedding. I tied the other end to the handle of my tin mug which I mounted on a pile of clothing. Thus, an invisible line ran the breadth of the hut between Ginger's bed and mine. He could approach neither Gramshaw nor myself without bringing my tin mug crashing on to the rock.

This relieved my anxiety very considerably. The corrugations at my back gave added assurance. For a couple of hours I played the time-guessing game, adding a system of scoring. When I was eleven points up, the game lost its savour.

The next thing I knew for certain was that I was staring at Ginger's boots, outlined on the luminous rock that was our floor. The boots were in movement and the toes were pointing towards Ginger's bed.

Ginger was on a return trip.

"Stand still, or I'll kill you!" I shouted, but I fancy it came out as a hoarse scream. I had my finger on the trigger before I gripped the torch.

The torch found his hands, which were empty.

"What—what—what's that!" cried Gramshaw, waking up. He turned his torch on Ginger. I dropped the revolver between my knees.

Ginger giggled.

"You'm thought I was the wild man. There ain't no wild man on this-yere island. Me. I jest bin down to latrine, an' I never saw 'un."

Like a cat, with total inaudibility, he went back to his bed.

"Sorry, Gramshaw!"

"All right, Clobbers old boy. All's well that ends well. Another two hours of shut-eye for me."

It did not occur to me to apologise to Ginger. Something had gone wrong, somewhere. The visual memory of Ginger's boots was clear-cut and unmistakable. Those boots had been walking into the hut, away from Gramshaw and the door. Therefore they must have passed my line of vision on the outward journey—if I had been awake.

I could have sworn that I had not fallen asleep. I could trace my train of thought up to the moment when I saw the boots. Yet I had to accept the fact that I must have fallen asleep, or into some barely conscious state between sleeping and waking. Why had I failed to hear the clatter of the tin mug?

I put out a hand in the darkness. The mug was still on top of the clothing. So the wool, rotten after its soaking in the sea, must have snapped at a pressure of less than an ounce. I was fingering the wool. I ran my finger along an inch or so—along a foot or so.

The wool had *not* snapped. It still stretched between the handle of my mug and the bolt-head on the opposite wall. At knee height from the ground.

To this paralysing fact I added another. Ginger had been substantially on the door side of the thread of wool when I had bellowed at him. When we had turned off our torches, he had made his little speech and had walked to his bed.

Therefore Ginger must have been aware of the trap: must have stepped over the wool on both journeys.

"Ginger knows we know!" I told Gramshaw, just before the heat next day—our first opportunity for private conversation. To that extent I was honest with Gramshaw. This was an essential fact, and I gave it him as soon as I could.

It was something of a damp squib.

"I thought as much, Clobbers old boy. I had nothing to go on or I'd have mentioned it. The modern rustic! They can use the latest modern machinery—they can mend it without being told how. Mixed up with a lot of common sense are all the old legends and superstitions of the soil—precivilisation and all that, I mean. They've kept a sort of animal intuition which we've lost. What makes you think he knows?"

I told him about my trap.

"I don't think that definitely proves he knows," said Gramshaw. "As a matter of fact, I heard you pottering about after I'd blown out the candle and wondered what you were up to, though I wasn't really interested. He heard you, too. With his instinct or intuition of what-have-you, he may have been able to tell what you were doing from the sound of your movements. By the way, he said he had come back from the latrine? Had he?"

"He had, for all I know!" And then, anticipating the obvious question, I lied to Gramshaw. "I watched him go straight out of the hut—you know how you can see a chap's feet outlined. I had my finger on the torch ready to snap it on and yell if he stepped an inch towards you. I was all keyed up waiting for him to come back. I heard and saw nothing until he was actually inside the hut and between our two beds."

How deeply I regret that petty, sordid little lie, which I told because I had not the dignity to confess that I had dozed! That lie is the foundation of my sense of guilt in respect of his death. The lie itself did no harm whatever—if I had told the whole truth, it would not have affected the sequence of events. The lie exposes me to myself as failing in my interpretation of the duties of friendship—reveals to me that, if my friendship had been as sterling as his, he would be alive at this moment of writing.

Gramshaw's turn for guard—my turn for a night's sleep. But I must make sure of the night's sleep. I rummaged among the bandages and antiseptics and found what I was looking for—a phial of medinal tablets.

Dose: one to two tablets, as prescribed by the physician.

No mere insomniac endured such a strain as I was enduring. I would make it two tablets. I counted a total of thirty tablets. That would mean fifteen alternate nights of sleep for me. A month. Beyond that there was no need to speculate.

I took the tablets with my tea that night. I was asleep within a few minutes. I felt a little heavy the next morning, but otherwise the experiment was a success. I did my night's guard without dread.

Then it was Gramshaw's guard again. I took another dose of medinal.

That is why I was slow-witted when I was awakened a couple of hours before dawn.

Again my sleep and my dreams seem to play a part in events. It is surprising but true that I was feeling the strain of that grisly threesome on the island more than Gramshaw, though I still had no fear of my own physical death.

I know, by inference, that I had been asleep some four hours before I had the nightmare. I dreamed that a preposterous, wild bogy-man, naked and covered in red hair, was standing over me and saying: "I can't kill you properly until you've moved your head away from that corrugated iron."

I woke and sat up. Outlined on the rock, near my bedding, I thought I saw a bare foot. My perspective muddled by the medinal, I counted the toes. Five! All correct! This settled, I yawned and dropped back on my pillow. I was stiff, stretched out my left hand beyond the bedding, so that it touched the rock.

It touched wetness, sticky wetness!

Still muddled, I flashed my torch at Gramshaw's bed. He was sitting up, his hands across his knees, apparently asleep. I smothered a laugh. (*Golden rule, Clobbers old boy.*) I would have to wake him and pretend I did not know he was asleep.

Meantime, this sticky wetness!

In the light of the torch it looked like ink. It was moving, trickling sluggishly towards my bed, from Ginger's bed. Then I bellowed.

"Gramshaw! Light the candle!"

"What—what—what! God, I've been asleep!"

"Light the candle, Gramshaw!"

His torch waved uncertainly. Then it found the candle. He was a long time lighting it.

"What's up, Clobbers old boy?"

"Ginger is not the killer. He has been killed. Look for yourself."

I stood away from the bed. He advanced on it, torch in hand. He caught his breath, looked from the corpse to me.

"The wild man!" he gasped. "It was true, after all. And I've let him get away!"

Would to God I had left it at that! Friendship failed. I was thinking only of my own safety.

"There is no wild man, Gramshaw. You killed Ginger—and all the others!"

As I spoke, I intended to press the trigger and kill him. But Gramshaw looked so extraordinarily—innocent! I let the moment go by.

"You're excited, Clovering, and don't mean what you're saying. But you'll apologise at once, or I'll give you a damned good hiding!"

The schoolboy's reaction! Reducing the whole multiple horror to the dimensions of what one chap may say to another before there has to be a fight! I could not press that trigger until he actually menaced me.

"You killed Ginger and the others. *Keep still!*"

He checked himself, caught sight of the revolver.

"You've got a gun. And you never told me! That's a bit of an eye-opener!"

"Go and sit down on your bedding, Gramshaw."

He hesitated, then turned his back on me and went to his bedding. He picked up a blanket.

"I'm going to put this over poor old Ginger," he said.

I waited until he had returned to his bedding, where he sat in a crouching position, braced against the wall. From the drawer in the table I took out two candles with my left hand, lit them from the burning candle and fixed them on the table.

Gramshaw was some dozen feet away and the other side of the table, but I did not like that crouch of his.

"Don't try to rush me, Gramshaw. I really will shoot—slap through the heart."

"You will if that thing is loaded." He was getting purchase against the wall.

"Look at that dartsboard," I invited.

I fired at it. The bullet entered nearly dead centre. The heavy wood splintered but did not crack. Gramshaw sagged as if I had fired at him.

"I have four live shells left. Keep that in mind, won't you!"

A brassy laugh broke from him.

"You'll shoot whether I rush you or not. You must—to save yourself."

That was a simple truth I had overlooked. I must kill or be killed. I must behave as Jim or Steeve or any tough would behave—unless I could find a compromise.

"Do you think I killed him?" I asked.

I could hear him taking a deep breath.

"If there is no wild man, Clovering, I know you killed Ginger. By your own reasoning, you also killed all the others."

He let the breath go, leaving himself panting.

"Let it be granted that I am the killer, Gramshaw."

It was a severe strain for him, but I could not spare him. His mouth twitched violently, as when we found the body of Titch.

"When the rescue-party comes, you will denounce me," I continued. "The bodies will be dug up and I shall be hanged."

He was steadier now. He nodded slowly, several times.

"But if I kill you, I shall have a sporting chance of getting away with it. Therefore it would be ridiculous not to kill you."

"Stop jabbering and shoot!" he shouted. "Shoot and get it over, you cripple-souled murderer! Shoot, damn you! What're you waiting for?"

To grip his attention, I pitched my voice as if I were making a point in a lecture-room.

"With that question, we touch bedrock. What am I waiting for? As a murderer, I have nothing to wait for. Nothing whatever!"

My tone puzzled him as much as my words. My own life depended upon my ability to puzzle him into thinking for himself instead of indulging in heroics. I went on:

"And now, *let it be granted* that you are the murderer, Gramshaw. If I don't kill you, you will kill me. We have exactly the same riddle, from the opposite angle. Why don't I press this trigger? What, in short, am I waiting for?"

"You intend to murder me, and I know it. I'm not afraid of death any more——"

"But I *don't* murder you, do I? That awkward fact keeps intruding." I could not hold Gramshaw at the point of that revolver until the rescue-party arrived. I now saw my only hope of escape from that dilemma. "You think you were asleep when I flashed my torch on you. I think you were in some intermediate stage of schizophrenic trance—or epilepsy or something. I know nothing of such things and don't need to. I am wholly certain that you are the killer. I repeat, why don't I kill you? The answer is that I need not—because I believe that you would never kill me."

"That doesn't make sense. If I'm the human monster killer you're trying to make me out to be——"

"You're also my friend, Gramshaw. You carried me out of that wreck. You protected me against those toughs, before I found my feet on this island, when they made a butt of me. That's pretty striking. We're such different kinds of man. You knew that my kind laughs at your kind, but you were too generous to care. Though I know you to be a maniac killer, I am absolutely convinced that you would never kill me."

"What's behind all this?" he demanded. Less roughly, he added: "I mean, I'm sorry, but I don't believe you."

"I know you don't." I was about to stake my life on my ability to deflect his murder mania from myself. For all I knew I might be attempting the impossible—perpetrating a psychological absurdity. Of one thing I felt certain, that the trick might work if I made it impressive enough. A plain statement would be useless. I must burn my suggestion into his imagination by any stage trick I could think of. I must shoot the idea into his head with the revolver.

"I've told you I have four live shells in this gun, Gramshaw. Before I count four, you will believe everything I have been saying." I paused to let that sink in. "First, take a good look at me. Feel your own muscles. Remind yourself how easily you could knock me out, then pierce my brain with that hammer—and how well I know it. . . . Stand by for the proof, Gramshaw. *Look at that dartsboard!*

"One!" I fired at the dartsboard. "Two!" I fired again. "Three . . . four!"

No more live cartridges!

"Am I a killer, Gramshaw? Am I afraid that you will kill me?"

I broke the chambers, ejected the empty shells and sent the revolver skimming and rolling over the ground to Gramshaw's feet.

I watched the revolver skimming and rolling. It was a good throw. It very nearly touched his feet. So nearly that my eyes were drawn to his feet.

Gramshaw's feet were in plimsolls, the laces neatly tied.

The foot I had seen outlined on the ground had been bare. I remembered counting the toes.

For some minutes I was but dimly aware of Gramshaw's presence, though the physical eye noted that he was sitting opposite me at the table and that he was talking.

" . . . So you mustn't think I funk it, Clobbers old boy. I'm willing—anxious—to apply to myself the tests you applied to yourself over Jim."

"Why not let it go at the wild man?"

"Because I must have certainty—and I can't have it unless we actually see the creature. The same thing is happening to me as happened to you when you suspected yourself of killing Jim. I want to know how you tested yourself—for innocent and guilty, I mean."

I hesitated. I was remembering the day we worked out the rations—Gramshaw's "blurry little sum". *Three and a half men for one year. Or one man for three and a half years.*

But he was asking me to assume that he was schizophrenic.

"If you really want to try it—begin by ignoring your own memory. Ignore, also, the pairing system." I told him about my own experiments which established that the attention of the other man was always intermittent. "You have to assume that you are a maniac murderer, and check off whether it is physically possible that you could have murdered any given one. I found that I could have murdered Jim, that I probably did not, because I would have had to do it all at the double and there was no time allowance for the transition—for Hyde to change back to Jekyll. And no time to hide the hammer."

"The hammer!" he repeated. "If I—if I did kill Ginger, the hammer will be in the hut." He slithered off the packing-case.

"If you find it, it won't prove anything except that either you or I killed Ginger—and we know that already."

"Suppose it were found in my bedding?"

"It would still prove nothing. How could you convince yourself that I—or the wild man, if you like—hadn't planted it there?"

"All the same, I'm going to search the hut."

He went to his bedding, shook everything out.

"It's not here!" There was an audible sigh of relief. He moved over a clear space towards my bedding.

"Search that too," I invited.

"No. You proved your good faith beyond the shadow of a doubt, Clobbers old boy, when you threw that gun away."

It was my turn to heave a sigh of relief.

"No good doing a job like this by halves," I said. "You needn't mind if I don't."

He searched my bedding, then examined the stove. It still contained the ashes left by the naval party and the green-silk nightdress put there by Titch. On the other side of Ginger's bedding there was no place of concealment. Along the wall opposite that against which we slept were the suit-cases and kitbags containing personal effects taken from the wreck. Beyond these, stacked in the corner at the door and by Gramshaw's bed, were my hatchet and the three fire-axes. He shifted them with much clattering, then turned to me.

"I know I haven't got it on me," he said, "but I want you to know it, too."

He took off his clothes, dropped them one by one on the rock. I felt constrained to do likewise, playing up to Gramshaw's self-dramatisation. Or was he putting on the act for my benefit? There was a spot in the hut which he had not searched. But no purpose could be served by telling him so. "We know now that it's not in the hut," said Gramshaw, as we re-dressed. I let it pass. The hammer might or might not be in the hut at that moment. The question is, "would there have been time to take it outside and hide it?"

"Difficult to say," I hedged. "My own observation begins with my starting out of a nightmare, dreaming that the wild man—a fantastic, ape-like creature—was killing me. I saw the outline of a bare foot on the ground. Being muzzy from the nightmare I just looked at it and lay down again. Very shortly afterwards I felt blood on the ground. Then I flashed the torch on you, found you were asleep——"

"That's the most sinister part of the whole thing, Clobbers old boy," he interrupted. "Me, going to sleep on guard. It's so unlike me—believing, as I did, that Ginger might have a go at you at any time!"

I was about to resume my tale when he burst out again.

"I *say*! Did you take medinal in your tea last night?"

"Yes."

"I *say*! Is it within the bounds of possibility—just the bounds of possibility, Clobbers old boy—that our mugs got mixed—they're all exactly alike—and that I drank your dope?"

"Yes." I did not believe it, but I thought it wise to agree. "You'd hardly notice the taste if you weren't looking out for it."

"And another thing!" cried Gramshaw. "That foot you saw! Did you say it was a bare foot?"

"It was a bare foot. I was dazed from the medinal—if I did take it—from the nightmare, if I didn't. I remember ticking off the toes. Sort of fatheaded thing one does, in that state."

He was up again, standing by my side,

"Look at my feet! Look!"

I looked at the hairy ankles protruding from the clean, neatly laced plimsolls.

"That proves something, doesn't it?" he cried. I nodded.

"It proves that Ginger was killed by the wild man!"

"Of course it does!" I said. I almost crooned it.

The hysteria broke, but in harmless form. He slapped me on the back. He shouted slogans. He danced. He flung himself down on his bedding and cried.

I did not believe in the wild man—nothing could make me but sight of him. But I had to admit to myself that I could not explain away that bare foot, of which I had counted the toes. I had been in a half-awakened state, but I had not dreamed that foot—I had seen it.

I rose from the table and stretched. Gramshaw needed something to steady him. I did not want him to have a drink, in that state.

"I'm going to make some tea," I said, and went out of the hut. Not until several days later did it occur to me that Gramshaw, having reinstated the wild-man theory, ought to have offered to accompany me, for our joint safety. I still do not know whether he actively believed in the bogy.

To me the schizophrenic, Jekyll-and-Hyde explanation still seemed nearly as absurd as the bogy-man. Such states of mind might be possible, for all I knew. In our case it was the swiftness with which the change occurred that challenged reason. Ignoring the murder of Titch, there were four murders— Jim, Pom, Steeve and Ginger—in which the transition, Jekyll-Hyde-Jekyll, must have taken place in a few minutes only— almost like switching coloured lights on and off.

I was ready to meet the theory half-way. Gramshaw might have an obsession, of which he was barely conscious. The focal point was the hammer, symbolising the battering down of obstacles. The obstacles were the men who were eating the rations which ought to be used to enable him to wait—*one man for three and a half years*—for rescue. When circumstances were such as to make a murder physically possible the obsession would flare up. Afterwards, he might forget the details of the act, as a drunkard or dope-fiend may forget the details of a debauch. That was about as far as I could go.

As I approached the hut, I trod heavily and whistled a tune, as I did not wish to startle him. There was no response from within. I pushed the rickety door open. And then, for the second time, I was gripped by physical fear.

Gramshaw was sitting at the table in the light of the three candles. In his hand was the double-headed machinist's hammer. He was turning the hammer on his wrist, striking at imaginary objects. Exactly as he had done that day when we were about to tackle the rations problem.

A boy with a toy, I had thought him then.

At sight of me, he held the hammer for my inspection—held it straight in front of him, with something approaching pride.

"D'you know where I found it?"

"I can guess. In the one place you missed—in Ginger's bed."

"You spotted that, did you! I thought of it at the time but I—felt I couldn't. As you said, it doesn't prove anything —except that the wild man left it in Ginger's bed."

He laughed weakly, then steadied. He was trying to make the hammer stand up on its haft.

"Let's face up to this wild man! We agree that human life cannot be sustained on this island except with what it brings to the island. In cold blood, as it were, one cannot believe in the wild man. But, look what we have to believe instead! Me as a complicated kind of maniac murderer—or you as ditto! Why, dammit, I'd rather stick to the wild man!"

"You're pushing my barrow," I said soothingly. "The foot I saw—which couldn't possibly be yours, because of the plimsoll—gives the wild man objective reality."

I turned away from the table.

"Don't turn your back on me!" cried Gramshaw. I stiffened in panic. "I mean metaphorically, Clobbers old boy!" He had perceived my mistake and his distress was painful to witness.

Presently, he went on: "I want you to play devil's advocate. Make the case against me as strong as you can. For Titch, there's nothing to go on. For Steeve, I could have slipped down from The Knob any time. What about Jim? Remember, Steeve was on the beach with me."

"Given that Steeve's attention was not fixed on you for a few minutes, beginning about six twenty-five, you could have killed Jim, returned to the beach and pretended, some five minutes later, that you didn't know why Jim hadn't turned up. Steeve, of course, could have done the same. While Steeve was alive the evidence was equal. . . ."

"And Pom?"

"You or Ginger could have killed Pom. Assuming you did —you faked that sprained ankle. When Ginger leaves you, instructed by you, you climb to the plateau, make for the boulders and slip along under cover to the fissure. You wait till Ginger has called us, wait until Steeve and I have left; then you go down the chimney to that shelf and call Pom to you. As soon as you've dumped the body in the sea, you sprint back. From the cliff above the beach you locate Steeve and myself looking for you. You slip down, under the boat, and offer us the tale of your having fainted."

"I *could* have!" Gramshaw was perfectly cool. "Is there any single item suggesting that I did—any of it—in any of the cases?"

"Nothing positive. But there's a fair amount of negative evidence. The only reason anyone had for believing you had sprained your ankle was that you said so. A sprained ankle swells. You, contrary to your custom, were wearing socks——"

"My feet were cold in the night—in the morning, I forgot to take the socks off."

"In the case of Jim, you stated in the log that you heard me hammering at a time when I was not hammering—which suggests that you were inventing details. In the case of Steeve, you say that you were woken up by the sound of an aircraft engine. I am a terribly light sleeper and didn't hear it. No one except you did hear it. Ginger had heard something, but refused to say that he had heard an engine. The weight of evidence is against the existence of that engine—but it set the stage for the murder."

This frank explanation was contrary to my policy. But I felt it necessary to let him know the strength as well as the weakness of the case against him, as it would be seen in court. While speaking, I watched him closely for excitement, but found none.

"That's a pretty strong case against me!" He spoke as if he were conceding a minor point. "I feel in my bones, of course, that I've never killed anybody. I suppose all maniacs do." He paused and went on: "The same applies to you— you feel in your bones that you've never killed anybody." He laughed nervously. "It's my turn to play devil's advocate against you."

"Then I suggest beginning with Pom," I answered.

"Right!" He was positively eager. "The agreed times, entered in the log, say that you were three minutes behind Steeve. I say that Pom did hear Steeve tell him to stop work. Steeve hurried up the chimney, to come to my aid. You called Pom on to that shelf. The time, too, might have been more than three minutes. Steeve didn't time you with a watch — he accepted three minutes when you suggested it. Anyway, three minutes would have been enough."

"That's ingenious, Gramshaw!" I was more than ready to encourage him. "But what about Steeve? Remember, I was in the glow of that fire. And you could see me all the time from The Knob."

"I could see you, but I did not watch you. You yourself proved that none of us watched each other continuously."

"True, but in the dark I could not tell *when* you stopped watching me. You might have had your eye on me in the moment in which I slipped away. It would never have been safe to slip away."

Gramshaw nodded thoughtfully.

"That more or less answers it," he admitted. "I see now that the case against me would be much stronger than the case against you. A jury would convict me. That is, they would if it lay between you and me—I mean, if there were no wild man."

"I'm afraid I have to agree with you there, Gramshaw." I was apologetic about it. "The real danger is that the rescue party may be no more able than we are to find him. If we can't produce that wild man, they'll laugh at us."

"You'll be all right!"

"I shall be in clover. All I have to do is give evidence against you!" I spoke with an irony heavy enough to ensure that he would not miss the point.

"You'll have no choice."

"Then I'll choose now. We'll stick together. There's only one course, Gramshaw. Bung that hammer into the sea, burn the log, remove the identification boards from the graves and keep our mouths shut."

"Clobbers! Oh, Clobbers old boy!" He protested, at some length, that I had a genius for friendship. He was, as I have said, a very emotional man.

Some minutes later, he took up the hammer and thrust it into his belt.

Dawn was breaking, and we set about our task. It took nearly two hours to carry the body to the crater and bury it beside the others in the sand—owing to the fact that I needed so many rests.

To lift the body in order to lower it into the grave, we both had to crouch. As we straightened up, staggering a little with our burden, Gramshaw's left foot slipped out of the plimsoll.

I made no remark. I pretended I had not noticed.

With our wooden handmade spades we covered in the grave. While we were doing so, I saw Gramshaw slip his foot back into the plimsoll without untying the shoe-lace.

"What about removing those boards?" I said, when we had finished.

"That 'ud be unsystematic. We'll have to work out every detail before we touch a thing. Carry on as usual in the meantime. By Jove, Clobbers old boy, look at that sun! The only good thing on this island is the sun in the early morning."

For some unaccountable reason, he appeared to be in good spirits. He chose a roundabout route for our return which brought us to the north-west side, near the fissure. He was chattering about fish.

"Poor old Ginger was a long way from a fool. That idea of drifting in the boat was fundamentally sound. What you could do when you feel like it is to lash four of those floor-boards, attaching half a dozen fish-lines. Drop it in somewhere about here." He pointed down at the sea. "The boards are more likely to be brought in than a boat, as they wouldn't catch the wind."

When we walked on I wondered why he had said "you" instead of "we".

I was walking in front of him—intentionally, though I knew he had the hammer in his belt. I believed myself to be safe, felt the urge to exult in my safety. I do not defend this act of folly.

"*Clovering!*" It was a hoarse shout. "Turn round, for God's sake!"

I swung round on my heels. Gramshaw's mouth was open, his lower lip stretched, like a child about to cry. In his hand was the machinist's hammer.

"That's better!" he gasped. "I was watching the back of your head. I—this hammer! I had a simply ghastly feeling that I was going to hit you with it! All over now. *Phew!* Stay where you are a minute."

He took half a dozen paces away from the cliff edge. Then he crouched, took three paces forward and flung the hammer with all his strength.

The hammer flew through the air, whistling. I watched it curve down to the deep water, saw the splash a perceptible time before I heard it.

"'At the bottom of the deep blue sea'," he chanted. "And what's more, it won't get there for several minutes. We're really standing on the top of an enormously high mountain. Nature is very wonderful when you come to think of it, Clobbers old boy."

As we walked on, Gramshaw began a roundabout apology.

"You know what happened to me with that hammer just now? Snake and rabbit! That feeling that you're about to do the very thing you're determined not to do. . . . Sometimes people who haven't a thought of suicide throw themselves from cliffs and towers—you know!—and women trippers who look over the side of the pier quite often throw their purses into the sea. Nothing in it really! There was no need for me to yell at you like that, upsetting both of us. Unpardonable behaviour on my part, Clobbers old boy!"

I made suitable response. It was the first time I had seen this kind of excitement in him.

"I suppose we're both a bit beside ourselves," he continued. He was leading the way, not to the hut but across the island. "Backwash from that awful conversation about manias and obsessions! Thank God, we've pulled through that all right! The luckiest thing that's happened, so far, is your waking up in time to see that bare foot. It's the kind of tremendous trifle that contains absolute proof in itself. Proof of the wild man, I mean."

"Don't let your mind dwell on it," I said, unable to resist the temptation to hand him one of his favourite platitudes.

"I think you're right, Clobbers old boy. Mustn't get morbid about anything. Remember what I said about the spirit of the island? You thought it bosh then, but you don't now, after all we've been through. Tell you what! If we think this thing is going to get us down, I'm all in favour of taking a chance on the open sea. Save all the water we can. Steer by the sun and the stars and keep sailing north."

I thought it a very silly idea. But it would take weeks of preparation, on account of water, so I pretended to consider it.

I was not surprised when he led the way to the boat. He contemplated his own lashing with admiration.

"Simple and effective, Clobbers old boy. I bet a sailor couldn't have done any better. You've only to take this end in your hand, double it through the loop and pull. A moderate shove will send her down the ramp and she'll float at full tide."

He gazed at the boat with affection, and climbed into it.

"There's a nasty little tear in the sail—a good two inches. We'll have to stitch that up, somehow or other."

While he was detaching the sail he chattered, whipping himself to the belief that an open boat was "in some respects" preferable to a liner.

"We might even use some of that corrugated iron to make a rough sort of cabin." He broke off, losing his train of thought. "I say, Clobbers old boy, did you see *two* feet or only *one* foot? I mean, you said you counted the toes of one foot. You saw the other foot, didn't you? Without taking particular notice of it?"

I could see no sense in the question, but I answered it accurately.

"No, I didn't see a second foot. As the foot didn't appear to be hopping, you can say that a second foot was connoted. Don't forget, I was half asleep or I wouldn't have counted the toes. What can it matter? We've agreed that the foot belonged to the wild man."

For me the incident of the foot lost its mystery when Gramshaw's foot slipped out of the laced plimsoll and back again, while we were in the crater. My answer was, therefore, intellectually dishonest. But I was cheating him solely because I believed it to be for his good. Indirectly, of course, for my own safety. I knew nothing of his mental condition, but it would obviously be wise to keep him as calm as I could and free from torturing doubts about himself.

He was absorbed in rolling the sail. When he had finished we carried it between us and stowed it in a corner of the stores-shed.

The heat was beginning and I was glad to rest. Gramshaw sat at the table making entries in the log. After midday I got up and read the log. As always it was accurate and scrupulous.

Fell asleep while on guard: Cl. agrees this may have been caused by my accidentally taking medinal.

There followed a complete record of events, including my own behaviour with the revolver, "our suspicion of each other as the murderer", dissipated by my relating the incident of the bare foot.

He recorded the time of our completing the burial of Ginger and then:

There is now no purpose to be served by continuing this log. Herbert Seiriol Gramshaw.

I wrote the report of Ginger's death, the fifth of its kind, and Gramshaw signed it.

At five we checked provisions by the stores list. It was at least clear that the hypothetical wild man had refrained from looting our stores. Afterwards, Gramshaw did an elaborate sum of his own which I pretended to check.

"You see what the figures mean, Clobbers old boy? We can increase the ration about twenty per cent—if we want to— and still hold out for fifteen months." He added: "Ironical, isn't it!"

I saw no irony, but I did see that he assumed we were in no danger from the wild man. We had not even discussed a new method of guard. He was in good spirits over supper for which we opened a tin of apricots as an extra. He wet-blanketed my suggestion that we should have a drink.

When darkness fell, I felt no qualms. I believed that my act with the revolver had been wholly successful—I believed that Gramshaw would never wish to kill me.

By routine, it was always he who blew out the candle. As usual, I settled myself on my bedding and lay down. Gramshaw blew out the candle which—again by routine—never left the table. He would blow it out and walk to his bed in the dark.

Tonight he did not walk to his bed. He remained standing by the table. The seconds lengthened into minutes. Then he spoke.

"Don't go to sleep!" His voice was hard and his voice incisive. "I want you to sit up. Don't use your torch."

"Righto!" I sat up. "What's the idea, old man?"

"Sit—as nearly as you can—in the position in which you saw that foot."

"I am in that position."

He moved from the table. Presently I saw a bare foot—a few inches from the spot where I had seen one before.

"Can you see my foot?"

"Yes. It's flat on the rock. The one I saw was bending a bit, so that the toes spread out."

"The act of walking," said Gramshaw. "Like this?"

"Nearly enough."

The next words came in a harsh, grating whisper.

"But you can't see my other foot! You can't see it! Even when I complete the step and you know where to look." And then, once again: "*You can't see it!*"

As a matter of fact, I could see it, sufficiently. That is, I could see the dark outline of the sole of the plimsoll. I could not see the canvas, because, having been pasted for weeks with powdered rock, it was perfectly camouflaged. But I could see, in black outline, the metal tabs at the end of the laces and the metal rings of the lace-holes.

"I knew you couldn't see it . . . You can't, can you?"

I did not like that excited repetition. I thought it would be unwise to contradict him. So I answered:

"No, I can't see it. But there's nothing remarkable in that. The canvas is almost as luminous as the rock and is therefore indistinguishable."

"I know. I thought of that at the time. But I had to make sure." He was speaking now in his normal voice. "Sorry to be such a curse, Clobbers old boy. G'night!"

The next morning we made a float of four floorboards, attached half a dozen fishing-lines and launched it in deep water. Gramshaw did nearly all the work and seemed to enjoy it. For the whole of the siesta period he sat at the table writing. We talked only about what we were doing at the moment. I failed to detect any mental strain on his part. I assumed that he had talked himself out yesterday and was feeling the aftermath.

I slept heavily that night. When I awoke at dawn, Gramshaw was not in the hut. I prepared tea and put out two biscuits each, as usual. I drank my tea and ate my biscuits, assuming that he had gone to look for the fishing-float—a toy which would prevent his mind "dwelling" on anything in particular. True, nothing had ever returned to the island on the next tide—the third and the fifth tide being the commonest. Gramshaw knew this. In a couple of hours I abandoned the theory and set out to look for him.

Though the plateau occupied about a quarter of the tiny island, I knew by experience that a team of six men in line would have to sweep the boulder area at least twice before they could be certain of finding an unconscious man. I spent most of the siesta in trying to accustom myself to the idea that I had seen the last of Gramshaw, now and again lapsing into a wild hope that I might be wrong. If only he would walk through the door—a string of fish in his hand and a platitude on his lips!

Before resuming my search, I had to draw off the water from the tray into which it dripped from the sailcloth and corrugated iron. This was done every day after siesta. As I took up the whisky bottle in which we stored the drinking water, I found a note tied round its neck.

Dear Clovering,

There is no wild man. That bare foot you saw all by itself was the only proof of the w.m.'s existence. The proof collapsed under my experiment on you with the plimsoll in the dark. You couldn't see my other foot last night for the same reason that you couldn't see it on the first occasion. We know now that the foot you saw walking from Ginger's bed was my foot.

I did not know the brain was capable of playing such a ghastly trick on a man's soul. I cannot do any more thinking. You will find me in the crater, beside Ginger. I have left papers protecting you (in the sponge fingers tin). I doped your tea last night with two medinal tablets. I am taking a dozen myself, which ought to do the trick comfortably. Best of luck, old man! The only thing that keeps me steady enough to do what I'm doing now is the knowledge that you believed our friendship was stronger than my madness. Thank God you meant what you said! I watched you and you were not afraid of me after you had dumped the gun. After writing this, I hope I shan't funk the medinal at the last moment. Before I actually swallow it I shall make one final test, though it isn't really a test because I know what the result will be.

Goodbye, Clobbers old boy!

He had not funked taking the medinal. The deep vein of gentleness in his nature had prompted him to dig his own grave in the sand. I was able to infer that he had done this in the dark. He had evidently begun digging too close to Ginger. The sand around the stick that marked Ginger's grave had been dug and replaced.

I had only to push the sand into the grave, leaving the wooden spade, which Ginger had made for Titch's burial, as Gramshaw's tombstone.

I went back to the hut, hugging the thought that the immediate cause of Gramshaw's suicide was my readiness to destroy the myth of the wild man.

That evening, when I went to the beach to collect sea-water for the condenser I found Gramshaw's float. Attached to the lines were three fish about the size of a herring, two very small ones and the bitten-off head of a much larger one. I dragged the float above the tideway. I did not know how to prepare nor cook fish and could experiment later. I trebled the supper ration and, as there was still a large store of spirits, drank myself into an optimistic stupor.

Nearly seven months passed since I finished writing the above. For four days I have been debating with myself whether to write what follows. Up to this point, every objective statement of mine is confirmed by the log or the reports signed by Gramshaw or the miscellaneous notes made by him. For what follows I can offer no proof. If a team of expert detectives were to land on the island today I do not believe that the examination of objects would reveal any clue that would confirm—or refute—what I am about to state.

Four days ago, in the early evening, I went into the store-shed for a carving knife with which to prepare fish, of which I now have an excessive supply.

Stepping inside the shed I had that half-pleased, half-irritated feeling I always experienced when returning to my rooms in college after they had suffered spring-cleaning, noticing that the furniture is all slightly out of place.

In the corner, where the shed touched the hut, there was a broad chink of daylight. Why had I not noticed that chink before? I stared at the chink for some seconds before I remembered that the sail, which Gramshaw had taken from the boat two days before his death, had been standing in that corner.

I must, I thought, have moved it absent-mindedly, having no intention of trying to mend it. There was something else out of place—missing, in fact—which I eventually discovered to be a case of canned meat, containing three dozen cans.

My immediate reaction was that of any unthinking house-wife. How *can* the sail have been moved? How *can* the case have been stolen? When there's no one but me on the island? There was a great deal of that sort of thing before I hurried over the plateau to the ledge where we had docked the boat.

The boat was no longer there. The boat had vanished—in circumstances in which the boat could not vanish. There had been no violent storm which might bring the seas up to the ledge.

Seas could have torn the lashing and smashed the boat on the rocks. But no storm—even if there had been one—no high seas and the rest of it—could have unfastened the lashing. The rope was intact. Someone had *taken this end, doubled it through the loop and pulled*.

The boat, in fact, had been launched.

That is all. As Gramshaw had pointed out, one man with a little knowledge could launch that boat at high tide. If there had been a wild man on the island he could have launched it, just as he could have committed the five murders.

Even at this moment the prolonged existence of a man on the island, whom we could neither see nor trace, seems as absurd as it ever seemed. As absurd as the belief that the sail, the case of canned beef and the boat can have left the island of their own volition.

My own power of reasoning has been impaired by my experience on this island. My sense of proportion—my ability to assess fact as would other thinking men—has been distorted. Nevertheless, a line of thought emerges which is hideously simple.

Gramshaw killed himself, primarily, because I accused him of the five murders. He accepted my "proofs" as valid, with the proviso that the existence of the wild man would nullify those proofs. By co-operating in destroying his belief in the existence of the wild man, I snatched away his hope. The launching of the boat compels me to suspect that I may have goaded an innocent man to his death.

Nine weeks later: Today an aircraft flew over. He saw me. With one of Gramshaw's white shirts, I was able to signal SOS. He circled the island, flying low. I repeated the signal. He dipped and flew off. Tomorrow I shall shave and dress myself decently and—I hope—hand this report to the officer in charge. I intend to do all in my power to assist his investigations.

"Usher, tell Mr. Clovering we are ready, please."

In the public gallery there was a low buzz of excitement. So far, it had been a day of glorious surprises. They had come to gape at a sole survivor and perhaps to hear tales of sharks and savages. They had heard a tale of murder and exhumations.

The Admiralty bulletin had been very bald. Clovering's affidavit had been treated as a secret document. Thus the newspaper men heard for the first time the facts jerked at them by the evidence of the airman and the naval witnesses. They were unable to assess the items in terms of the conduct of the sole survivor.

The witness "box" was a table on which had been placed a small wooden frame. Clovering took the oath by reading aloud from a printed card fixed to the frame.

After formal evidence, deemed to have included the reading of his affidavit, Clovering was questioned by counsel representing the shipping company. They were very polite to each other. Clovering readily agreed that his statements about the indiscipline of the ship's company were hearsay. On that understanding he would withdraw them.

Next came counsel retained by Gramshaw's widow, briefed to do what he could towards clearing her husband's name.

"Mr. Clovering, am I right in saying that there were upwards of nine craters and a hundred boulders on that island? And that the boulders varied in size from that of a large molehill to, say, the dome of St. Paul's?"

"I think that is a fair description."

"Did you examine every one of the larger boulders to discover whether it might be hollow—whether it might in fact mask a cave?"

"No."

Pressed on the possibility of there being a cave on the island, Clovering gave an open answer. There might be one—there might not.

"If there had been a cave, occupied by a man living as you lived, on stores saved from a wreck, such a man could have lit a fire for his condenser without you or any of your party being aware of it?"

"If the cave were in the northern part of the island—yes."

"Now, Mr. Clovering, I am about to ask a purely formal question of which I know the answer. Did you launch that lifeboat yourself?"

"No."

"Your affidavit states that it could not have been launched by weather conditions. How do you escape the conclusion that the boat was launched—I will not say by a wild man—by a human being whose presence on the island was unknown to you?"

"That is my own inference."

"You agree, do you not, that if there had been a—wild man—on the island, it would have been possible for him to have committed all the murders?"

"Yes. But please let me add that I have no positive evidence of an unknown man's presence, except the launching of the lifeboat."

"Thank you, Mr. Clovering."

102

Counsel sat down. The possibility of the wild man's existence had been definitely established. Clovering's grudging admission enhanced the reality of the wild man by excluding the suspicion that he himself was trying to put over a tall tale. There was a lull in the proceedings until the chairman asked the Attorney General:

"Have you any questions to put to the witness, Sir Brian?"

The Attorney General rose. He was a large man with a bird-like face and a thin piping voice that was itself not un-birdlike. He never looked at a witness until he reached the end of a sentence.

"Mr. Clovering, at the time when you wrote your version of events on the island, you had access to the log and other documents authenticated by Gramshaw? Was it in your mind that your report, if it was to be believed, must never conflict with a statement of Gramshaw's?"

It was a hostile question, but Clovering was unperturbed. There would be many more. On the island he had prepared himself. He knew that the Attorney General would take the premise that any single statement might be a lie, covering guilt. Clovering's policy would be to answer with the same frankness with which he had written.

"Oh yes, Sir Brian. I frequently checked my account with his."

"Would it be an exaggeration to say that you wrote your account *round* his account?"

"It would be inaccurate. I wrote first, then checked."

"Do you believe that Gramshaw was schizophrenic?"

"I had, and have, no knowledge of the subject. I *guessed* that he could not be, because of the rapidity of the transitions. But at the last I wavered a little."

"Your guess was confirmed, in your absence from court, by psychiatric experts. Neither in Gramshaw's handwriting nor in your own account of his behaviour is there any symptom of schizophrenia nor of any other mental abnormality. Yet he killed himself because you convinced him that he was schizophrenic?"

"That confirms my statement that I was, unhappily, the immediate cause of his death."

"Mr. Clovering! In his farewell note to you Gramshaw writes: 'I shall make one final test'. Your account offers no comment. What was that final test?"

"I don't know."

"Did you make any effort to find out?"

"No. I assumed it would be a subjective test—a test of his own mentality."

"As Gramshaw was not schizophrenic you ask this tribunal to believe that he planned this abominable series of murders and secreted the hammer for that purpose?"

"Certainly not: I have given reasons for myself believing in Gramshaw's guilt. It is not my affair if the tribunal should decide that the wild man was the killer."

"*Ah-h!* That—wild—man!" Sir Brian was mouthing the words. "The shadowy figure of that wild man hovers over this court, in instant readiness to checkmate any move against yourself. Gramshaw might have committed all the murders. The wild man might have done so. And *you* might have committed all the murders, Mr. Clovering?"

"Admittedly. But only on the assumption that I am myself schizophrenic without knowing it." He added: "I am not concerned to prove that it was impossible for me to commit the murders. I have reported circumstances showing that I did not."

The chairman who had frowned frequently during the last few minutes now expressed his dissatisfaction.

"Sir Brian, I feel it incumbent upon me to remind you that this is not a criminal court. I have listened with profound astonishment to your questions. I cannot divine their purpose."

"My immediate purpose, sir, is to discover the witness's view of his own mentality during his sojourn on the island."

"Then I shall warn the witness. Mr. Clovering! You need not answer any question of which the answer might tend to incriminate you if it were used in evidence elsewhere."

Clovering bowed acknowledgement.

"I think, sir, that Mr. Clovering is wholly confident that no question of mine could evoke an answer that would incriminate him." He turned to witness. "Mr. Clovering, have you ever been a voluntary patient in a mental nursing home?"

"No."

"Have you ever been subjected to examination by a mental expert?"

"No."

"Now carry your memory, please, to that hammer. That double-headed machinist's hammer which you say you believe to be the symbol of Gramshaw's obsession and the instrument employed in each of the murders. You were alone when you first saw that hammer, were you not?"

"Yes." Clovering answered mechanically as if to a formal question.

"Up to the time of the shipwreck, your interests had been academic. You were not interested in carpentering tools?"

"Not in the least."

"Yet, at first sight, that hammer seems to have caught your interest. You describe it in some detail. You note that it is the only object in the hut in a state of perfect preservation?"

As Clovering seemed to regard an answer as unnecessary counsel continued:

"The second time you saw that hammer, you and Gramshaw were about to work out the rations?"

"Yes."

"In spite of the grave business in hand, the hammer again interests you. You give it considerable space. You write down Gramshaw's description of it as a machinist's hammer with a double preen. You watch Gramshaw toying with it—'striking at imaginary objects' you say. Does not that passage suggest that already that hammer was associated in your mind with violence?"

Clovering smiled tolerantly.

"That passage, Sir Brian, means only what it says."

"When you found the body of the man you called Titch and examined the wound, you immediately *assumed* that the hammer had been used. And you made a similar assumption in regard to the other four murders?"

Clovering hesitated.

"I see that I must accept your word 'assumption'. I certainly never obtained scientific proof. But in the circumstances the assumption carried moral certainty."

"I am at present suggesting only that the hammer had some psychological fascination for you—such as you ascribe to Gramshaw—and that this fact distorted your judgment?"

"Possibly! But you are putting the cart before the horse. After the murders had been committed with the hammer—as I believed—I did regard it as a gruesome object. To say it fascinated me is an exaggeration."

"When did you last see that hammer?"

"When I was on the cliff-head with Gramshaw—as described!"

"Your description of that incident is rather—may I say?—colourful. Are we to take that description literally?"

"I see no objection to your taking it literally."

"Then I will do so. I will put to you the points of that description. Please answer 'yes' or 'no'. Did you see Gramshaw throw that hammer into the sea?"

"Yes." The tone indicated slight surprise.

"Did you hear it 'whistle through the air' as he threw it? Did you see it 'curve down to the deep water'? Did you 'see the splash a perceptible time before you heard it'?"

"Yes."

"Did Gramshaw then—'chant', I think you said—'at the bottom of the deep blue sea'? And did he add: 'It won't get there for several minutes'?"

"Yes."

"Are you surprised to learn that that hammer has been recovered and is in one of the boxes on the exhibits table here?"

For the first time Clovering's calm was threatened. He gripped the wooden frame, displacing it. He recovered himself, replaced the frame before answering:

"I am very surprised indeed!"

Sir Brian opened the box, took out the machinist's hammer to which a label was attached by a string. He placed the hammer on the edge of the frame on the witness table.

"Before I ask you to identify this hammer, it is only fair to warn you that, during your absence from court, it was identified by the three naval ratings who recovered it. You will find a mark, which was engraved on the island, in the presence of witnesses, by a ship's artificer." Sir Brian paused. "Mr. Clovering, is this the hammer which you have told us you believe to be—er—the symbol of Gramshaw's obsession, and the instrument employed by him in the murders?"

"Yes."

Sir Brian picked up one of the smaller cardboard boxes.

"In this box"—he removed the lid—"is a plaster cast of the wound which caused the death of the first victim—the man you knew as Titch. Will you please fit the hammer to the cast of the wound?"

Clovering betrayed not a trace of unease as he did as counsel asked.

"To my inexperience, it seems to be a perfect fit," he said.

"That is indisputable," said Sir Brian. "It can leave no doubt that the man Titch was killed with that hammer."

Sir Brian handed witness another of the small boxes.

"This is a similar cast of the wound of the last victim— of the man you knew as Ginger. Will you repeat the act of fitting the hammer, please?"

With the same courteous indifference, Clovering applied the head of the hammer to the plaster cast—with the same result.

"Thank you, Mr. Clovering. It is therefore equally indisputable that the man Ginger was killed with that hammer. Your assumption is proved to have been correct in respect of these two murders. Now *this*"—Sir Brian removed the lid of a third cardboard box—"is a similar cast of the wound of the man known as Steeve. I'm sorry to trouble you again."

Again Clovering took the plaster cast, but the courteous indifference was lacking. He applied the hammer-head, but this time his fingers perceptibly fumbled.

Sir Brian watched the fumbling for some twenty seconds and then:

"It doesn't fit, does it?" he said. He opened one of the larger boxes, took out a fire hatchet and handed it to the witness.

"Will you try this, please? It is the hatchet taken from the hut. Try the hammer end—not the blade."

Clovering took the hatchet and applied the hammer end.

"That's better," exclaimed Clovering, recovering his poise. "Yes—it fits."

"It *fits!*" echoed Sir Brian in an ecstasy of agreement. "The hatchet fits the wound of the man we will continue to call Steeve. It fits, as you will find, the wound of the man called Pom. And it fits the wound of the man called Jim. *On the other hand*, the machinist's hammer fits the wounds of Titch and of Ginger. Have you any comment to make upon that, Mr. Clovering?"

"Only that the wounds are all rectangular—that the difference in the aperture is extremely small and would be even less easily observed in the actual wound."

"I put it to you, Mr. Clovering, that you killed Titch at night, in the open, with the machinist's hammer. I put it to you that, unable to burden yourself with a hidden hammer as well as a hidden revolver, you killed the other three men with the hatchet—which you could always carry openly without incurring suspicion?"

"You need not answer that question, if you do not wish to," interposed the chairman.

"Thank you, sir, but I am quite willing. There is no ground for counsel's assertions. I did nothing of the kind."

"I put it to you," persisted Sir Brian, "that you murdered the man Ginger—using the hammer a second time, because the hatchet was at that period in Gramshaw's keeping during the night—close to his bed?"

"You pursue your own fantasy, Sir Brian. I repeat that I have killed no one with any weapon whatever."

"If your conscience was wholly clear, why did you take an elaborate precaution to prevent a working-party from looking for that hammer?"

"I took no such precaution! I was certainly surprised, a few minutes ago, that the hammer had in fact been recovered."

"Because you had seen it thrown into the sea?"

"Yes—in very deep water."

"I will concede the depth of the water, Mr. Clovering. Let me tell you that, under your skilful persuasion, Gramshaw believed that he had committed all the murders with that hammer. His final test—of which you failed to grasp the significance—was to make sure that the hammer fitted the wound of Ginger. For that purpose Gramshaw himself disinterred the body."

For the second time, Clovering gripped the frame of the witness "box", and again displaced it.

"That hammer, Mr. Clovering, was not recovered from the sea. It did *not* whistle through the air, as you so vividly described. Gramshaw did *not* remark that it would be several minutes reaching the bottom of that admittedly very deep water. Gramshaw—a few minutes, perhaps, before he took the fatal dose of medinal—left that hammer beside the body of Ginger, where it was found by the working-party, who . . ."

But—as the chairman had reminded Sir Brian—it was not a criminal court. There was no warder within arm's reach of Clovering to prevent him from swallowing the crystal of cyanide.

THE KYNSARD AFFAIR

THE KYNSARD AFFAIR

I

THE CLUE TO the Kynsard mystery was the life-and-death story of Gibbern, the fat-headed murderer. His fat-headedness had helped him in the first instance—he killed his wife in a manner so lacking in ingenuity as to attract no initial suspicion. He would never have been caught if he had not been such a little ass of a man—fundamentally, an honest ass.

This element of honest asininity—this childishly simple murder—awakened the interest of all classes. There is reason to believe that more than one man said to himself: "That's the blue print for murder. Gibbern would have got away with it if he hadn't been an honest ass. Now I, as it so happens, am not an honest ass. Therefore . . ."

The Kynsard affair followed with somewhat indecent haste.

On the morning of Gibbern's execution there was the usual crowd outside the prison, the usual handful of enthusiasts demonstrating against capital punishment. After the notice had been posted—eight o'clock, nowadays—Local Superintendent Halsdon, satisfied that there was no likelihood of disorder, was walking back to his station when he spotted a small Morris saloon car illicitly parked in a blind alley, formed by the prison on one side and a factory on the other.

The July sun was playing on the windows of the car, wet from recent rain, so that he could not immediately see inside. The doors were locked. He noted the registration number, and was turning away when a cloud reduced the dazzle.

He whipped out his control key and opened the door. Sprawling over the back seat, under a rug and a newspaper, lay a naked woman, dead. Head and face had been battered. Even so, he could see that it was the face of a comparatively young and comely woman. Auburn hair too! He perceived that she had been dead for some hours.

The corpse, as such, did not unnerve Halsdon. He was in full possession of his faculties. He knew it was foolish to speak to a corpse—still more foolish to say:

"Hi! D'you think I was born yesterday!"

His imagination was struggling to fit his discovery into his own pattern of human behaviour, even at its most eccentric, most maniacal. Here was gross absurdity. Not because a woman lay murdered in a car, but because the car had been parked at that spot.

Gibbern's wife had been found in a car, battered to death, in circumstances which suggested the work of an unknown pervert. Here was another woman, battered to death, found in a car parked at the nearest possible point to the gallows on which Gibbern had just paid his penalty. Could a maniac have committed murder as a practical joke? But even a maniac would insist that a joke should have a point, however maniacal. This joke had no point because, after the verdict, Gibbern had confessed. That body in that car at that spot and at that hour was a sublime insult to human intelligence.

Perhaps he reminded himself that a policeman must consider murder, not as a metaphysical riddle, but as a murder. He ran the few paces to the main road and beckoned to a constable. With the constable beside him, he drove the car to the mortuary adjoining the district police station.

It was assumed that this was not a local murder. Better to call in Scotland Yard sooner than later.

Detective-Inspector Turley had handled the Gibbern case. He was in the middle thirties, but looked ten years older— which was an advantage in many ways. After sticking for some years in the lower grades he had been recognised as an able man, possessing the talent of encouraging the talents of others and co-ordinating the results.

Beside him in the car sat his aide, Detective Constable Rawlings, a promising youngster, short-listed for promotion. Following was the nucleus of a staff.

A few minutes after Turley arrived, the doctor was ready to make his report.

"There were two blows on the face, inflicted before

death," said the doctor. "There were three blows on the crown of the head, the second of which caused death. She has been dead about twelve hours. Subject to microscopic confirmation, I would say the weapon was of wood with smooth edges.

"Aged 24 to 28; wearing a wedding ring. Height approximately five feet five. That auburn hair is natural, but it has been tinted up. A good-looking girl I should say—straight nose, well-shaped jaw. Hands long and narrow: she wasn't a typist, nor a pianist. No operations, but she had a small accident some time ago necessitating a couple of stitches." He added a technical location of the scar.

"Where do they keep that, doctor?" asked Turley.

"Say an inch and a half above the waist-line," smiled the doctor. "I've—er—cleaned up the face a bit—surgically, I mean—so that her people will be able to recognise her. If you have to publish a photograph, it will be all right. A good man, choosing his angle, could get a perfectly natural photograph."

"What staggers me, Mr. Turley," said Superintendent Halsdon, when the doctor had gone, "is the car being dumped there. Gibbern! Same sort o' murder! Looks as if the murderer was a maniac sort of hypnotised by Gibbern and couldn't keep away."

"Could be!" agreed Turley politely. "Have you done anything about the car?"

"Registered owner—Miss Elizabeth Trotwood of Cranebrook Mansions, West Central."

"Elizabeth Trotwood!" ejaculated Turley. "That's a new one! Ever read Charles Dickens, Super? 'Betsy Trotwood'— character in *David Copperfield*. Looks like the name's phony."

"Her ration book will settle that. I've sent a man to Cranebrook Mansions, believin' you'd approve, Mr. Turley."

"Quite right! Let's see the doctor's description again."

Rawlings, knowing what would be wanted next, handed his chief the official Missing List. Turley quickly found something.

"This looks like it, Super. 'Height five feet five, auburn hair, grey-green eyes, aged 26. Distinguishing marks, nil. Reported at six last night by husband, Arthur Kynsard, barrister-at-law'—I know of him: does a lot of railway work in the courts—'further inquiries by same at midnight and eight-fifty this morning.' There's his home address in St. John's Wood and chambers in Lincoln's Inn. You might ask him to call."

While Turley was retiring to the room that had been placed at his disposal, with an outer room for his staff, there came a ring from Halsdon's man at Cranebrook Mansions.

"Okay, sir! Flat taken in the name of Elizabeth Trotwood. Description tallies—auburn hair and the rest of it. These are small flats but not cheap. From what the caretaker has let fall, I'd say they're mostly love-nests. All quiet and orderly. Where good-class City men come to see the special girl-friend. Trotwood has a friend. But the caretaker doesn't know his name nor anything about him. Description: middle-aged, shortish, fattish, with a loud voice; laughs a lot. Any orders, sir?"

"Find where the Morris car was kept and try and pick up something from the garage. Don't be too long. The Yard have started and we don't want to overlap."

By which he meant that the Yard would get the credit, and might just as well do the work.

Within twenty minutes a high-powered Chrysler drew up and a constable stepped forward to investigate.

"My name is Kynsard."

"Right, sir. The superintendent is expecting you." The constable knew why: to register sympathy, he opened the door of the car. He was mildly surprised to notice that the rear was stacked with unframed pictures. The gentleman didn't look that sort. One picture caught his eye—a modernistic Medusa, the snakes about the head looking like corkscrews.

"Second door on the left, please, sir."

Kynsard was tall, slender, alert, in the early thirties. His physical appearance was an asset to him as a barrister, for he looked like a youthful version of a Lord Chancellor. Broad jaw, long thin lips, wide-set eyes, heavy lidded, and massive brow.

"Is my wife here, Superintendent?"

"Well, we don't know that it is Mrs. Kynsard——"

"You said there had been an accident. If she is here and not in hospital, it means she is dead."

"Now look here, sir! You may be alarming yourself for nothing, and I hope you are. We asked you to call because the description is like the description you gave the Yard of your wife. But in these cases, it's nothing for us to call a dozen or more people who've all given a close description, and quite often it turns out not to belong to one of 'em."

"Yes, of course!" He smiled—it was a good smile that was often effective in court. "Thank you, Superintendent. You've helped me to pull myself together. This sort of work can't be pleasant for you—I mustn't make it worse."

"That's all right, sir. If you feel steady, we'll go and get it over."

Kynsard lagged a little when following the local superintendent across the yard to the mortuary. Then he braced himself, the broad jaw thrust slightly forward.

A sheet had been placed over the body, covering it to the chin. Kynsard gazed down at the face. He turned to the superintendent and nodded slowly.

Outside the mortuary he spoke.

"That is my wife, Superintendent."

"I'm very sorry—very sorry indeed, Mr. Kynsard!"

"Thank you. How was she killed? It didn't look like a road accident."

"We think—in fact we know, sir—that the poor lady was murdered. And I'm afraid that, after you've signed the declaration, we must ask you to see Inspector Turley. He'll want all the information you can give him."

II

Dealing decorously with stricken relatives was a part of Turley's routine. Part of his routine, too, was to begin by suspecting a husband when a wife was murdered. True that a barrister would probably think of a safer way of shedding an unwanted wife. Perhaps this wife was not unwanted.

This kind of witness would certainly be out of the ordinary. For one thing, a lawyer would know that, as husband, he would be top of the list of suspects. He would know the difference between suspicion and evidence, and would not trouble to impress his innocence on the police.

After an exchange of civilities, Kynsard sat back in his chair, arms folded, waiting for Turley.

"Are you quite certain that deceased is your wife? I ask, because a painful mistake is sometimes made on these occasions."

"Quite certain!"

"In the description you filed at Scotland Yard, you stated that your wife had no distinguishing marks?"

"None!" He amended: "Unless you would count a small scar a little above the waist. She cut herself there some years ago."

"Did you look for that scar?"

"No. It wasn't necessary."

Identification being settled, they could begin.

"Well now, Mr. Kynsard, you'll know the kind of detailed information I want."

"You'll find I shall need your help—I've done very little criminal work." After a moment's pause Kynsard, as it were, opened his case.

"I last saw my wife yesterday morning when I left for chambers, about nine twenty. Over breakfast, I had mentioned that I was not appearing in court and she suggested we should have lunch together. I agreed, and she said she would book a table at Blainley's, in the Strand. She got up and telephoned there and then.

"When I turned up at Blainley's, she was not there. I took up the reservation and had lunch by myself. I ought to have been alarmed then—she had never done that sort of thing before—but, frankly, I was merely annoyed.

"I arrived home a little before six, just before our cook-general left. She works from ten until six—the only staff we have—we've put part of our house out of use. She was indignant because my wife had not been home all day and there was no food in the house, and Mrs. Tremman—my wife's mother—was coming to dinner.

"Now, my wife didn't make that kind of mistake. I was pretty certain then that something must have happened to her, So I rang Scotland Yard.

"Mrs. Tremman turned up about seven. We were soon working up each other's anxiety. I'm afraid I made myself a bit of a nuisance to your people. Mrs. Tremman concentrated on ringing the hospitals. I drove her home after making my last inquiry of Scotland Yard—round about midnight. That's all I can tell you."

"What about dinner?"

"Mrs. Tremman foraged and found some canned stuff— we had a scratch meal in the kitchen."

Very clear and concise for a bereaved husband, thought Turley.

"As far as you know, was the deceased carrying any considerable sum of money?"

"As far as I know—no. From my knowledge of her habits I'd say that it's extremely unlikely. She has an account at the local branch of the Metropolitan Bank. She hated jewellery and wore none."

"I'd like to check up at the Metropolitan. The usual housekeeping account, I suppose?"

"Rather more than that. In addition to what I handed her, she had eight hundred a year of her own."

"Had she control of her capital?"

"Nothing there, Inspector!" Kynsard smiled. "Income derived from a trust created by her father's Will, in favour of his wife and daughter. The only person to profit by her death is her mother—who gets the eight hundred a year. I doubt whether my wife has made a Will. If she has, it can only cover cash in her current account and her personal belongings—clothes, gadgets and pictures."

"Valuable pictures?"

"No. Bought as a means of helping her hard-up artist friends. She's always trotting them round to obscure exhibitions. The back of my car is loaded with alleged masterpieces at the moment."

"Artists!" exclaimed Turley, as if he had uncovered something. "Any extra-special artist friend?"

"Not among the men." Again Kynsard's smile smoothed a rough passage. "I think I know how to go on from there. Our marriage was not a success. But we both made the best of it. We were polite and considerate—at least, she was, and I hope I was."

"You never discussed divorce?"

"In effect, no. Neither of us wanted somebody else—I'm too busy for gallivanting. In fact, it was the volume of work I have to get through that was partly to blame. I'd no time to afford her reasonable companionship."

"So she spent a good deal of time—not in your society?"

"Of course! But she always told me where she had been—and always gave all the details. She was—vivacious and rather voluble. I'm convinced there was no man in her life. She had a special woman friend. Nearly all her chatter was about this friend."

"That woman might be useful. Can I have her name and address?"

"I don't know it. Barbara—that's my wife's name—had the common trick of spattering her conversation with first names. 'I was just leaving the art school with Madge when Leonard ran after us'—that kind of thing! I never knew who was who—and I never cared enough to inquire. In the jumble of first names, one stands out through constant repetition. The name of Betsy. That was the special friend."

Elizabeth—Betsy. Charles Dickens. Betsy Trotwood. The phony name. Turley was groping for the link.

"If you can remember anything at all about Betsy that would help us to pick her up——?"

"Wait a minute! There's some damn silly key-word!" Kynsard stroked his chin, then exploded: "Titania! Titania Underwear! About three months ago my wife showed me—in one of those glossy women's weeklies—an advertisement photo of the usual pretty girl, grinning in cami-knicks, or whatever they call 'em at the moment. She said the girl was Betsy and asked me if I didn't think they were like each other—which I didn't. Presumably, the Titania people will be able to help."

"That's fine, Mr. Kynsard!" Turley made a note. "This girl is a professional model, then?"

"She may be. But I rather fancy she's an artist who occasionally does that sort of thing for pocket-money. She probably has other resources. For instance, she has a car—a small Morris saloon. Frequently lent it to Barbara, as I more or less monopolise our Chrysler. I've seen the Morris two or three times in our garage when Barbara had borrowed it."

"As far as you know, had your wife an appointment with Betsy yesterday?"

"Not to my knowledge."

The details of the car, reflected Turley, would be published in the later editions.

"Mr. Kynsard, the deceased was found in a Morris saloon owned by Elizabeth Trotwood."

"'Trotwood!" echoed Kynsard. "'Betsy Trotwood'! It sounds as if she'd been reading Dickens. Not that it matters. I suppose it must be the same Betsy. Does she admit knowing my wife?"

"We haven't had time to contact her."

Turley's intuition warned him to break off, now that the link had been dropped into his hand. The caretaker at Cranebrook Mansions had given a description which tallied with that of Barbara Kynsard. This part of the case, he thought, was going to be easy.

That the girls were one and the same was at least a working hypothesis. Kynsard knew it, or did not know it. If he did know it, his pretence of ignorance would strongly suggest his guilt. No more questions until more facts had been gathered elsewhere.

Turley was making the routine speech of thanks for helpful information, when Kynsard interrupted.

"I can give you a small point relevant to my wife's movements—though technically it's hearsay. Before I came here, Mrs. Henson—that's our cook-general—told me that my wife must have left the house in a very simple house-dress and wearing indoor shoes. No hat or coat. No bag."

Turley was impressed.

"That was before ten, or your maid would have met her? What was the simple house-dress like?"

"I don't know." Kynsard's tone was bitter. "I have absolutely no eye for women's dress."

As Kynsard left the room, young Rawlings appeared in the doorway.

"Plenty for you, Rawlings. Get hold of the man who shared that flat in Cranebrook Mansions: we want to swop yarns with him. And check this tale with Blainley's restaurant in the Strand." He gave details.

"Very good, sir. There's a queer customer in with the super. Said he might be able to help us, but he'd talk only to the inspector in charge. He looks as if he'd got something."

A minute later Turley heard footsteps and a rasping, cackling laugh in the corridor. The local superintendent opened the door for a shortish, tubby, middle-aged man. His clothes were expensive, as was his attaché-case, but the effect of gentility was negatived by a diamond ring.

"Luck's in! It's Detective Inspector Turley!" he exclaimed, on a laugh. "Saw you just after you'd given your evidence in the Gibbern job."

"What is your name?" asked Turley.

The other turned round, noted that the local superintendent had gone and that the door was shut.

"I read about this little affair in the noon editions. So's not to waste your time and mine—that car she was found in! Is it a Morris Saloon, registered number DV 2165?"

"It is," said Turley. "I must have your name."

"Girl under thirty, auburn hair—sort of greeny eyes—about an inch taller than me? Let me finish. Got a small scar about here?" He pointed to the beginning of the outward curve of his person.

"Correct. Sit down, please, and tell me your name."

"I'll tell you more than my name—which is Flanch, Samuel, fruit and vegetable wholesaler, Covent Garden. I'll tell you *her* name—Elizabeth Trotwood—called her Betsy. You're wondering why I'm walking into trouble like this. I'm not such a mug as to keep anything back when you boys mean business. *Ha-ha!*"

The laugh was a nervous affectation. Turley recognised the type—crude, inclined to flashiness of dress and manner, but commercially respectable.

"Keep going, Mr. Flanch," he prompted.

"That poor kid was my only bit o' fun, Inspector, and I don't want the missis to know. Get me?"

"Queering your pitch wouldn't help us."

"S'right! I ran a flat for her—in Cranebrook Mansions, West Central. Bought her that car. Paid this bill only yesterday for her clo'es . . ." He smacked down a receipted bill. "Cor, I shall miss her! She was a good sort, Inspector, apart from—well, she was a good sort."

"Wait a minute!" Turley had rung his bell. "Rawlings, this gentleman is Mr. Flanch, who shares the flat in Cranebrook Mansions. Take him to see if he can identify the body. Then p'raps you'll come back here, Mr. Flanch."

III

Some five minutes later Rawlings returned.

"He identified her as Trotwood, sir. Took him a minute or two, but he was in no doubt about it."

"Well, where is he?" demanded Turley.

"He was a bit flattened out. Broke down outside the mortuary—said he must step across the road and have one before he could tackle you, sir."

After a couple of double brandies, Samuel Flanch was ready to face his ordeal. His anxiety now seemed to be focused on his wife.

"You think I've been deceiving my wife, Inspector, and you're quite right, if you look at it the wrong way. But it was for her own good. She's an invalid and it would be bad for her health if she thought I'd been telling her lies. Now, I've come forward of my own free will to save you trouble. And one good turn deserves another, eh?"

Turley reassured him and put the usual questions.

"I last saw Betsy three nights ago—Monday, that was. We had a bit of a row—that's why I haven't seen her since, though I was going to make it up. Showed you that bill, didn't I?"

"What was the row about?"

"You're muddling me, Inspector, if you don't mind me saying so. Better take things in their proper order." He opened his dispatch-case. "Look here. I popped in at that flat this morning before I came on here—thought this might be wanted."

He produced a women's weekly magazine, folded back at a full-page advertisement in colour.

Turley gazed at an attractive young woman in Titania underwear.

"That's Betsy! Good-lookin' kid, eh? And mind you, you don't want to go thinking things just because she's dressed like that—they're only sort of stage clothes, if you look at it the right way. These girls are skilled workers and there's no hanky-panky about the job."

"You were going to tell me why you quarrelled."

"I'm telling you. Those clo'es! In those studios, it's one thing. What I didn't like was, she went and ordered herself a couple o' sets same as she's wearing in that picture. It didn't seem decent to me, and I told her so. Yesterday, I thought p'raps I was being a bit pernicketty, so I paid the bill and meant to give her the receipt last night.

"I got to the flat about six. She never turned up. I was riled because I had to wait alone in the flat till eleven. It was no good going home earlier. You see, I'd told my missis——"

"Quite so! Had Betsy gone out in the Morris?"

"Must of! I looked in at the Tythrop Garage this morning, before I came on here. Car wasn't in its place. I reckoned there was just the chance she might have lent it to a particular friend of hers—a girl, I mean—who used to borrow it, off and on."

"Who was the friend?"

"Last kind of friend for a kid like her you'd think of! Class! A lady! Wife of a well-known lawyer an' all! I don't hold with mentionin' names, only you're bound to find out. I gotter think of myself in this mess." Flanch lowered his voice. "Mrs. Arthur Kynsard—Barbara, they call her. How those two came to be friends—search me!"

Turley nodded. Everything seemed to be adding up. In each phase of her double life, the girl referred to her other self as her "friend".

"Did Betsy tell you that, Mr. Flanch, or did you find it out for yourself?"

"Both! She told me, but I thought she was swanking. One day, she showed me one o' those toff's papers. 'Here you are, Sam,' she says. 'Don't you think she's like me? Everybody takes us for sisters', she says."

"Were they alike?" asked Turley.

"Not so's you'd notice. You can see for yourself, if you'll give me a minute." He turned back to the attaché-case and this time produced the *Illustrated London News*.

Turley was shown a three-inch flashlight photograph of a woman in furs beside a man in evening dress. *Mr. and Mrs. Arthur Kynsard were among the guests of the management at the re-opening of the Cosmopolitan Theatre.*

Turley looked again at the Titania advertisement in the women's magazine. The lusciousness of the coloured display was distorting. He covered the cami-knicks with blotting paper and concentrated on the head.

"There's a resemblance, all right," he muttered.

"It was her husband that interested me," said Flanch. "You see, a group of us thought we'd have a smack at the railway over some charges they'd clapped on us. He appeared for the railway. Shall I forget him! After he'd done banging at me, I had to step out and have a couple."

Turley opened on another line.

"Do you know whether Trotwood was her real name?"

"I didn't bother myself or her with that kind o' question. Why should I care? Come to that, I shouldn't wonder if it turned out she'd got a husband tucked away somewhere."

"Would it surprise you, Mr. Flanch, if I were to tell you that Betsy Trotwood and Mrs. Barbara Kynsard were one and the same person?"

"Surprise me!" A rich, throaty laugh rumbled round the room. "It wouldn't surprise me, because I'd know you were talking through your hat—begging your pardon—I'd know you were mistaken in your supposition. Why, look at those photos! You can say they'd be mistaken for sisters, but that's only girl's chatter. Anyone could tell they're not the same girl. Style, for one thing. You can't see that Mrs. Kynsard standing up in front of a lot of all-sorts to be photographed in her whatsernames."

Turley could draw no immediate conclusion from the photographs.

"Mr. Flanch. You will read in the later editions that, before you came into this room, Mr. Kynsard identified the body as that of his wife."

"*Did* he!" Samuel Flanch lolled back in his chair, contorting his features in profound bewilderment. When he spoke, it was Turley's turn to be surprised.

"Well, he can have her! I gotter forget poor Betsy, and that's as good a way as any. Besides, it lets me out."

Turley was not satisfied.

"Are you ready to believe that this girl you knew as Betsy must have been Mrs. Kynsard—leading a double life?"

"I gotter think o' my missus now!" ejaculated Flanch. "I came here of my own free will to help you out. And now you tell me it's all set without me butting in." He repeated: "That lets me out."

"It doesn't let you out!" snapped Turley. "We don't care who she is, except in so far as it helps us to find who killed her. When I first suggested to you that she might be Kynsard's wife, you laughed. How did you know I was talking through my hat?—that was what you said."

"And I apologised for being so rude, if you remember," evaded Flanch. "I was the one who was talking through his hat." He bounced to his feet. "I'm going to hop it, Inspector, if you've no objection to same. If that gentleman says she's his wife, it's okay by me. What's the good o' me kicking up a lot o' dust saying I don't think she is?"

"One minute! Was Betsy a professional model?"

"I shouldn't say she was a regular professional. There was that one firm that used to photograph her—and that wasn't every week." He added: "I've got an idea she used to sell artists' pictures on commission—or try to. One time, the Morris was bung full o' such pictures, and she told me she was helping her friend Barbara to sell them—or exhibit them or something. Looney pictures, mostly! There's one in the bedroom now, standing against the wall. Girl's head with snakes coming out of it. Gives me the creeps."

"Was she in a job?"

"Shouldn't think so. I wouldn't call her greedy, but she did cost a bit. Never had any cash of her own." He added: "I knew her nature, but I didn't know much else about her, nor where she came from—sort of posh orphanage, maybe. We'd meet mostly at the flat—go out for dinner—have a day together in the country sometimes. She was a pally sort."

Turley had finished with Flanch for the moment. He made a few enquiries of the local superintendent, then called Rawlings.

"Cami-knicks! Panties! Step-ins! You wouldn't know what I mean, but the Titania Company will show you. Look at this ad. That's Trotwood, that was! Pick up anything you can from Titania about her. Ask 'em to lend us the original photographs. If there's one of her decently dressed, so much the better. Try *Illustrated London News* for the original of this photo of the Kynsards. Ask the Tythrop Garage, near the flat, for all they can give you about the Morris."

"I'll go myself, sir."

"You won't. There's a bit o' diplomacy waiting for you. Get this. Deceased is probably Kynsard's wife and Flanch's mistress. Same girl. But Flanch doesn't believe she was Kynsard's wife. He's pretending he does believe it, because he's scared stiff his wife will find out about the girl and he wants to step out of the case.

"You'll say—or you ought to—that what Flanch does or doesn't believe doesn't matter. Quite right, boy! But it is just possible they're not the same girl, so we've got to check."

"Meaning that Kynsard or Flanch might have given a phony identification, sir?"

"It doesn't have to be phony. May have been made in good faith. But it's odds on their being the same girl. If Betsy and Barbara are not one, you have two girls looking much alike, each having a scar on the tummy made by two stitches—at exactly the same spot. All the same, it's short of absolute certainty.

"Assuming there are two girls like each other—and remembering that the doctor admitted he had tinkered the face up a bit—Kynsard may have suggested to himself that it was his wife. He came here in an agitated state, expecting to find his wife. So we'll have an independent identification. The Kynsard girl's mother—Mrs. Tremman. She may be at Kynsard's house. I want you to go personally, smooth her over and get her to come here and identify."

IV

Arthur Kynsard lived in a house that had been built for his great-grandfather. It had the advantages and drawbacks of a mid-Victorian mansion. Though barely four miles from Buckingham Palace, it stood in its own acre, with outbuildings which had formerly housed three horses, two carriages and a coachman with wife and family. As it was almost impossible to obtain a gardener, the garden created the illusion of extreme poverty. Rambler roses blocked the paths to the one-time tennis and croquet lawns, now a tangle of matted grass and seeding thistles. Kynsard had to content himself with keeping the carriageway clear of brambles.

Returning from the police station, Kynsard drove in by the rear gate, opening on what had been a lane in 1870, had become a side-street, and now, through bombing, again bore the semblance of a lane.

Mrs. Tremman, his mother-in-law, sat in the bow window of the drawing-room, watching the open gate of the miniature drive.

Margaret Tremman was a very young fifty—could still carry auburn hair. She was clever with dress. In recent years, enforced exercise in the form of housework had given her flesh a firmness it had lacked in the thirties. She had an intuitive grace of body which enabled all but very young and very old men to ignore her age.

In temperament, she was of the type that brought vitality to the drawing-room in the days of middle-class ascendancy. As a mother, she had been guilty of all those common failures which no one notices except the child. Deeply, if unconsciously, jealous of Barbara, even at school age, she had systematically kept the girl younger than her years.

As a mother-in-law, she had been a success. Kynsard thought her decorative and amiable. He approved of her, being unaware that she fancied he was attracted to her.

Kynsard, entering the house through the kitchen quarters, was in the drawing-room before Mrs. Tremman knew he had arrived.

Her eyes searched his face. The woodenness she found there told her the essential truth.

"She's dead, Arthur?"

He took her hand, slender like Barbara's, enveloped it.

"I won't try to break it gently—you aren't that sort," he said. "Barbara has been killed." He added enough detail to head off irrelevant questions.

"Oh! Like that awful case everybody was talking about! Gibbern! They ought not to be allowed to print such things."

She prattled while she tried to grasp that her daughter had been murdered. Presently she looked up at him.

"You knew!" she exclaimed.

He shrugged, said nothing.

"You knew this morning. Before you went to the police station—before the police rang up."

"Yes. I think I knew even before that. Last night, while I was trying to go to sleep, I had the feeling that it had happened."

Mrs. Tremman said it was a terrible shock. She said everything which she believed she ought to say. She told a meandering anecdote bearing on telepathy.

"But it's funny you should get a thought-wave from her. You and poor Barbara weren't very close, were you!"

"No! It wasn't a complete success, Margaret."

"Poor boy! I guessed it, of course. I was always grateful for your loyalty to her, Arthur."

She waited in vain for him to say what a good mother she had been. She sighed and cried a little, albeit gracefully. She reminded herself of her many kindnesses to her daughter and of her forbearance. Youth was charming but exasperating. It would be hypocritical to deny that poor Barbara had been difficult. As a mother, she had been robbed of her natural authority when her husband tied up the property in that ridiculous trust. He had believed that it would be Barbara who would eventually enjoy the double income. Well, he was wrong!

"This is the police, by the look of it," said Kynsard as a car turned into the drive. "They'll probably keep calling here at all hours. I'll see them in the dining-room."

"If they should want me, you can tell them I'm not being hysterical," she said.

"You're being very brave. I always knew you would be if anything happened."

He really was a very dear boy, she thought, as he left the room. And so clever, with a successful career stretching before him. It was good to reflect that her brother had been of great help to Arthur by briefing him so often for the Railways. True that her brother had said that Arthur was a lucky find. But the fact remained that she herself—indirectly—had brought him the most lucrative part of his practice. She stood in front of the massive Victorian overmantel and adjusted her make-up, resolving that she would not cry again. She had barely finished when Kynsard returned.

"I say, Margaret—I'm awf'lly sorry—but the police want you to go with them to identify her."

"I don't mind. I'm living on my nerves, I suppose. Anyhow, I intended to see her. Don't look so worried, dear."

"It's worse than you think. I won't have them taking you there unprepared." He put both hands on her shoulders. "Barbara's face was injured—there's a slight distortion which might give you a shock."

"You were silly enough to say just now that I'm a brave woman. I'm not really, but I have a certain self-control. I promise you I won't break down or anything."

"There's more in it than that. The distortion—I was in some doubt myself for a few seconds. Of course, I satisfied myself—completely and absolutely—that it was Barbara."

"I shall be able to do the same."

"Yes, but—there's something I must tell you which has been kept from you. Do you remember, in our first year, you gave her for her birthday a magnificent set of scissors in a crocodile case?"

"I remember, certainly! But what *are* you leading up to, Arthur?"

"When we went down to Devonshire that year she took the scissors with her."

"Why? She wouldn't want them on holiday."

"Never mind—she took them. And she had an accident. Ran the point of one of them into her chest—look at me—about where I'm pointing. There was a doctor staying in the hotel. He put stitches in, and by the time we came back to Town it was more or less all over."

"But why did you have to make a mystery of it? I've never known poor Barbara suffer in silence."

"She said you'd be upset, because the scissors had been your gift. Some superstition about scissors and knives bringing bad luck."

"What utter nonsense! She knew I wasn't superstitious—in that way!"

"I didn't go into that. The point is that the scar remains. And if the police ask you for identifying marks on the body it is better you should know. Otherwise——"

He broke off.

"Otherwise?" she asked.

"Otherwise, Margaret, the police may ask you to make a second visit, to make sure—and start a debate about it on the spot—and that, my dear, would tear your nerves to ribbons and make you ill."

A smile spread from her lips to her eyes and enveloped him.

"Dear Arthur! You do take such care of me! But you're simply not to worry about me. I'll remember what you've said. Are you coming with me?"

"I think you'd better go with them. The Chrysler is still bunged up with those pictures. I'll clear them out now. Pick you up at the police station."

A minute later she came back into the room.

"They're not quite ready to start. That young detective is talking to Mrs. Henson. I wonder what he's bothering her about—she'll give notice if we aren't all very careful. He asked her to take him upstairs!"

"Only checking up. The police check every statement you

make. Be careful not to give them any more information than they ask. For instance, that point about the scissors! You can volunteer that statement, because it's part of the identification. But if you add—unasked—that you actually got the information from me, they'll come back to me to re-check—then back to you."

"You're over-anxious, Arthur," she said. She added, talking partly to herself: "I can't think why Barbara didn't want me to know. It can't have been for the reason she gave you."

Kynsard stayed with her until she left in the police car. On his way to the garage, he was stopped in the hall by Mrs. Henson, the cook-general, a prim, embittered widow of thirty.

"Is Mrs. Tremman going to stay here, sir?" The question veiled a threat.

"Certainly not! She'll leave after lunch. I suppose you can put up something for us—it needn't be anything special?"

"Yes, sir. I've found the ration books." She lowered her voice. "Have they caught the man yet?"

"No. But they seem to think they will. As I daresay you know, the car has been traced to a friend. A Miss Betsy Trotwood. I've never met her myself, though I believe she has been here in my absence. Do you know anything about her?"

"I've never seen her. But Mrs. Kynsard often mentioned her—she used to gossip a good deal about where she was going and who was coming to see her. That young detective asked me about her and I told him what I've told you. . . . *Ooh!*"

"Thought of something, Mrs. Henson?"

"Day before yesterday we were bringing down those pictures—same as you've got in the car now, sir. And Mrs. Kynsard said: 'Before I forget, I must tell Betsy about George's —"Methoosah"'" it sounded like, meaning one of those pictures. And when I came down to the hall I heard her on the telephone saying you were taking some pictures in the Chrysler and she said: 'In that case, you'd better bring the Methoosah here, and they can all go in together.'"

Kynsard nodded. It was the way Barbara talked. Mrs. Henson had unconsciously imitated her.

"If the police ask you again, it would be as well to mention that you heard Mrs. Kynsard speaking on the phone to Miss

Trotwood. After lunch, when Mrs. Tremman has gone, I'd be glad if you'd help me bring those pictures in. I'll stack them in the garage now. I must hurry or I shall keep Mrs. Tremman waiting at the police station."

v

After lunch, Margaret Tremman was in no hurry to go home: they adjourned to the drawing-room—cosy in spite of its size and its jumble of periods. Arthur Kynsard had been unable to do anything to the house. Some of the furniture bought by his great-grandfather had survived better than the Edwardian additions, which seemed flimsy and pretentious in the era of austerity.

Since returning from the police station, they had not spoken of Barbara. Margaret was intrigued by Arthur's demeanour. Was he grieving at all, she wondered.

"We are holding ourselves in—that will create a complex," she said. "Don't you want to know how I got on at the police station?"

"If you're sure you feel like talking about it," he invited.

"The police were very gentle and sympathetic. But they did ask one or two irritating questions, and I was glad you had told me about the scissors. Thank heavens that part of it is finished!"

"But it isn't. If they don't find the man in a few hours, they will trace Barbara's own movements as far back as they can, interview all her friends——"

"That's what I'm afraid of. It was all a little awkward. They asked me if I knew a friend of hers called Betsy Trotwood. In spite of everything, I nearly laughed. I don't suppose the police read Dickens."

"She's real! Dickens took his names from London shop-fronts. You'll find them nearly all in the telephone book today."

"Arthur, did you ever meet Barbara's Betsy Trotwood?"

"I never actually met her."

"Nor heard her voice? Nor saw her handwriting? Nor met anybody who knew her?"

"True, but irrelevant."

"You know I'm never irrelevant! When Barbara was a little girl and had been naughty, she never denied outright what she had done. She always said 'Betsy' had done it. An imaginary projection of herself. It was Betsy who broke things and lost things. Betsy who stole the jam. Not that she ever did really steal jam—children didn't before the war—but you know what I mean."

"The Betsy you're talking about," said Kynsard, "never had any toys of her own. *This* Betsy has a Morris saloon, which Barbara used to borrow. It's been in the garage here more than once. It was registered to Elizabeth Trotwood. It was the car in which Barbara was found. Mrs. Henson believes she heard Barbara speaking to Betsy on the telephone."

Margaret thought it over.

"Betsy did have toys—the toys Barbara was tired of. And Barbara could be heard talking to Betsy."

"You're on the wrong line, my dear," said Kynsard. "I've never seen the Trotwood girl, but I can show you a photo of her." He went to the bamboo paper-rack—a survival from the 'nineties—rummaged at the back of it, then laid an out-of-date weekly before her, showing a full-page advertisement in colour.

"Titania! I wear that myself. But what—is *this* the girl?—the model?"

"That is the real Betsy Trotwood."

Margaret looked more closely at the photograph, then laughed.

"Well, old boy, that seems to me to prove that I'm right, not you!"

Kynsard glared at her in bewilderment.

"If you look at that photo closely," she explained, "you'll see that this girl is remarkably like Barbara herself. The nose is not quite the same. And this girl's teeth are a wee bit more prominent. And the auburn is redder than Barbara's, but that may be the colour printing. I daresay you know, by the way, that Barbara tinted—the natural colour faded when she was twenty-three."

His fixed glare disconcerted her.

"I mean"—Margaret tapped the advertisement page—
"this is a real young woman, of course! But I don't suppose
for a moment that her name is Betsy—still less Betsy Trotwood. And I don't suppose Barbara had ever seen her, except
in this advertisement."

He turned his back on her and paced the room.

"Have you forgotten," he demanded, "that Elizabeth
Trotwood is registered as the owner of the car? It's a futile
discussion. The police will look up that girl——"

"And find she was Barbara—Barbara making her dream
life partly real, identifying herself with an unknown girl
physically like her. Arthur, we're being rather absurd about
this. I want to tell you something about yourself which I'm
afraid you won't like very much. May I?"

"Go ahead."

"You don't want to believe that this Betsy Trotwood
business was a waking fantasy, because you shrink from
admitting to yourself that poor Barbara was just a little bit
mentally unbalanced. Her father was a pronounced eccentric
—as I found to my cost."

"Well, I'm damned!"

"I don't mind your being damned, dear boy, but I do mind
your being offended."

"I'm not offended!" He gave a sharp laugh. "You've got
hold of the butt end of a truth the wrong side up. I *did* think
she was insane. But I've known for two years that she was
not."

"How could you be sure?"

"I had her examined. She didn't mention it to you, because
she didn't know." With calculated effect, he continued: "Did
she tell you about Lady Maenton and the mechanical mouse?"

"I didn't know you knew the Maentons."

"We don't—*now!* Your brother very decently introduced
us. Maenton was likely to be useful to me. We got them to a
cocktail party, here. Barbara was at her best—witty and
gay and looking lovely. Lady Maenton was sitting where you
are. I was over there. I heard some chatter about mice..A
minute later there came a shriek from Lady Maenton. Barbara
had loosed a toy mouse—a thing that goes by clockwork, runs

round in a circle. And Barbara was roaring with laughter—
expecting everybody else to laugh with her."

"Oh, Arthur, I'm so sorry!" Margaret Tremman was profoundly shocked.

"There had been one or two practical jokes before we were
married. I was—well—puzzled. On our honeymoon she
played some childish trick with my shaving tackle. Three
months after we got back here, the mouse episode occurred. I
was more alarmed than angry.

"In our first year, this nursery-age joking became a feature
of our life. She used to buy mechanical contraptions at a toy
shop—things that unexpectedly squeaked or popped or
squirted water. I used to lose my temper sometimes. A day
or two after we'd made it up, something would go pop in the
bathroom—or when I opened my brief-bag in chambers
there'd be some jack-in-the-box effect. And we had to laugh
about it when I came home in the evening.

"When she had 'flu—you remember?—we'd been married
two years then—I conspired with old Dr. Watkins to call in
Sir William Turvey, pretending he was a gynaecologist. He
came twice. Put her through his hoop—me, as well—made
me tell him all I could about her."

"Did he ask about her heredity?"

"Not exactly. Home influence."

"I hope you gave me a good character?"

"He told me that she was as sane as he and I. He explained
that nearly every adult has layers of juvenilism. He instanced
middle-aged men who were always hanging round their
old school—intelligent women who secretly dress dolls and
play with them. There was no treatment. The only action to
be taken was to warn her not to make a fool of herself to anyone but me.

"I duly warned her. She didn't take it seriously—thought
I was being 'stuffy'. That meant I couldn't let her loose among
professional connections. We had to remodel our habits. That
was the beginning of the estrangement. She joined an art
school—made her own circle of friends—including Betsy."

"Including Betsy!" echoed Margaret, with a tolerant
smile. "Did she stop the practical jokes at home?"

"Yes. Oddly enough, I missed them. They were damned irritating, but they did show that she was happy. There was only one more—about three months ago—and then, like a fool, I lost my temper over it."

"She told me," put in Margaret. "You were absorbed in reading that awful Gibbern case. And she got herself up in your wig and gown——"

His thoughts slid away. It was the wig-and-gown joke that had given him, to his own astonishment, an impulse to murder his wife.

For a moment he had shocked himself. Then he laughed it off. The murder impulse was probably felt by thousands of decent persons of both sexes who never did anything to express the impulse in action. Why, he himself had once felt how pleasant it would be to murder an ill-tempered judge who had bullied him! And one of the waiters at Blainley's! And now and again Mrs. Henson! Occasionally some non-criminal did turn the impulse into action. Some thirty or forty persons a year in the whole country. Gibbern had been one of those.

But Gibbern was an ass—an honest ass who had committed himself to lying and couldn't put the lies over. A sensible man would stage his murder so that he need tell no lies. He would build the murder into his own routine.

In the days that followed, he pursued the idea as an idle exercise. In the practice of murder, there were two main methods. The first was to conceal the body. The austerity era made this easier than it used to be. On the fringe of London there were still a number of bomb-shattered houses, factories and other buildings which had not been cleared—could not be cleared for yet another five years or more.

There was, for instance, the wreckage of that cider factory —with a flooded basement—which he had often noticed when driving to Rubington, where Barbara's mother lived.

But that method would not be useful to a husband who wished to murder his wife. If the concealment were successful, he would eventually have to apply for leave to presume death. Moreover, concealing the body was inartistic as well as dangerous. It fell into the category of the unplanned murder

—at best, only to be used as a desperate device if something should go wrong with the plan.

Gibbern's idea was sound. Make no attempt to conceal the body. Let it be found—and have your tale ready.

The exercise developed into a work of art, constructed of common sense and an exact knowledge of the rules of evidence. He soon perceived that to have a tale ready would merely be to repeat Gibbern's mistake.

There must be no tale at all. No statement of fact that could not be proved. No theory of the crime.

Gibbern had been unable to distinguish between suspicion —which automatically falls on a husband—and evidence. He had been unable to endure being suspected and had tried to dispel suspicion by explanation. It was the job of the police, not of Gibbern, to explain how Mrs. Gibbern came to be murdered.

Suppose he himself wanted to murder Barbara. The time to choose would be between breakfast and the arrival of Mrs. Henson. And up to the moment of murder there must be no unusual behaviour, requiring special explanation. In placing the body for discovery he would not say he had done this or that, which he had not done. He must be able to describe his own movements truthfully, simply omitting to mention the presence of a corpse.

That was the formula. Have only one thing to remember— Don't mention the corpse.

Moreover, Gibbern had shown anxiety about his "missing" wife too soon. He had failed to create circumstances justifying anxiety.

Now if, say, he had asked his wife to telephone for a table for lunch . . .

" . . . and although I'm her mother I never blinded myself to her faults. And I say her vanity would never have let her do it. Don't you think I'm right?"

Margaret Tremman had been prattling on—he had not the least idea what she was asking him.

"I don't follow how the vanity comes into it."

"She would have been conspicuous in the street in that dress and in those awful old shoes. Mrs. Henson says one toecap had come partly unstitched but Barbara wouldn't allow her to throw them away. I have the same weakness myself for an old pair. I wouldn't let you see me in my house-shoes for the world!"

"Hm! That's a riddle for the police!"

"If she was enticed out of the house like that, I can tell the police that the murderer had no eye for women's clothes."

"Good heavens!" He regarded her with what might have been admiration. "That's very astute of you, Margaret."

"Not very!" she protested. "And, anyhow, it's nonsense! You couldn't 'entice' Barbara to go out like that. She'd make you wait while she changed."

Margaret was pleasantly aware that she had reclaimed his full attention.

"It's my opinion," she continued, "that poor Barbara was killed in this house—or in the garden, it might be—before Mrs. Henson arrived."

For a time he said nothing. Then:

"Possibly you're right. For myself, I haven't the ghost of a theory of how it all happened."

VI

The local police were successful in the one assignment with which Detective Inspector Turley entrusted them—the movements of the Morris car in their own district.

The first three hours had yielded a series of negatives. A number of persons passing the spot at relevant times during the night had failed to notice a parked car in the blind alley. Suddenly the negatives coalesced into a positive. The last person who had *not* seen the Morris car was a constable whose spell of duty finished at eight in the morning.

He had "taken up a position" at the mouth of the blind alley as the clocks were striking seven-thirty. He had remained there until approximately a quarter to eight.

Therefore the Morris had been driven into the blind alley between seven forty-five—when the crowd was collecting outside the prison—and eight five, when Superintendent Halsdon had found it.

At five thirty Detective Inspector Turley held a conference in his room at Scotland Yard. Present were his two
chief subordinates, Wallsend and Swilbey, both detective-
sergeants—also young Rawlings, who arrived just in
time.

"We'll hear what you have to say first, Rawlings."

"Morris car, sir. Taken out of the Tythrop Garage by
Trotwood at twenty to seven last night. Mileage total then
thirty four thousand three twenty six."

"Huh! Why the blazes do they keep a log of their clients'
mileage?"

"Not of every client. Only those who complain about the
tyres supplied by the Tythrop. Trotwood complained recently.
The day before yesterday they fitted two new ones. I telephoned Superintendent Halsdon, who gave me the present
reading—three thirty three—approximately seven miles. I
checked distances on the map. Tythrop to the prison, five
miles. Tythrop to Kynsard's house, three miles. Kynsard's
house to prison, four miles. All calculations to the nearest
mile only. At that, the reading is consistent with the car having
been driven from Tythrop to Kynsard's house and from there
to the prison."

"Good bit o' work, Rawlings!" Turley was inclined to be
formal at these conferences. "It doesn't make a lot of sense
at present, but that's not your fault. Did the garage tell you
how she was dressed?"

"The man said he didn't notice anything special about her
dress, except the nylons. She had the ordinary woman's bag
in one hand and an unframed picture in the other, which
she put into the car."

Turley made a note. Rawlings went on:

"Clothes and underclothes, sir. At Cranebrook Mansions I
could find no trace of the house-frock nor of the old house-
shoes in which Mrs. Kynsard is believed to have left home
before ten o'clock."

"I was at the flat when he came," put in Wallsend.
"Helped him search. They certainly weren't there."

"That ticks that off," said Turley. "Mrs. Kynsard didn't
go to the flat and change."

"Shoes same size," continued Rawlings. "One pair identical—in lizard skin with the back part of the shoe cut wedge-shape. Other clothing—two walking-suits, one pinafore frock, two evening dresses. Coney-skin coat. Underwear, night-dresses, shoes and stockings, which I have listed. In a cardboard box with Titania trade markings I found one—'set' I think they call it, sir—similar to that shown in the advertisement."

"That links on," said Turley. "Flanch said she had bought two sets. Maybe she was wearing the other set."

"A point about the Titania line, sir. When I was at Kynsard's house this morning I got the servant to take me to Mrs. Kynsard's room. There was no factory stuff there. The underclothes were art-and-crafty. The girl told me that Mrs. Kynsard had them hand-made by sort of artist people. Very fine work it was."

"Nothing in that!" said Turley. "The girl was running two personalities. Art-and-craft for Kynsard—glamour for Flanch. What about you, Wallsend?"

"Not my lucky day, sir!" Wallsend was a temperamentally gloomy man who would report his own successes as if they were failures. "It's a two-roomed flat with bathroom and kitchenette. Clean and well kept. I got nothing out of it. Not even a bit o' the girl's handwriting. The caretaker hadn't seen her for ten days. He's not a porter—lives with his wife in a basement flat, not on Trotwood's staircase, either. He doesn't see the tenants except by chance or when there's some complaint."

Turley turned up the notes on his interview with Flanch. "'Girl's head with snakes in bedroom'?" he read aloud.

"Snakes in the bedroom, sir?"

"The chief means a picture," cut in Swilbey. "I've seen that one, sir. Got it in my report." Presently Swilbey was explaining: "I've been working on the Morris. A few women's things in the dash-boot—lipstick and the rest of it. Checked with Kynsard's maid. Same lipstick. Galley proofs of the catalogue of an art exhibition. Seven items have underline saying 'lent by Mrs. Arthur Kynsard'.

"Now there were a lot o' pictures in Kynsard's Chrysler

yesterday. He pitched them out of the car at lunchtime today, and in the afternoon the maid helped him carry them back to the house—they're not heavy but they're awkward to carry. They were stacked up in the morning-room. I counted 'em. There were eight, not seven. And one o' them was a girl's head with hair looking like snakes."

"Let's see those catalogue proofs," said Turley. He glanced down the long strips, without immediate result.

"What about trying under 'Medusa', sir?" suggested Rawlings.

"Ah! Here we are. 'Medusa. Artist: George Penton'. We'll get that picture and ask Flanch if it's the one he saw in Betsy's bedroom.

"You, Rawlings, remind that garage man that the girl was carrying a picture and ask him if he noticed any snakes— only don't put it that way. If that girl was carrying those snakes at that time it looks as if she went straight to Kynsard's house. I'll take care of that end myself. Keep going, Swilbey."

"Continuing the Morris, sir," resumed Swilbey. From a pocket case he produced a theatre ticket issued by an agency —a stall for the matinee next Saturday at the Parnassus Music Hall. "That was on the floor by the driving seat, might have dropped out of the dash-boot. I checked at the agency. Two stalls were ordered on the phone yesterday by Flanch and were delivered at his warehouse at approximately three fifteen. The warehouse was shut. Flanch was standing outside waiting for the messenger. As a rule, the agency would issue the two seats on one ticket. Flanch asked 'em to make out two tickets."

"Three fifteen!" echoed Turley. "Flanch says he didn't see the girl yesterday. Looks like we're getting a move on."

"Maybe, sir. Flanch couldn't have sent her that ticket by post—it couldn't have reached her before she took the Morris out at six forty. He might have sent a messenger—I haven't seen him about it—thought I'd better report first. I've sent a man to find out Flanch's office hours."

"Right! You can see Flanch about it. Don't frighten him." Turley planted his elbows on the notes and dossiers and leant over his table.

"Now, boys, we have enough to get started. We'll take the

identification first. So far, the photographs have carried us nowhere. I sent 'em to the experts, all lumped together. The Titania one; the one of Mr. and Mrs. Kynsard together; two cabinet photos of Mrs. Kynsard from her house; and the death photos. I asked the experts to say whether the photographs were of three girls, of two girls, or of one girl. Opinion is about equally divided as to whether there are two girls or one girl. Only one expert said there were three girls. Another expert thought he saw some difference in the teeth. I'm having a dentist take a cast of the jaw and teeth of deceased.

"Fingerprints of corpse. None in Mrs. Kynsard's bedroom. The housemaid, expecting the police, had cleaned up before we came. Two clear prints on the toilet things in the flat at Cranebrook Mansions. That's a clue that it's the same girl; but it's not evidence, because they are stated to have been friends. If that's true, Barbara—Mrs. Kynsard—may have been to the flat at any time except when Flanch was there.

"Now, we've been paying too much attention to this question of one-girl-or-two. We're going to settle it in here, right away. Until further orders, you, Swilbey, will go ahead on the assumption that Barbara Kynsard and Betsy Trotwood are the same person. That means you'll concentrate on the Barbara line. Don't be frightened of that house-dress and those shoes. Barbara may have bought a new rig-out unknown to the maid.

"I want you, Wallsend, to work as if you *knew* there were two girls. Your first job is to find Trotwood—alive or dead. That means you'll be keeping a wide eye on Flanch, in close liaison with Swilbey. So far, Flanch has no alibi.

"Swilbey, you've got a deadline at six forty, when your Barbara Kynsard took the Morris from the Tythrop. She may have been killed a minute or so later. She may have been alive for an hour or so. That's the best the doctor can do for us.

"Now for Kynsard. He was in his house talking to his maid at six. Talking to his mother-in-law, Mrs. Tremman, at seven. Mrs. Tremman was with him until about midnight, when he drove her to her house in Rubington.

"Forward of the six-forty deadline, there's only the twenty minutes' gap—beginning six forty—in Kynsard's alibi—

unless he's in conspiracy with Barbara's mother, which is obviously punk. If you can't trace the Morris from the Tythrop, you'll have to work back of the deadline."

"That suits me, sir." Swilbey chuckled. "And as Flanch is an honorary husband, as you might say, it works out on the Gibbern model. Kynsard or Flanch. One of 'em faking a pervert murder."

"Some of you boys ought to've been poets," grinned Turley. "I didn't say anything about Gibbern. Only, that Morris didn't travel very far. Never left the built-up area. Hardly gives a maniac a fair chance."

VII

"That lets me out!" repeated Samuel Flanch as he walked from the police station in search of a taxi. He repeated it several times in the hope of convincing himself. It was a great pity that he couldn't make a yarn of it in his trade club. "Hi, taxi!"

On the whole, the interview had run along the lines he had planned, until that extraordinary business about Betsy being Kynsard's wife. Might be a good thing—might really let him out. After all, it didn't matter what they called her. The Inspector had not questioned any of his statements. Kynsard saying she was his wife didn't upset anything he had said about her as Betsy Trotwood.

Retrospectively, he listened to his own voice, talking to the inspector. The dress bill—yes; the time he went to the flat last night—the general circumstances of the flat and his relations with the girl—if the police checked up, it would come out a hundred per cent okay.

There was that bit about his missing her, about her being a good sort. No means of checking that sort of thing. He laughed so loudly that the driver glanced over his shoulder.

He became grave, almost wistful. Come to think of it, he *would* miss her. He had said she was a good sort: even that was true, in a way. And that she was pally. Funny how it happened sometimes that when you thought you were telling lies you were really telling the truth.

It was eighteen months, as near as made no matter, since he had picked her up outside that art place in Chelsea. Full of surprises from the first, she had been. And full of surprises to the last, if you cared to put it like that.

He had been surprised when she accepted his invitation to come and have a bite at the Palais de Danse, surprised again when he found that she could hardly dance at all and so thought that he was very good.

When he kissed her, he guessed that she was an errant wife, a bit inclined to be ashamed of herself until you jollied her out of it. Lemonade was what she drank, except sometimes, when she would take all the gin you'd let her have, and then she'd be solemn as an owl and a bit of a nuisance. Meaning to say that she would only have a drink when she felt her nerve was failing.

The best-looking kid he had ever had to do with, and the jolliest, most times. There was something about her—made you sort of forget everything.

Never knew where she came from. Nor where she thought she was going to, until she told him—and that spoilt everything. He didn't think she was a Londoner. He judged by her speech, which was a mixture of Cockney and posh, with a bit of Scotch and maybe a splash of Irish—she had probably travelled about a bit and lived with different kinds of people.

For all he knew, she might have been a little queer in the head. That would account for the last fortnight, which had been a bit thick.

Those eighteen months had slipped by like winking. No more fun now! Why had he cried like that at the police station? Must have been in love with her in a sort of way. Cor, what an end to everything! There wouldn't even be anything to remember except the nightmare of the last fortnight, when she had suddenly demanded that he should fix a divorce and marry her.

"What part of Covent Garden d'you want, sir?"

"This'll do."

He crossed "the Garden" from the end of Henrietta Street, took out his latchkey and admitted himself to his one-room office. There were a few letters on the floor, which he picked up and put in a green canvas bag kept for that purpose. The room, like most of its kind, was sparsely fitted—gave no indication of the prosperity of its tenant. A writing-table, wall maps of railways: two telegraph boards—on which were pinned notices from the railways and the haulage companies.

He sat down at the table, took from a drawer a small notebook, with entries in pencil, and checked his figures. Presently his eye was caught by an envelope, creased, under the ornamental corncob that served as a paperweight. On the envelope was scrawled in his own handwriting *Me*. He stared at it, unable to remember anything about it.

The envelope bore the imprint of a theatre-ticket agency. Inside was a single ticket for a stall for the matinée at the Parnassus on Saturday.

He remembered now. They were to carry on as usual for a bit, while he explored the question of divorce and marriage. He had given her the other ticket, telling her that he expected to turn up late. She was to take a seat, and he would join her as soon as he could.

Shan't go by myself, he reflected. Give the ticket to somebody. No, that was the kind of thing that often led to a lot of trouble. He lit a match and burned envelope and ticket.

After half an hour with the notebook, he locked up and walked two hundred yards to his warehouse on the other side of Long Acre. It was a small affair, employing six hands and two male clerks. He opened his letters, none of which required individual attention and passed them to the senior clerk. The business, except for the buying, ran more or less automatically.

He went out to lunch, returning to the warehouse to keep an eye on things before closing at three o'clock. He was preparing to leave, when a man walked in whom he guessed to be from the Yard.

"Mr. Flanch? I'm from the Yard. Shan't keep you a couple o' minutes. Check up, you know. You start early in your business, I believe?"

"This morning," said Flanch, "I got here about half-past six, half an hour late, as I'd had ignition trouble. Bloke's mending it now. Tuesdays and Thursdays I'm here much earlier—generally about three. My business is rather specialised and I mostly know what's coming."

"And you were here in the warehouse for some time?"

"No. Just looked in and went over to my office in the Garden. Part of the time I was in the market, buying."

"Were you buying, for instance, between seven thirty and eight thirty?"

"No." Flanch was uneasy. "It's a bit of a job to remember when you tie it down like that. Part of the time I was in my office—don't remember any callers about then. I stepped over and had a bit o' breakfast at that place at the corner. I'm a regular there, though that won't help you much, as there are a good few others."

"That's quite all right, Mr. Flanch, and thanks very much."

It was a pity, thought Flanch, that the police couldn't get it over in one sitting. Thanks very much and all that! Some men would find it getting on their nerves if there was going to be too much of it.

At three o'clock he abandoned his intention of going straight home. He went to the club and ordered tea, gossiped until the mid-afternoon editions arrived.

"Murder Maniac's Victim Identified." "Well Known Barrister's Wife." "Mystery Girl Missing." Two papers republished the photo of Kynsard and his wife, from which a third, the *Echo*, had cut out Kynsard.

But Flanch's immediate interest was on the "mystery girl".

The police are anxious to get in touch with a glamorous photographer's model who has the Dickensian name of Betsy Trotwood. Miss Trotwood (picture back page) bears a striking physical resemblance to the murdered woman. This, coupled with the fact that they were known to each other and were on friendly terms, is believed to be of importance. Miss Trotwood is missing from her flat in Cranebrook Mansions, W.C., and so far all efforts to trace her have failed.

On the back page was the same photograph of Betsy "by courtesy of Titania Ltd." He grimaced. A strain of prudery made him hate those photographs—even if the whatsernames were only a sort of stage-clothes.

He settled down to reading the accounts. They agreed as to the facts, which were meagre, but differed in the trimmings. All accepted the maniac theory. The *Echo* alone emphasised the "macabre note" of the car having been parked at the prison wherein Gibbern was being hanged.

They had started an intensive search for Betsy. Well, he had known they would, as soon as the inspector showed he believed Kynsard's identification. That meant that his own courageous visit to the police station had been wasted. The police would keep on bobbing up at him, asking questions about her. Sooner or later Louie, his wife, would tumble to what was going on.

Funny, he thought, how his deep love for Louie hadn't been touched by his feeling for Betsy. The latter must have been, he supposed, simple lust with a bit o' soft stuff on top. He had blubbered like a kid outside the mortuary—because it came to him suddenly that Betsy had given him a lot of fun.

Poor Louie was nothing to look at now—had been physically non-existent for ten years, apart from her paralysis. And that, he told himself almost daily, was his fault.

The paralysis had resulted indirectly from a car smash, their first car. He himself had been publicly exonerated. Indisputably, the accident had been caused by the drunkard who had run into him. But Samuel Flanch believed that he would have been able to dodge the drunkard if he had not himself "had a couple" at the last stop.

He had escaped with a few scratches, but Louie was condemned to a pair of crutches for life. She had never reproached him because she believed what the judge had said when he sentenced the drunkard. He did not guess that she had found compensation in her own way. In fact, his gentleness and solicitude made her regard him as an ideal husband. He was aware only of a lively sense of guilt—of a hopeless indebtedness to his wife.

"I couldn't find anything wrong with your ignition, Mr. Flanch. And your feed's all right, too. Sorry I'll have to charge you five bob for the examination."

"That's all right, boy. These things happen. Why I remember once. . . ."

He spun out the anecdote, having discovered an inexplicable reluctance to hurry home.

He had a pleasant, roomy house, with a well-kept garden, on the outskirts of Golders Green. With his prosperity he had not changed his point of view. Thus he was one of the tiny class in England which alone had no difficulty in getting servants and gardeners and the like. Nothing would induce him to regard his servants as anything but additional members of his family. He ate with them, quarrelled with them and chaffed them, with complete spontaneity. Each side would have been shocked at the idea of giving or receiving notice.

Driving into the small garden garage was a close fit, and you had to wriggle out afterwards. He looked round for his wife, then went into the house through the kitchen.

"Oh, there you are at last, Sam!" exclaimed Ella, his housemaid. "Louie's been expecting you for an hour or more."

"Couldn't get away. She ought to be sitting in the garden on a nice day like this."

"Well, she isn't, that's all! She's in the little room."

The little room was her particular sitting-room, but it contained an armchair for him.

"Couldn't get away before!" he breezed. He bent and kissed the prematurely wrinkled face. "Wot cheer, me old china!"

She made no response. On her lap was the mid-afternoon edition of the *Echo*. Well, of course she would have read all about everything! For a gentle, mild woman, she had an astonishing interest in murder cases—liked discussing the details over and over again. But why was she looking so gloomy over this one?

He dropped into the armchair.

"Anything gone wrong, Louie?"

"I got something on my mind," she answered.

Her hands were strong and deft. She turned herself in her chair, so that she could see the door. "I don't want Ella to hear what I'm saying."

This looked bad.

"Something on your mind, eh!" Samuel Flanch laughed immoderately. "All right, then! Out with it."

"I don't know how to out with it, and that's part of the trouble. Sam, I've been reading the paper."

He felt his heart thumping, took out a cigarette but did nothing with it, fearing his hand might be trembling. These long silences were breaking his nerve.

"That maniac murder, d'you mean?"

She nodded.

"Well, old dear, what about it?"

She was looking out of the window.

"We don't often have to put things into words with each other, so it's difficult to begin," she said. "Right now, I'll say I've got nothing to complain of. You've been as good to me, and as kind, as a man can be to a woman. And I'd give up my life for you, Sam, and anything else that would do any good— and be glad in the bargain, if it helped you."

"Look here, Louie, you're scaring me stiff! What's it all about?"

"I'm only asking you this, so that I can help you if you need help." The *Echo* slid from her lap to the floor. She pointed down at it. "Did you kill her, Sam?"

"Cor strike O'Reilly!" The laugh this time was a positive bellow. "If that doesn't beat the foot-an'-hand! Fancy you going and asking me a thing like that!"

She looked at him hard. Under her gaze, he laughed again.

"It was the way you talked about Gibbern." She was explaining, not apologising. "Every night from when they first had him up, and we were talking about it in here, you used to say he was a rabbit who lost his head. He'd got a good idea, you said, and he'd thrown it away because he was a rabbit. It was such a good idea, you said, that a man could do it all over again and still get away with it, if he wasn't a rabbit. And in the paper it says this murder *is* almost the same thing over again. And left up at the prison, too!"

So that was all! The cigarette was twisted and unsmokable. He took out another and lit up.

"Most people talk like that about a good murder," he said. "You say to yourself, 'Now if I'd been doing this job I'd have taken care to do so-and-so'. It's a sort of game. Why, you were talking like that as much as I was!"

Again her eyes rested on his. He grinned at her until she looked away.

"Very well, Sam!" she said. "Let's say no more about it." She was not looking at him any more. She was again looking into the garden, fixedly, meaninglessly. The silence lengthened—with it, his unease. After some minutes he asked:

"You haven't got anything else on your mind, by any chance?"

"I haven't anything else bar the murder on my mind," she answered with unwonted precision. "But I haven't been quite straightforward with you."

She paused for a moment, looked confused.

"Sam, I know about Miss Trotwood! I know you've been her lover—if you can call it that—for eighteen months. And I don't mind. I know the best of men can't help their nature. And me being like this——"

"Chuck it, Louie!" he begged. The reminder of the accident was unbearable. He shifted in his chair, put one hand over his eyes, like a shamed child.

"All right, old girl! I'm sorry you know about that. It seemed more decent, in a way, not to tell you. But I never took anything from you to give to her."

"I know you didn't, dear. There's nothing to worry about there. Years ago I told myself you would do something o' that."

"It was a bit thick, telling you lies about business, but it had to be done. I was pretty careful with that part of it. I suppose you guessed up a girl. Women always do." He reflected. "But what I'd like to know, now we're talking about it—who told you it was that particular girl?"

"Miss Trotwood herself! She came to see me last Thursday."

"Oh my God!" Samuel Flanch collapsed. The cigarette fell from his hand. Presently it burnt through to his knee and he smacked it out.

"She told me she wanted you to marry her because she was going to have a baby. She said you had asked me to fix a divorce, which of course I would have done—but you told her I wouldn't agree, and you wanted another week to talk me over. And the week was to end today, but she didn't think you meant to do anything about it."

"The baby was a bluff!" he muttered.

"I think she believed it, Sam, whether it was true or not. I thought she was a nice girl. Well behaved and well spoken. I was very sorry for her, in a way."

Samuel decided that admission would be the safest course.

"I did tell her all that. I'd decided to drop her and I wanted a bit of time to wind things up." Suddenly his depression vanished. "Anyway, she's done a bunk! If you read the paper again, you'll see the police want to find her, because she's like the other woman. They were friends. They'll probably call her on the wireless tonight—make out she's lost her memory."

The laugh came back. Louie waited until it had died away.

"She told me something she said she'd never told you. She was married herself. To a man in a good position who didn't love her, so she didn't love him. She said he would be glad to divorce her as soon as she asked him."

"That may be true for all I know or care. She's gone. The flat's empty."

"I think her husband is Mr. Kynsard."

As he said nothing, she went on:

"I tore off a piece of the newspaper and put it over Mrs. Kynsard's furs. She was very like the girl who came to see me."

"They *are* alike. That's what's worrying the police. But they're not the same. They were friends, I tell you."

"Well, Sam, I hope you're right. But you didn't know she had a husband, so I don't see how you can know who he was or wasn't."

What a fool he had been to deny that Betsy was dead! It was the way Louie had put it to him. He had started telling lies to prevent himself being suspected of the murder.

Just like Gibbern, the rabbit.

"And it does seem funny," continued Louie, "that she has run away, after coming to see me like that. And me telling her I'd do whatever you asked me about the divorce."

"I don't see it's funny at all," he protested. "She couldn't keep up the bluff about the baby, so she took herself off. Blurry good thing, too! I'm through with her. I'm through with fooling around with girls—I've learnt my lesson!"

He could not leave it at that. Like Gibbern, he felt the irresistible urge to explain.

"You've got it inside out, matey! If that girl is Mrs. Kynsard, she can't be Betsy. How do I know? I told you they were friends, didn't I? Paper says so too, doesn't it! All right! I tell you, I've heard Betsy talking on the telephone to her friend, Barbara Kynsard. You can't ring yourself up on the telephone and talk to yourself." He bellowed with laughter. "That's a good one, eh, Louie?"

Louie made no answer. He saw that she did not believe him. Wiping the palms of his hands, he went out into the garden.

VIII

Margaret Tremman lived in a comfortable brick bungalow in the prosperous suburb of Rubington. On returning, she cleared off arrears of housework. Dusting the furniture assisted a process of mental stocktaking. Today marked the end of a phase in her life which had disappointed her. A new phase was beginning, with an income doubled by the death of Barbara.

"I won't give way! The feeling of shock will pass," she told herself, and felt that she was being rather splendid.

A self-centred woman, too vain in her womanhood to pretend that the loss of her daughter would darken her life, she hoped for a second marriage or, as next best, a sympathetic friendship, with passionate moments. She shrank from the word "lover", which connoted furtive week-ends and a vague shabbiness.

Part of the process of not giving way was to prepare herself an evening meal: she was still in the preliminary stage, when Detective Inspector Turley arrived unexpectedly. He was not her kind of man, but she was sensitive to the suggestion of toughness behind that mild and even—yes, sympathetic—manner. So she took him into the drawing-room and gave him coffee.

Turley opened with the unscrupulous assertion that women's dress was always a stumbling block to Scotland Yard. Mrs. Tremman believed him, and was soon expounding the significance of Barbara's house-frock and unmended shoes.

"As I told my son-in-law, I firmly believe that my daughter met her death in her own house. Or at least in the garden. Almost anything could happen in that garden. It's such an awful wilderness. Of course, Mr. Kynsard can't help it, but——"

"At what time would you say it happened?"

"Why, it *could* only have happened between her husband leaving for chambers and the arrival of Mrs. Henson at ten."

Dead end! The doctor had stated definitely that death could not have occurred until the early evening at the earliest. Turley dropped that line.

"It's your opinion that Mrs. Kynsard was leading a—second life—as Betsy Trotwood?"

"I gave you my reasons. I may be wrong, of course."

"And you may be right. We have not found that you are wrong. But we have found that the woman known as Betsy Trotwood was getting into that car—the car in which your daughter was found—at twenty minutes to seven last night." He added: "She took it out of the garage in Central London and drove away in it herself. How does that fit in, Mrs. Tremman?"

Margaret Tremman came as near to gaping as she would ever permit herself.

"At twenty to seven!" she repeated. She became abstracted, and presently explained: "I'm trying to think what time it was when I arrived at their house. The six fifteen from here—a wretched train!—is due at St. John's Wood Station at six fifty. I got a taxi at once, which is wonderful nowadays. If the train was punctual I must have been talking to Arthur—that's Mr. Kynsard—about seven o'clock."

"Why is the time so important?" asked Turley with deliberate naïveté.

"Oh, it doesn't matter in the least, because it all came to nothing."

Turley had had experience of that kind of conversation and merely waited.

"Arthur opened the door to me and paid my taxi. I saw he was preoccupied. In the hall he told me about Barbara, pretending he wasn't alarmed, which he was. He talked a lot about dinner, to cover his anxiety—he never notices what he or anybody else eats. I myself wasn't worried at that time because, of course, I knew Barbara much better than he did. She often used to forget when we had guests coming. So when he said he thought he heard Barbara I thought he had too."

She had lost her way again. Turley tried an indirect question.

"Did *you* think you heard Mrs. Kynsard?"

"I thought I did, but I wasn't positive. Besides, I wasn't all keyed up and listening, as he was. He said: 'I think I hear the garage doors.' They're the kind that make a grinding noise, you know. 'I'll be back in a minute!' I went into the drawing-room and waited. As he didn't come back at once I assumed that Barbara *had* turned up and that they were having a row about it in the garage."

"Did you have to wait long?"

"Ever so long! Twenty minutes, I should think."

"Didn't you feel like going out to see what they were doing?"

"I have always tried to avoid being the traditional mother-in-law," she simpered.

"No one could call you that, Mrs. Tremman." Turley saw she had taken it, and went on: "The traditional mother-in-law would have asked some sarcastic questions about being kept waiting for twenty minutes. Especially as Mrs. Kynsard was *not* in the garage—nor anywhere else, as I understand it?"

"Oh, I never make a fuss over little things like that! Arthur looked so pathetic when he had to tell me it was a false alarm. And he'd got himself so dirty that I sent him off to wash."

Turley tried to look as if a plum had not fallen into his mouth.

"You see, when he found that the garage doors had not been opened, he wondered what had made the noise. He thought someone might be prowling in the garden—an obviously stupid suggestion! But the poor boy was a mass of nerves by then. Soon he suggested I should ring up the hospitals."

"What was he doing while you were ringing up?"

"I don't suppose he was doing anything—probably wandering about the house and looking helpless. He's a brilliant lawyer but not very clever at anything else."

So he was not beside her at the telephone.

"How many hospitals did you ring up?"

"I didn't count. About half-an-hour's worth. Then we had a picnic in the kitchen. And then we preyed on each other's nerves until about twelve, when he drove me home in the Chrysler. To show you what a state he was in, he made me promise to ring him at a quarter to one, by which time he expected to be home. It's only about six miles to St. John's Wood, though it takes such a shamefully long time in the train."

"Did you ring him up?"

"Yes, but he didn't answer." There was more coming. "So I rang again about one, and all he said was that there was no news. I think he felt lonely. He made a very long story of how he'd had some engine trouble on the way home and had to leave the Chrysler at the garage and walk home. As it's only one minute's walk from the Three Stumps Garage, he needn't have been so sorry for himself. It was just that the poor boy didn't want to be alone with his thoughts."

Or perhaps because the poor boy wanted to establish an alibi, thought Turley. Yet, as an alibi, it didn't seem to fit in. The Morris might have come to the house at seven. Kynsard might have committed the murder while Mrs. Tremman was waiting in the drawing-room. If he had done so, he could gain nothing by proving that he had driven straight home after leaving Mrs. Tremman. Turley had picked up a line, but no more.

The sun was still shining when he reached Kynsard's house.

"I would like to see the garage, Mr. Kynsard. Mrs. Tremman told me you thought someone was trying to get in at about seven last night. What exactly happened?"

"Nothing," said Kynsard as they stepped into the garden. "I thought I heard the garage doors. As I had left them locked, I assumed that my wife had borrowed the Morris again and was putting it away."

Kynsard unlocked the panel doors. The runners, travelling on rusty rails, emitted a shrill groan.

"That's loud enough!" exclaimed Turley. "And I should say it's not above thirty yards to the house. I wonder what *did* make the noise you heard?"

"So do I," said Kynsard. "They make the same noise when they're being shut. I thought at first that I must have heard them being shut. I sprinted to the rear gates—at the end of this drive there—that give on to the lane. They were open, but I had left them open myself. There was nothing in the lane. I scouted about the garden, though I hardly know why. Then I unlocked these doors and looked inside. In effect, everything was as you see it now."

The garage could have housed six large cars. The Chrysler stood near the centre. On the concrete floor were a large number of tracks and oil drips. It was as if Kynsard parked his car in a different position every time he returned.

The garage was dirty and ill-kept. At the far end an upright iron-runged ladder gave access to the upper quarters.

"Did you look up aloft?"

"No. I haven't been up there since I was a small boy— and I imagine no one else has. If you want to go up, I don't guarantee those rungs will hold you."

"I'll chance it."

While Kynsard waited below, Turley climbed the ladder. Dust was thick upon the upper floor and there were no footprints in the dust. Nevertheless, he explored a one-time hayloft and four small living-rooms in an advanced state of decay. He reckoned Kynsard was right in saying no one had been there for many years.

Down the ladder. At the foot, he shook some of the dust from his hands. The reverse angle of the light revealed something he had missed.

He pointed to a patch on the concrete floor, almost dead centre, bent over it.

"This has been scrubbed—and very recently!" he announced.

"Has it!" Kynsard laughed. "How amazing!"

"It has been scrubbed," repeated Turley. "Have you any idea why, Mr. Kynsard?"

"None whatever! To me, frankly, it's incredible. It's almost impossible to get anything scrubbed nowadays."

A lawyer knew when not to answer questions, reflected Turley.

"You'd like a wash and brush-up, wouldn't you? You're pretty well covered in dust, for which I feel I ought to apologise."

Turley accepted the offer, and they went back to the house. When Turley returned to the hall after cleaning up, there was a knock on the front door.

Kynsard opened it to a strikingly handsome young man in a shabby sports suit with a flowing tie and a confident manner.

"Mr. Kynsard, presumably. I am George Penton. I am very sorry to intrude upon you at such a time, sir. I have been given to understand that the late Mrs. Kynsard was very kindly sponsoring a small work of mine for exhibition at the Rantoul Galleries."

Kynsard nodded.

"I'm afraid that arrangement will fall through. What can I do for you?"

"If I'm not being a plague, could I have my picture back? A Medusa, you know!"

"Come and pick it out, will you." To Turley, Kynsard added: "Excuse me a moment, Inspector."

Turley contrived to place himself within earshot of the morning-room. He heard Penton ask:

"I say! Is that chap a police inspector? Good lord! Could I slip out by your back door?"

"I'll chance being disbarred and give you free legal advice," said Kynsard. "It never pays to run from the police unless you've committed a murder and mugged it."

"The police," grinned Turley, entering the room, "only want to know where you live, Mr. Penton."

"I live in what's left of Theobald's Road, Number——"

"Then I'll give you a lift back if you like, and I can put you through the third degree while I'm driving."

With his Medusa under his arm, Penton got into the police car.

"Darned thirsty weather!" remarked Turley when he had driven out of the neighbourhood. "What about a beer?"

"Sorry, I'm broke! I can't buy back."

"That's all right. We'll have one on the Government."

Penton insisted on bringing his picture with him, attracting a certain amount of attention. Turley piloted him into a corner of the saloon.

"Here's mud-in-your-eye! When did you last see Mrs. Kynsard?"

"I've never seen her. A friend told me that she was good at influencing dealers. And the friend——"

"A friend with auburn hair?"

Penton looked miserable.

"I see you know the whole story!" he exclaimed. "Look here, I wish you'd tell me why she's bolted. Yesterday evening she never gave me the slightest hint. In fact, we had another date."

"Suppose we begin at the beginning. You tell me what you know about Betsy and I'll see if I can contribute anything."

"You've contributed some excellent beer!" Penton took a long, grateful swig. "What do I know about her? Virtually nothing. She's one of those girls you feel you've known all your life, and that's all you ever do know about her. She picked me up about a fortnight ago when I was carrying the Medusa. She said: 'Oh, do let me look!' and then we went back to her flat, which is run for her by a greasy sort of chap, but I always went before he came, so I've never seen him. She knows something about painting."

Turley endured while Penton explained how much and how little the girl knew about painting.

"And she offered to push your work, did she?"

"I don't know about pushing. I don't know that I would care to be pushed. One is not, after all, a toothpaste. If one's work is any good, one asks only that it should be seen. This means crawling round people who are influential enough to get one's work inserted in someone else's exhibition. Otherwise, one is never even approached. How many people have got Betsy's guts?"

"There you beat me!" confessed Turley. "I gather she was getting you an exhibition through Mrs. Kynsard?"

"Certainly not! The most she could do was to wangle me in with a mixed crowd of impressionists, many of whom, between ourselves, are absolutely n.b.g. All the same, I jumped at it. Dear Betsy, as I daresay you know, is hopelessly unbusinesslike. No method! She got me listed in this exhibition and then did nothing about it. As late as yesterday afternoon I was horrified to find my picture still in her bedroom. She said: 'Oh heavens! Barbara reminded me and I forgot again. I'll have to take it round this evening.'

"As it was pretty close to the greaser's time, we got up and left the flat, with the Medusa. We had a drink in the Red Lion, and I persuaded her to give the greaser a miss and come back and dine with me after she had delivered the picture.

"She refused to let me go with her, giving the absurd excuse that I looked too shabby. I wondered what was really in her mind, and now I know—unless you are going to tell me I'm wrong."

"Let's have your theory first."

"My *facts* first!" said the artist. "You know perfectly well she can't have had anything to do with the murder of Mrs. Kynsard. Betsy wouldn't have taken the trouble to deliver my picture if she had been mixed up in some garish plot to spoil the exhibition."

"Why did she bolt, then?"

"It's my belief that she suddenly felt she couldn't stand the greaser any more—that she must make a clean cut at once, while the mood was on her, and get in touch with me later on. She knew my address.

"But I only thought that out this afternoon, and I hope you can confirm it. Last night I felt so rotten when she didn't turn up for dinner that I decided to get drunk. It's none too easy to get drunk nowadays. It cleaned me out. Hence my warning that I couldn't buy any beer."

"The Government invites us to have another," said Turley. The Government, he decided, was getting value for money. "Can I have a look at your picture?" he asked, when the mugs had been refilled. "Ah! That's the kind that makes you look twice and think a bit. I shall have to take this away with me. It's a pity the Government doesn't buy pictures, but I daresay we could squeeze out a small rent for the loan of it. And if you'd like a quid on account—here it is."

"Do you know," said Penton profoundly, "that until this evening, I've had a totally wrong idea of the police. Tonight, my vision has been broadened. Here's a health unto His Majesty!—which means thanks awf'lly for the quid, old man!"

As Turley entered his room at the Yard, the house telephone rang.

"Heard you'd just come in, sir," said Swilbey. "Flanch will be here any minute."

"Have him sent here. And come right along yourself. I've been horning in on your assignment."

By the time Turley had given his facts, Flanch was announced and Swilbey took over. In his senior's presence he used the suave approach.

"Sorry to drag you up at this time, Mr. Flanch, but you said you didn't want us to call at your place." He produced the agency ticket for a stall at the Parnassus for next Saturday's matinee. "Can you tell us anything about that?"

Flanch took the ticket, read part of the inscription aloud. He knitted his brow to indicate an effect of memory.

"There!" Samuel clapped his knee and laughed. "I'll be forgetting my own name next! I bought that for Betsy. One for myself too. A few of us are giving a farewell lunch to one o' the boys on Saturday and I reckoned I might be late."

"When did you give it to her?"

"You win! Blamed if I can recollect."

"It's important, Mr. Flanch. Let's see if we can help you. When did you buy the ticket?"

"I ordered both by telephone. Girl brought 'em along— but which day it was, search me!"

"It was yesterday," said Swilbey. "The girl delivered it to you outside your warehouse, where you were standing waiting for her. And the time was close on three fifteen."

"Wait a minute—don't tell me—I've got it now!" Samuel was showing animation. "I didn't give it to her—leastways, not into her hand. I left it in the flat for her when I was in there waiting for her. Wrote a note to that effect—with a bit o' soft stuff about making up our row. Dessay you found that too, unless she had the sense to burn it."

Swilbey waited until Samuel had finished laughing.

"You left that flat at eleven?"

"S'right!"

"So she couldn't have picked it up before eleven! She was dead before eleven, Mr. Flanch."

Samuel licked his lips, then plunged in.

"Before we go any further, who was dead?" he demanded aggressively. "You say Betsy. Mr. Kynsard says Mrs. Kynsard."

"So your only answer is that you were mistaken when you identified the corpse—marks on the chest and all? Your only answer is that there are two women? Is that the alibi, Mr. Flanch?"

"Who's talkin' about alibis!" blustered Samuel. "And now I come to think of it, I don't remember seeing that ticket and the note I'd written with it—I don't remember seeing it on the table when I came back from buying those cigarettes. That would be about seven forty-five, as I told the inspector this morning."

"You didn't tell me anything about buying cigarettes," said Turley. "You told me you entered the flat about six and left it about eleven."

"Well, if I didn't happen to mention it, I apologise, that's all!" whined Flanch. "I came of my own free will to tell you what I thought might help you. When it's a matter o' murder, you don't keep your mind on buying fags and theatre tickets."

"Did you find a tobacconist open at seven forty-five, Mr. Flanch?"

"I knew they'd be shut. I went to a pub——"

"What was the name of the pub?"

"Gimme a minute—the big one on the corner of Crane-brook Street—the Spread Eagle."

Samuel waited, alert for the next question. But no question came from the detectives. Only a silence which Samuel was unable to endure.

Again that irresistible urge to explain.

"Look here! It's all quite natural if you look at it the right way. I got there at six. I was riled she wasn't there—stamped about a bit. Then I thought I'd go home and cook up a tale for the missus, washing out the other tale. I put the ticket ready for Betsy and wrote the note. Thought I'd give Betsy another ten minutes and turned on the radio. After a bit I found I'd got no more cigarettes. Then I went out, same as I told you. You can't go into a pub just to buy fags, so I had a couple o' Scotch. Then I changed my mind about going home. When I got back to the flat I didn't notice the theatre ticket had gone. You started talking about it and I remembered it had gone."

"All right!" Detective Inspector Turley paused, lit a cigarette, taking a long time over it. "As you say, Mr. Flanch, it's all quite natural if you look at it in the right way. Sorry we had to trouble you to come up to Town. If Detective Sergeant Swilbey has no more questions, we needn't take up any more of your time."

Samuel's jaw dropped. His forehead glistened. He was too astonished to feel anything but fear.

"Well—if that's all——" the laugh broke out again. "If that's all, I'll say good night, gentlemen."

"Good night," chorused the detectives. It took Samuel quite a long time to rise, walk to the door and open it. The silence so oppressed him that he closed the door behind him with reverential gentleness.

Swilbey shrugged, by way of protest at letting Flanch go.

"Flanch gave that ticket into Betsy's hand," he asserted.

"We know that, but we don't know at what time."

Turley nodded assent.

Swilbey went on: "You've instructed me to regard the two girls as one girl. Okay! Betsy-Barbara takes that picture along at six-forty. Betsy-Barbara's mother and husband are waiting for her to turn up for dinner. Don't tell me she drove home, dumped the picture and then drove off again. That would have spoilt all her double-life stuff. So if there's only one girl, it points that Kynsard killed his wife in his own garage about seven."

"That's about what I'm thinking," agreed Turley.

"You're thinking *that*, sir?" Swilbey was taken aback. "What about that picture? Kynsard wouldn't have left that lying about for us to pick up. Being a lawyer, especially, he'd have known it was dynamite."

"Hm! Ought to have kept my mouth shut," grinned Turley.

"And another thing, sir! If Kynsard's guilty and Flanch isn't, what's the point of Flanch telling us those lies? What's he hiding? That he saw Barbara-Betsy about six-forty and gave her a theatre ticket? Why shouldn't he? Yet there he was in that chair, sweating blood to make us believe he didn't see the girl at all that night."

"Have it your own way!" grinned Turley. "Suppose there are two girls, if you like?"

"If there are two girls, Barbara is murdered and Betsy disappears. What say Flanch and Betsy murdered Barbara, laying that picture as a trail to Kynsard?"

While Turley was pondering his answer, Swilbey added:

"Take it that way, and you get Kynsard acting reasonably. He hears the garage doors, same as he says. Those two slip the picture into the Chrysler and as they can't get away before Kynsard comes, they hide. He thinks there's someone prowling in the garden and he's right. That explains why he didn't destroy the picture."

"*If* there are two girls! *If* Betsy and Flanch murdered Barbara!" Turley shook his head. "Cutting out the 'ifs', we have one girl and one picture. I'm going along myself now to get Kynsard's views on modern art—with snakes on!" Turley chuckled. "If Wallsend finds a real Betsy, we'll try that line of yours."

Kynsard had found Barbara's diary—was beginning to study it intensively when Turley reappeared.

He received his caller with a resigned smile and took him into the drawing-room. Turley declined the offer of a drink.

"Then you'll find I'm quite good at coffee. Black or white?"

"Black, please." Turley was glad of the diversion. Here was the most difficult man he had ever tackled. The technique which generally brought results from the criminal classes would be useless. Moreover, it would be a waste of time to try to trap this man, who was himself a skilful cross-examiner.

"I'm on the track of those pictures you were to take to the exhibition."

"Then I'm not much use. I was merely the carrier. We loaded them up the night before last. I was going to take them last night as soon as I came home. I don't even know when the exhibition opens."

"You don't drive to chambers in your car?"

"It's quicker by Underground."

"How many pictures were there?"

"Half a dozen or so. I didn't count."

"The catalogue says seven ' lent by Mrs. Kynsard '. Would that be about right?"

"I should think so."

"They were loaded into your car on Tuesday evening, remained there throughout Wednesday and today until this afternoon?"

"They remained in the car until I left to collect Mrs. Tremman at the police station. I took them out before starting. Shortly after three this afternoon Mrs. Henson and I brought them into the morning-room."

"You'll wonder why I'm pressing you about these pictures——"

"Not really! I know you have to plough up an immense amount of ground. At a guess, you're trying to trace Betsy Trotwood through those pictures. Betsy was concerned with the exhibition in some way. Mrs. Henson heard my wife speaking to Betsy on the telephone about it."

"If it isn't troubling you too much, Mr. Kynsard, would you mind counting those pictures standing against the wall in the morning-room?"

Within thirty seconds Kynsard returned.

"Seven," he announced.

"Add the one which that young artist took away when I was here and you get eight."

"Correct. A Medusa treated impressionistically."

No more skirmishing, decided Turley. Give him a straight wallop and see what happens.

"That Medusa was being loaded into the Morris car—by the lady calling herself Trotwood—at twenty to seven last night."

"Really! Then how the devil did it get here?"

"That's what I've come to find out, Mr. Kynsard."

"I wish you luck, Inspector."

"At twenty to seven," continued Turley, "that Morris started from Cranebrook Street. Plenty of traffic about at that time. It would take about twenty minutes to cover the three miles. At seven approximately you think you hear some-one in the garage. You go out to investigate——"

"And find no one!"

Turley said nothing.

"A most eloquent silence, Inspector!" Kynsard laughed good humouredly. "So you believe that I found the fair Betsy in the garage, that after taking delivery of the picture, I promised I would never tell anybody that she had brought me that picture. And even when this horror descends on us and the police want to know everything we can tell them—even when Betsy herself absconds—I go on stoutly denying that Betsy brought me that picture of the Medusa."

No skirmishing. No fencing. Try another wallop.

"If there's no explanation from you, Mr. Kynsard, I think you know as well as I do what view our legal department is likely to take."

"I don't. I can't for the life of me see a legal point in it anywhere."

"They may say that Mrs. Kynsard turned up here in the Morris at seven and that you killed her."

Kynsard rose from the sociable on which he was lounging. The daylight was fast fading. He switched on the centre light, returned to the sociable, and sat with the light full on his face.

"Inspector! That seems to me such an outrageously *silly* remark that I'm sure we must be at some cross-purpose. I must have missed something. Did you, or did you not tell me that, at twenty to seven, *Betsy Trotwood* got into that Morris with that picture? You did? And it was *Betsy* who took twenty minutes to drive here? At what point does my wife come on the scene?"

"Our case is that Betsy Trotwood was Mrs. Kynsard."

"Oh-h! Mrs. Tremman's theory of a substitute personality, which she expounded to you this morning!"

"In the Betsy Trotwood personality, she had a lover," said Turley. "The lover identified the body of your wife as Betsy Trotwood."

"How damned unfortunate!" exploded Kynsard. He had the air of a man exasperated by a vast annoyance. For a minute or more, he seemed oblivious of the detective's presence, following his own train of thought. "I apologise for saying you made a silly remark. You have an uncomfortably strong *prima facie* case."

"I'm glad you appreciate that, Mr. Kynsard. You'll realise that it's absolutely essential to give me an answer about that Medusa."

"But I don't know the answer—any more than I know who scrubbed that bit of the garage floor—if it was scrubbed. Just a minute! Let's see how strong your case is. I'll take your assumption that Barbara equals Betsy Trotwood. Then, Barbara turns up at seven *with* the picture, *in* the Morris. I go out to the garage, remain there long enough to murder her. Weak spot! How do I know she's going to turn up at that time? Why take the enormous risk of murdering her there and then in a most hurried and unprepared manner when I could have chosen my own moment? Let that pass. Let all the weak spots pass. Stick to the strong ones. I club her to death—then there's your point about the washed floor. I wash the bloodstains—probably dry up the mess later with petrol."

"Run the Chrysler in and out to cover the tracks of the Morris," put in Turley.

"I cover the tracks of the Morris. All this mopping up being done, of course, after I've driven Mrs. Tremman home at midnight. From seven until after midnight the body of my wife remains in the garage, while I act a natural distress at her non-appearance. Ring up Scotland Yard—*Phew!* That's a bit risky, Inspector. Incite Mrs. Tremman to ring the hospitals. After taking Mrs. Tremman home, I get back here about one——"

"Why does it take you so long to do a double journey of twelve miles on a clear road?"

"My exhaust manifold came loose. I cobbled it up, but it came loose again in the last half mile. I did a stretch of the main road making a row like a machine gun. As I was afraid of flame under the bonnet, I put her in the Three Stumps all-night garage at the end of the road, and collected her in the morning. But let's get on with my hypothetical murder.

"Having arrived, I say good night to Mrs. Tremman on the telephone, telling her not to worry, and so on. Then I slip out into the garage and mop up as described. I'm wondering how the devil to get rid of the body. (I'm a bit of a moron, Inspector, to land myself in a hole like that, but let that pass, too.) I have about two hours before daylight. I suddenly remember that Gibbern is being hanged in the morning. This gives me an idea. I strip the body to suggest a maniac murder and put a maniac's flourish on it by dumping the car at the prison. Hm! That's a *prima facie* case all right."

The man was extraordinarily good at taking wallops, thought Turley. Give him one more.

"By a chance, we happen to be able to prove that that Morris travelled approximately seven miles after leaving the Tythrop Garage. It's three miles from there to your house and four miles from your house to the prison."

"That gives you a useful little dovetail!" said Kynsard admiringly. He sat back and sighed. "Damned unfortunate for me! Mrs. Tremman's substitute-personality nonsense unexpectedly backed up by that other identification! That identification, by the way, will break under cross-examination —don't forget that scar on the chest. In the meantime, I suppose you will arrest me on suspicion?"

"I can't avoid it, Mr. Kynsard, if you don't give me any kind of answer."

"I'm grateful for your personal attitude, Inspector, but I can't make any answer except a string of denials, not one of which I can substantiate."

"Don't let's worry about substantiation in the first instance," pleaded Turley. "If you'd only give me your own version of how that picture got there——"

"I haven't a version——"

"—I needn't necessarily proceed to arrest."

"I don't see how you can dodge arrest," said Kynsard thoughtfully. "Of course, I don't want to be arrested. But, after all, it won't amount to much."

As Turley muttered his astonishment, Kynsard explained:

"Let's look at this thing in its proper proportions. You have a *prima facie* justification for arresting me on suspicion. I shall give you twenty-four hours, and then I shall demand a charge or release. If I am charged with the murder of my wife, I shan't even bother to reserve my defence. I shall tear your case to pieces in the magistrate's court. How and why? Because your case is based on the *supposition* that my wife led a double life as Betsy Trotwood. On that supposition, it's a cast-iron case. If my wife got into that Morris at six forty with that picture, you will doubtless succeed in hanging me. But she did not. Betsy Trotwood, a different person, got into that car."

"Come to that, Mr. Kynsard, my view of the case is the same as yours," said Turley, with some unease. "But so far you haven't proved that Betsy is a different person."

"I don't have to. You have to prove they're the same, and you think you can do it with this lover's identification, and the rest of it. Now I cannot, of course, know for certain that my wife did not have a lover, though I regard it as extremely improbable. But I have the complete moral certainty that she was not Betsy Trotwood.

"It is only some twelve hours since you found the body of my wife. In that short time, you cannot have established independent evidence that Betsy Trotwood never existed. Unfortunately, I have no relevant information about Trotwood. But I decline to believe that a woman—who has a lover, you say—a photographer's model and so on—can disappear without leaving any evidence of having existed. I know, Inspector, that you will make every effort to find Trotwood. And I believe that your efforts will be successful—and that you will torpedo your own case."

Turley admitted to himself that he was wavering. He could safely use his discretion in the matter of arrest. This type of man would never run away.

"I'm sure I hope we shall, Mr. Kynsard. In the meantime, we have not a single lead to Trotwood's separate existence."

"Nor have I. Half a minute, though! Before you arrived this evening I unearthed a diary of my wife's. Let's look through it together."

The diary had a cover of tooled leather, the whole about the size of a passport—an expensive article.

On the inside flap was an inscription in a round curly hand:

B. with love from B.

Turley turned the pages of the diary, noting only the handwriting.

"That's not your wife's hand!" he exclaimed, pointing to the inscription.

"No, it isn't! I never noticed that. A hundred pounds to a biscuit it's Betsy's."

Turley turned forward to the latest entry, of two days ago. Kynsard was looking over his shoulder.

A. horribly polite about taking pictures.

"She means me," explained Kynsard. "Makes one feel rather a pig!"

Turley went back through a week of trivialities.

"'B. paid back £5—wish she hadn't—has to get money from that man'," Turley read aloud.

"Begins to look like Betsy, doesn't it?" suggested Kynsard.

Turley had turned back five weeks—with sporadic allusions to "B"—before he came to a decisive entry.

"We've got something here!" he exclaimed. "'June 5th. Met B. at Astorelle's. Her appointment went wrong. Let her have mine, as she has to be photographed tomorrow.' Who's Astorelle?"

"I don't know. Hang on!" Kynsard left the room, to return with the telephone book. "'Astorelle Limited. Posticheurs. Ladies' Hairdressers'.'" Kynsard's laugh betrayed excitement for the first time. "If the management have recorded that incident—if they remember two auburn-haired women chattering in a friendly flutter, my mother-in-law's theory will collapse. And so will your case, old man!"

"And I shall be as pleased as anybody," said Turley. "Can I take this diary with me?"

"My only objection is that, in the event of my being charged, that would be real evidence for the defence. You must remember, you gave me a bit of a shock just now. I don't want to be too cockahoop. Copy all you like, but I think I'd better hang on to the original."

Turley thought it over.

"Very well! We'll try Astorelle's first."

IX

Turley's second conference was held at midday, some twenty-eight hours after the discovery of the body.

"What about Astorelle's, Wallsend?"

"Proof that there were two girls, sir. But that was my assignment anyway. We haven't really gained anything." Wallsend was as gloomy as ever. "It's a posh place. Line of cubicles, with an operator in each, and the guv'nor walking about seeing everybody's satisfied. The regular clients stick to a particular operator.

"On June 5th, Trotwood and Mrs. Kynsard came in together—having met outside, the guv'nor thought. Trotwood had made a mistake in her date and Mrs. Kynsard said Trotwood could have her appointment—they were both regulars for the same operator. Trotwood's hair-do used to go on Mrs. Kynsard's account, but was itemised separately on Mrs. Kynsard's bill. The guv'nor showed me the books. He said the girls were much alike to look at, but not so's you wouldn't know one from the other—he'd have thought they were sisters. But the girl operator who did them both said she knew they weren't sisters. Girls talk a lot when they have their hair done, the operator said, and Trotwood's was a different class o' talk."

Turley decided that the evidence was conclusive. He turned to Swilbey.

"We shall have to alter the wording of your assignment. The girls are not the same girl."

"The murder is the same murder," returned Swilbey. "The assignment I'd like is what I said last night. Flanch, with Betsy as accessory, killed Barbara Kynsard."

Turley was doubtful.

"Motive isn't our business, of course, but I must say I always feel more comfortable when I know what it is. Anyway, take your own line there, Swilbey. Wallsend, no change— you're still on Betsy."

"Yes, and I ought to have picked up something by now, sir," moaned Wallsend. "When Betsy left the Tythrop Garage she must have gone up in smoke, as far as I can see."

"According to Flanch," Turley reminded him, "Betsy went back to the flat about six forty-five. She picked up the theatre ticket and said: 'Now I'm going to bolt for it without taking any of my clothes, so as to give Sergeant Wallsend a proper headache.' Flanch doesn't know we found the ticket in the Morris. You go on from there, keeping in step with Swilbey."

When reports from all sources had been considered, Turley summed up.

"I don't want you all to kid yourselves that this is one of those open-and-shut cases where you can't go wrong." When the mutterings had subsided, he went on: "Led by me, you believed that Barbara and Betsy were one. We know now they aren't. They weren't so much alike that anybody commented on it until they were asked about it. The bashing and the doctor's tinkering-up may have produced a sort of third face, so that those who knew Betsy would say in good faith: 'That's Betsy, though the face looks a bit different due to the bashing', and those who knew Barbara would say the same —er——"

"*Mutatis mutandis*, sir?" suggested Rawlings.

"That's about right, boy. The corpse was identified as

Barbara by her husband and her mother. Both volunteered that statement that there was that scar on the chest, though the corpse was not inspected below the chin. Anyway, husband and mother! You can't beat that. You don't have to. The jury will believe them and no one else. Hold that thought.

"Flanch identified her as Betsy. Before going to the mortuary he also volunteered the statement about the scar. How did he know that Mrs. Kynsard had that scar? He denied that Betsy could be doubling as Barbara. But when I told him Kynsard had identified the body as that of his wife, Flanch withdrew his own identification.

"We don't have to answer these questions. We just have to find evidence of how Barbara Kynsard was killed. We don't even have to find Betsy Trotwood, as far as this case is concerned. But looking for her may take us somewhere. And when we find her, she may tell us something. That's the set-up."

"What the newspapers call 'clues'," muttered Wallsend miserably. "We got a plateful o' clues and no evidence."

Rawlings waited long enough to give Swilbey a chance to speak and then:

"That scar, sir. Barbara may have been living a double life without any special reference to Betsy. I mean, it's just possible she may have had an affair with Flanch. He's a wolf if ever there was one! And if he got gummed up between the two girls——"

"Huh! Sell that to the films!" snorted Swilbey. "What say Barbara told Betsy about her scar, and Betsy passed it on to Flanch? Maybe Flanch killed her for a better reason than that!"

Rawlings subsided. No one was ready to support the theory that Flanch had been Barbara's lover.

The inquest was held on the next day. After formal evidence had been given, including evidence of identification by Kynsard and Mrs. Tremman, the inquest was adjourned for a month. On the day following, the funeral took place.

In those three days Samuel Flanch lost a stone in weight. The strain of waiting for the police to have another bang at him was breaking his nerve. He had all the answers ready, but no one came to ask the questions. There was no means of explaining anything to anybody.

On the fourth day after the discovery of the body, Samuel arrived home unexpectedly in the early afternoon. A spell of fine weather had set in. Louie was in the garden.

"Ha! There's me old trouble-an-strife! I want you to come inside, mate. Got something for you to sign."

He raised her with practised gentleness from the pseudo-rustic bench and slipped her crutches into position.

In the little room he produced a formal-looking document of abnormal size. On the wall was a tradesman's calendar. He took it down to act as a table, gave her his fountain-pen.

"We'll want Ella to be a witness."

"I must know what it is I'm to sign, Sam."

"Read it, then, if you don't trust me." The laugh was as vociferous as ever.

She adjusted her spectacles, opened out the document.

"I don't understand it—it seems a lot of rigmarole to me."

"So it is! I didn't want you to bother your head with it, but as you feel that way about it, I'll tell you."

He had been jolly for the first time since their conversation about Betsy. Now he became solemn.

"First you gotter listen to a bit o' talk. Serve you right, old dear, for askin' questions. Know what I told you the other night about me being through with girls? I meant it, all right. Only, I started thinking. You know what I am and I know what I am and I don't trust myself with a bit o' skirt—me going up to Town every day and staying all hours. My place is here with you—doin' a bit o' gardening in summer. Out of temptation's way, if you understand me. Told you I'd learnt my lesson."

"But what about the business, Sam?"

"I've sold it!"

"Oh dear! How're we going to live without the business?"

"You know, Louie, you always were one to ask silly questions! D'you think I hadn't thought o' that? I got thirty thousand quid for the business. Thirty thousand jimmy-o-goblins! That's more'n you'd any idea I was worth, isn't it?

—and you're wrong, because I'd have got more if I'd waited. Wanted to get it off me chest."

"But why were you in that hurry?"

"Cor, let me finish, will you! We're not going to put thirty thousand pounds on a horse. We'll neither of us ever see it. It's already gone to an insurance company. Joint life annuity. You don't know what that means. It's the rigmarole there in your lap. It means they're going to pay me seventeen hundred quid a year. Knock off income-tax—gives a thousand a year and small change over. About what we're living on now, first an' last. Wait a minute! If anything happens to me, you get the seventeen hundred—that's to say the thousand odd— every year as long as you live. You can live to be a hundred —they'll go on paying and smiling just the same."

"Why should anything happen to you? And what sort of thing?"

"There you go! Who said anything was going to happen to me! I said *if*. I can live to a hundred too, if I want to. All you gotter do is sign here. Makes you a party to it. Hi, Ella!"

Mrs. Flanch signed without comment. Ella, perceiving that some grave family business was being transacted, witnessed the signature in a silence that radiated general disapproval.

When she had left the room the silence held, making Samuel feel that he had done something disreputable.

"Cor blimey! Here I've given up the business I built up from nothing, made you comfortable for life and you don't even say 'thank you'."

"You've made me very *un*comfortable," she said. "You'll soon get tired of gardening, and I don't know what you think you're going to do at home here in the winter—— Oh, what does it all *mean*, Sam?"

"Just what I told you it means, and nothing else. What's the matter with you, Louie?"

Her voice was barely audible as she answered:

"I'm frightened."

Samuel's head had ached steadily for the last twenty-four hours. He pressed his hands over his brow.

"You got to pull yourself together, mate, or we shall both go looney. Don't talk—listen! We been married twenty—

twenty-four years. In that time I've told you lies about being at business, et cetera, when I was really with Betsy. It was the same lie every time, dressed up—ought to count as one lie only."

"You needn't count it at all, because I knew it. You were always so straight with me that I knew at once when you did tell a lie."

"Have it your own way. You'll know whether I'm lying now: *I—did—not—kill—Betsy—Trotwood!*"

"I believe you, Sam!" She added: "Do the police think you did?"

"I dunno!" The admission was torn from him. "I dunno what they think, and that's a fact!" He got up, placed the document she had signed in its envelope. "I'm going out to register this." He added over his shoulder: "Whatever they think or don't think, you'll be all right for money."

The next day the war of nerves ended with a polite request by telephone to call on Detective Inspector Turley at Scotland Yard.

In the last few days, Samuel Flanch had made the discovery that he was a sensitive man, that he reacted to the moods of others, that his peace of mind could be affected by commonplace objects. No one could call him starchy, yet he felt he had lost something worthwhile when Detective Inspector Turley called him "Flanch" instead of "Mr. Flanch".

Turley was not being tough. He simply looked up when Flanch was shown in, then looked back at the papers on his desk. He said, almost absentmindedly, "Sit down, Flanch," and took no further notice of him for something like three minutes.

On the desk were photographs of Barbara Kynsard, living and dead. Nothing in that! A photograph of Cranebrook Mansions. Of Tythrop Garage; of the pub at the corner, and a long shot of the street. Samuel found himself trying to add up the photographs. He started violently as his eyes were drawn to the wall behind the inspector. Perched on a shelf was that looney picture of a girl's head with snakes. He felt the creeps coming back in a more disturbing form.

Towards the end of the three minutes, Turley spoke on the house telephone. "Waiting for you," he said. He pulled another lever and again said: "Waiting for you." A third lever, "Come along, Rawlings."

Detective Sergeant Swilbey came in, then his colleague, Wallsend. Both sat down without even glancing at Samuel. Then young Rawlings arrived with a dispatch-case and sat at the desk opposite Turley. Samuel furtively wiped his hands on his jacket. He remembered that all his life he had been, perhaps, a little over ready to call other men rabbits.

Turley swivelled his chair and faced Samuel.

"So you thought you could tell us what it was good for us to know, and leave the rest out! That's what the small-time crooks do."

"I never did! I approached you of my own free will——"

"We've heard that one. Of your own free will, you told us the corpse was Betsy, when you knew it wasn't."

Samuel Flanch let out a long breath as if from a blow in his middle.

"How long have you known Mrs. Kynsard?"

"Never seen her in my life. I told you I hadn't."

"How did you know about that scar?"

Samuel made a hissing noise as if he were reclaiming the breath he had lost.

"I didn't know. I knew Betsy had a scar, like I described. If her friend Barbara had one too, it wasn't my fault."

Turley and the detectives exchanged glances but no word was spoken.

"We'll leave that for a minute. You gave us a little poem about what you did at that flat on Thursday night. You went out to get cigarettes; you left the theatre ticket on the table with a love letter; and when you came back, after getting the cigarettes, Betsy had been in and out and taken the ticket. You'd better listen to Detective Sergeant Wallsend."

"Time of Flanch's entering the flat unknown, believed to be about six." Wallsend was reading from his own report. "Radio started in flat about six fifteen, turned on very loud. Mr. Richards, occupying flat below, at or about six thirty, ascended to No. 17 intending to request that radio be lowered.

He knocked several times but could get no answer. He tried again at nine and at nine thirty with the same result. The radio continued until close-down, and started again at six next morning. It did not cease until eleven, when Flanch was seen to enter the flat and remain there for a few minutes."

"Don't say anything yet, Flanch," put in Turley. "We're going to show you how you stand. Carry on, Wallsend."

"Tests established that both the bell and the knocker can be distinctly heard throughout the flat while radio is playing at its loudest. Summary of Flanch's movements: Was in flat before six thirty, but had left it by then and did not return until the following morning. Movements unknown between six thirty and eleven forty approximately, when he returned to his home. Next morning, he arrived at his warehouse at six thirty, half an hour later than usual, saying this was due to ignition trouble. Denied by garage mechanic. Between seven and nine in the morning, movements unknown."

Turley resumed charge of the proceedings.

"We know you met Betsy round about six forty and gave her that theatre ticket. We don't know why she bolted. We don't know what you or she or both of you did with the Morris. But you can see that we're considering the possibility —mind, I only say possibility—that you, in that Morris, met Mrs. Kynsard and murdered her, and that Betsy bolted because she didn't want to give evidence—that you hid the Morris with the body until something after seven in the morning and then took it to where it was found."

"Cor-strike-o-Reilly!" The laugh bellowed a sudden confidence. "That's a mountain out of a molehill if you like, Inspector!" The four unresponsive faces chilled him. "I've been a fool—I can see that, now it's too late. Not sure I hadn't better keep my trap shut."

"That's up to you. You sold your business yesterday for spot cash, didn't you?"

That, guessed Samuel, would justify arrest. No good telling them about the joint annuity. Might make it worse.

"I'll take a chance," he said. "I did go out for cigarettes, same as I said. Didn't think about that radio. When I was having my drink I stood by the window, with one eye on the

Tythrop Garage. I saw Betsy come from the opposite direction
—that's to say, not from the flat. She was carrying a picture
and she went on to the Tythrop.

"I wasn't going to rush after her. I finished my drink and
took it easy to the Tythrop. She was coming out, in the
Morris. I stopped her with a bit o' chaff, but she was stand-
offish. I put a foot on the running-board, and tried to sweeten
her up. She said she didn't want the ticket. I put it in the
dash, telling her she could give it me back later if she didn't
want it. She said she'd been trying to find Barbara, but
couldn't. She was going to take that picture and put it in
Kynsard's Chrysler along with the others, and she'd see me
on Saturday at the Parnassus if she felt like it. That wasn't
good enough for me. I jawed a bit. Then she said she wouldn't
be back at the flat till late. I said: 'A boy-friend, p'r'aps',
and she let in the clutch and I had to jump for it. I didn't
believe it was a boy-friend——"

"Why not?"

Samuel hesitated.

"I dunno. I just didn't. I thought she was going to spend
the evening with Barbara. I went back to the pub and had
another. Then I got the rats. I don't suppose it's much good
my telling you what I did, because I can't prove it. I went
up to the West End and picked up a girl—wouldn't know her
again if I saw her. Got back home a bit after half-past eleven
after looking in at the Tythrop—told me the Morris hadn't
come back.

"Next day, when the early editions came out, I didn't think
at once it was Betsy, but I wanted to make sure. I nipped
over to the flat. Turned the radio off, same as the sergeant
here said. I saw Betsy hadn't been back—I looked over her
things. She'd gone away in what she stood up in. I was pretty
sure it wasn't a boy-friend, as she hadn't taken even a small
suitcase. Not her style with a boy-friend.

"Thought I'd better go to the police of my own free will,
in case they asked me funny questions. On the way I thought:
'It's a pity I saw Betsy those few minutes last night. It wouldn't
do any harm to leave that bit out.' That's where I made my
big mistake."

Samuel had lost his momentum. In the silence, his hands troubled him again. He looked from Turley to Swilbey, to Wallsend, even to young Rawlings. A blurry set o' wooden images! Lumping great men, all these Scotland Yard dicks were. Must be six foot apiece.

Detective Inspector Turley began to speak, without looking up from his blotting-pad.

"Your first tale is that you didn't leave the flat between six and eleven. We catch you with that theatre ticket, and you give us a second tale. We catch you through the radio complaints, and you give us a third tale. Where's this lying going to stop, Flanch?"

"I wanted to keep out of it. Those lies couldn't do you any harm. You'd have found out Betsy went out with the Morris without me telling you."

Swilbey cut in.

"Flanch, we want Betsy."

"I dunno where she is, and that's a fact!"

"Someone's taking care of her, and you said yourself it isn't a boy-friend. She's side-stepped two appeals on the radio. She has no clothes, you say, except what she stands up in. She bolts without even stopping to pack a suitcase. Can you sweat up any reason for that, Flanch?"

Flanch licked his lips but failed to achieve an answer.

"You're right, it doesn't look like a boy-friend," pressed Swilbey. "It looks like a girl bolting from the police."

"I told the inspector I don't know much about her. She may have been up to something without me knowing."

"And don't forget she bolts within an hour of her friend Barbara being murdered. And don't forget the friend was found in Betsy's car."

"Here, draw it mild! You can't put it over that Betsy killed Mrs. Kynsard."

"I'm putting over that she knows the bloke who did, and that he's keeping her out of the way."

"Meaning me, eh? Cor, that's a good one!" Flanch loosed a laugh.

"In your tale number three—don't let me get muddled over your tales, Flanch—I mean the one where you're standing beside the Morris talking soft to her. She's been robbing the till, you think, and has it in mind to bolt. Why didn't she talk soft back, and tap you for a spot o' cash for her travelling expenses?"

"I dunno why she didn't, but she didn't."

"She didn't bother, eh? She just thought: 'I've got to run from the police and hide myself. I haven't time to pack a suitcase—I've only time to deliver this beautiful picture to oblige a friend'."

Flanch found himself glancing at the picture. If he had been told that the face of the Medusa was believed to have turned living men to stone he would have accepted the legend as a news item.

Turley glanced at Swilbey and took over.

"She had a boy-friend, Flanch, but she didn't bolt with him. We've found him. They spent the afternoon together in the flat. And they meant to dine together as soon as she had delivered that picture."

"Well, she did the dirty on me, that's all, me paying for the flat!" He added viciously: "That's if she *did* have a boy-friend!"

"The point is, she was enjoying herself with him and meant to rejoin him for dinner. If she was afraid of the police—before six-forty—she had plenty of time to pack a suitcase."

When Flanch made no attempt to answer, Turley spoke to Swilbey.

"You can take him along to your room and go through that West End tale. He must get corroboration. Otherwise, we won't wear it." Turley added:

"One more question before you go, Flanch. Can you produce anybody to confirm your statement that Betsy had that scar?"

"Have a heart, Inspector. It was below the evening-dress line—you couldn't even see it when she was only wearing those Titania whatsernames."

"Did she ever go to a doctor for anything?"

"Not as far as I know."

As soon as young Rawlings was alone with Turley he made a suggestion.

"That alleged scar of Betsy's. We know that Betsy was a bit of a hanger-on. Barbara paid for Betsy's hair-do's. Barbara may have sent Betsy to her own doctor or dentist or both."

"Good enough! But mind you don't get under Swilbey's feet. Ask him if you can approach Mrs. Tremman—she's more likely to know than Kynsard—then tackle the doctor or dentist or masseuse or anybody else who messes these women about."

On the next day, as Turley was about to go out for lunch, Rawlings reported in some excitement.

"That scar follow-up, sir! No masseuse. Barbara's doctor had never attended Betsy, but Barbara's dentist had. I showed him what I showed the doctor—photo of the scar and the other documentary stuff. And he made a tooth problem of it, sir."

"D'you mean the scar was a bite?"

"Look what he says about Betsy's teeth."

Rawlings produced three dentist's charts—a card with a printed diagram of the upper and lower jaw, with dentist's markings in ink indicating individual variations of the patient's teeth.

"I got him to mark the charts so that I shouldn't mug the point, sir. This one, *Barbara (D)*, is the chart made from the cast taken from the corpse by another dentist. *Barbara (L)* is Barbara's teeth when her dentist treated her six weeks ago. *Betsy* is Betsy's teeth when she was treated a fortnight ago, the visits being charged to Barbara's account. Look what he's written on Betsy's card, sir!"

Turley studied the chart, with difficulty deciphered the dentist's handwriting.

"Medusa-multiplied-by-a-million!" he exploded. "I must take this to the chief superintendant. And he'll run it up to the great white chief. I'll get 'em both before they go out to lunch. Wait here until I come back."

Within a quarter of an hour Turley returned. To Rawlings he looked like a seasoned old boxer staging a come-back. He went to the house telephone.

"That you, Swilbey? . . . Out to lunch, is he? Well, you

know where he is, don't you? Right! Go after him and tell him to pull Flanch in."

He turned to Rawlings, beaming.

"You've done a job o' work, young feller-me-lad! You'd have shown more tact if you had let Swilbey put this up to me. Don't worry. If you've broken the rules, I'm going to keep you company.

"I don't suppose you've ever read Sherlock Holmes. Don't —until you're drawing your pension. Meaning we're going to do a spot of deduction—but it's not to be taken as a precedent, mind! What did they teach you at college! Get facts and don't guess. If you feel you must guess now and again, always begin by guessing that a perfect alibi is a fake."

"Neither Flanch nor Kynsard has a perfect alibi, sir."

"Quite right, but I wasn't thinking of the men," said Turley. "I was thinking of the cars. This case pivots on cars. Take that poor little Morris. There's a murder-car for you! Not a hope anywhere! Even its own meter rats on it and tells us how many miles it travelled on its murder-trip.

"Take Flanch's Ford. Alibi dead rotten. It might have been almost anywhere at any time.

"But take Kynsard's Chrysler. It's the one car in London that couldn't possibly have been mixed up in any murder. Betsy knows it's in the garage, with pictures inside it. She tells Penton and she tells Flanch, and she's right. It's in the garage when Mrs. Tremman arrives for dinner. It stays there until it takes her home at midnight. And then, dammit, in case you might wonder what it was doing in the small hours, it can prove it was in a public garage—with old Medusa's snakes and a sunset or two in the back—suffering from an open exhaust manifold. Exhaust manifold my foot! Anybody can open it with a screwdriver in about forty seconds. See what I'm getting at, boy?"

"No, sir. If all that is true——"

"It is true. We've checked every minute of the Chrysler's time."

"Then how can the car itself have been used in a murder?"

"The answer," said Turley, "is a Medusa." He laughed in a manner reminiscent of Flanch at his loudest.

"I don't know *how* the Chrysler was used," he went on. "We'll find out. After lunch, you're going to drive me from Kynsard's house to Mrs. Tremman's bungalow. You'll want a stop-watch. And ask the superintendent if we can borrow a girl. She needn't have had any experience, but she must be a lightweight."

X

Margaret Tremman told herself that it was her duty to prevent Arthur Kynsard from moping and to see that he was properly looked after during the period of readjustment.

She would have been shocked to the marrow if she had suspected herself of desiring the husband of her dead daughter. For beneath her vanity was a fundamental decency. She believed that she enjoyed his warm regard, tinged with romanticism once removed.

It was becoming her custom to turn up for dinner with her own rations and sundry unrationed items, to the purchase of which she had devoted time and thought, supplementing Mrs. Henson's inadequate effort to provide him with a decent evening meal.

Detective Inspector Turley was aware of this. He timed his moment carefully—so carefully that, with the aid of young Rawlings playing Boy Scout in the garden, he was knocking at the door as they were crossing from the dining-room to the drawing-room.

Through the open door of the drawing-room, Mrs. Tremman heard Kynsard greet the inspector. She sighed, because it meant that her evening with Arthur would be broken up.

"I'd like to see Mrs. Tremman as well, please."

"Then come into the drawing-room. Have you had any luck with Betsy Trotwood?"

"We've found her," answered Turley from the doorway.

"Good evening, Inspector." Mrs. Tremman was greeting him as a personal friend. "I heard what you said. Is her name really Trotwood? It can't be!"

"We don't know, Mrs. Tremman. She is dead. Murdered!" He paused, glanced at Kynsard and learnt nothing. "This afternoon the commissioner ordered the arrest of Flanch, the man who was living with her."

"How horrible! How perfectly awful!" exclaimed Mrs. Tremman. "It must be the same maniac."

"It's horrible, but it's also very troublesome for us," said Kynsard. "I was counting on Betsy to clear up that irritating little riddle of the picture. Medusa's head, wasn't it?"

"That's what I've come to talk about," said Turley. Mrs. Tremman motioned him to a chair. He placed his bag rather clumsily between his feet. He opened in the tone of one making a speech.

"In a murder case, it generally happens that a number of innocent persons tell the police a number of lies. And suppress information that appears to be trivial but turns out to be important. Their object is to avoid being called as witnesses. Our difficulty comes in getting them to amend their statements without making them feel they have lost dignity."

Margaret Tremman jumped in.

"If I have misled you, Inspector, I shan't feel it undignified to apologise."

"I'm glad, Mrs. Tremman. Please carry your mind back to seven o'clock last Thursday. Mr. Kynsard told you he heard the garage doors. You told me you *thought* you *might* have heard them. I'll tell you now that we know they were opened about that time. Are you still uncertain whether you heard them?"

This was merely a shaker. The vital questions were to come. He had calculated that in Mrs. Tremman lay the exposed flank of the formidable antagonist who knew so exactly what he could say, and what he could not say, with safety.

"As you put it like that, I suppose I must have heard the doors."

"Thank you, Mrs. Tremman." He turned towards the sociable, where Kynsard was sitting. "Mr. Kynsard, we know also that Betsy Trotwood delivered that picture—the Medusa —at about that time. Would you care to amend your statement that you did not see Betsy Trotwood? It's a matter of great importance to the man we have arrested."

"I have nothing to add, Inspector, or to withdraw."

"Did you see the picture when you were in the garage?"

"I didn't notice it."

"But you surely would have noticed it if—say—it had been propped against the wall, or against the side of the Chrysler? You were looking, you said, for an intruder, or traces of an intruder."

"I suppose I would have noticed it. But I did not."

Mrs. Tremman could perceive only that the men were in some difficulty and felt she must rise to the occasion.

"I see what must have happened!" she cried. "We heard the doors being *shut*, not opened. The girl was shutting them and slipping away, after putting the picture inside the Chrysler. So of course Arthur didn't see it!"

"Yes—er—yes!" said Turley thoughtfully. "Do you agree, Mr. Kynsard, that that is a feasible explanation?"

"I agree that it's a feasible explanation. Whether it happened so is another matter."

"Your continued denial that you saw either Betsy or the picture convinces me that she did put it in the Chrysler," said Turley. "That saves Flanch."

He waited for three seconds and then: "It's my painful duty, Mr. Kynsard, to arrest you. You will be charged with the murder of the woman known as Elizabeth Trotwood. The official warning is unnecessary in your case, but I am required to give it."

Mrs. Tremman hovered on the brink of laughter while Turley was reciting the warning. Her sense of proportion was slipping. It was impertinent to speak to Arthur like that! Arthur seemed to think so too. She waited for him to say something devastating.

"This is great, Inspector! I am charged with the murder of Elizabeth Trotwood. I submit to arrest under protest and have no statement to make."

"Arthur! Is the inspector serious?"

"Yes, my dear! Uncomfortably serious." He got up. "I'm afraid you'll have to see yourself home."

Mrs. Tremman stared at the inspector. He stared back at her, rather rudely. She remembered with disgust that she had thought him clever and sympathetic.

"I am sorry, Mrs. Tremman, but unless you can answer my questions satisfactorily I must arrest you, too, as accessory. And the warning I gave Mr. Kynsard applies also to you."

"Arrest *me*! For murdering Betsy Trotwood?"

"For being accessory, Margaret," cut in Kynsard. "That means helping me to commit the murder, or to cover my traces."

"But if you didn't murder Betsy Trotwood, how can there be any traces? Oh, do let's talk sensibly! What must I do, Arthur?"

"I don't think the inspector will allow me to advise you. No doubt he would like to. But he has his regulations to consider."

"I can look after my regulations," said Turley. "If Mrs. Tremman wants your advice on her position, I've no objection to your giving it."

"By courtesy of the inspector, this is your position, Margaret. If you answer his questions to his satisfaction, he will probably not arrest you. If you fail to satisfy him, your defence will be the weaker."

"But I haven't got a defence and I don't want one!" protested Mrs. Tremman. "And I do hate not answering questions—besides I want to ask one or two myself. Why does he think you killed Betsy Trotwood?"

"He won't tell you. The police have to tell me everything they know, as soon as they can get it typed, but regulations require them to play the oyster at this stage."

"If Mr. Kynsard would confine himself to giving legal advice and leave police regulations to me, we could get on," snapped Turley.

Turley was playing for high stakes. Kynsard would never make the mistake of supplying positive evidence against himself—if left to himself. The attack had been launched on the exposed flank. Kynsard, for all his cleverness, had fallen into the trap of consenting to advise Mrs. Tremman. In his own house! There could be no allegation of police coercion.

"Mrs. Tremman—a few seconds after Mr. Kynsard went to the garage, did you *think* you heard a scream?"

"D'you mean a man's scream? Or a Betsy Trotwood's scream?"

"If Trotwood was a normal woman, I think she screamed, though possibly she fainted."

"At sight of my son-in-law? It's getting sillier, Inspector. Do you expect me to believe that he rushed at her and killed her—a girl he had never seen before—like a maniac murderer?"

"Not like a maniac!" The woman's irrelevancy was forcing his hand. "It's such an unlikely thing to happen, isn't it, Mrs. Tremman? It's so unlikely that it can have only one possible explanation. He killed her—a woman he had never seen before—to save his own life."

Turley glanced at Kynsard. He was leaning back against the mantelpiece in an attitude of boredom—too knowledgeable to wish to impress his innocence on the police.

Turley continued: "We know that Betsy came here and delivered a particular picture. We know that she wished to put it with the other pictures in the Chrysler. In finding a place for this rather large picture, she disarranged the other pictures. At that point Mr. Kynsard came in. She had seen what was underneath those pictures. It was her life or his. Do you understand now, Mrs. Tremman?"

"No," she answered bluntly. "What was under the pictures?"

"The body of your daughter—whom he had killed between nine and ten that morning. He put the body in the Chrysler and covered it with the pictures. It remained there all day. It travelled behind you when he drove you home. Did you not know this, Mrs. Tremman?"

"What a perfectly abominable thing to say to me!" Mrs. Tremman knew she was losing her grip of a situation that defied the traditions of her lifetime. "Arthur, can't you stop him?"

"We don't want to stop him. You must answer his question. Did you know that the body of poor Barbara—murdered, as he says, by me!—was in the Chrysler?" With skilful inflection he made the question sound childishly absurd. "Give a plain answer—just 'yes' or 'no'."

"No. Of course not!"

Turley pointed a finger at Mrs. Tremman.

"Then why did you falsely identify the body of Elizabeth Trotwood as that of your daughter?"

"*Don't answer*, Margaret!"

With that interruption, Turley knew that he had made his second gain. Through Mrs. Tremman he would wring a definite admission from Kynsard.

"Inspector, if you will ask whether Mrs. Tremman *believed* the body she examined to be that of her daughter, I will advise her to answer."

"Of course I did! I should not have been so upset if it hadn't been poor Barbara!"

As he asked his next question, Turley had his eyes on Kynsard.

"Do you remember stating to me—and signing the statement—that there was a scar on your daughter's chest?"

"I do. So there was!"

"When your daughter was alive, did you ever *see* that scar on her body?"

Kynsard cut in quickly.

"Tell the inspector exactly what happened, Margaret—give him the full circumstances. Keep nothing back, or he will arrest you."

As he spoke, Kynsard glanced at Turley, smiled and gave the ghost of a bow, acknowledging that the other had scored. But if it was an acknowledgment, it was also a defiance. He still believed he could win in the courts.

"I had not seen it. But I knew it was there, because Mr. Kynsard told me just before I came to the police station. I must explain that——"

"He doesn't need any more, Margaret. I confirm that answer, Inspector. I think that disposes of the charge of being accessory to my alleged crime—or rather crimes."

"Not quite. There's another question coming."

"I feel as if I were in the middle of someone else's nightmare!" cried Mrs. Tremman. "I don't believe a word you're saying, Inspector. But—if Arthur killed Betsy, why should he want to pretend she was Barbara?"

"Look how successful that trick was, up to this evening! At this moment, another man is under arrest. Kynsard killed Barbara first. He had the colossal nerve to leave the body in his own garage for fifteen hours. That gave him a safe method of carrying the body away—as well as all those hours in which to work up her 'disappearance'. First, he could use you as cover when transporting the body. Secondly, by timing the movements of the Chrysler, he could create the illusion that it was impossible that he could have disposed of a body.

"He forgot that Betsy had a key to the garage. She discovered the murder—and he battered her to death with a mallet. He ran the Morris—parked in the lane—into the garage. Before he left for the police station in the morning, Mrs. Henson unconsciously revealed his blunder over the house-dress, which enabled not only the police but you yourself to see that your daughter was almost certainly killed in the morning at home.

"That must have shaken him, though it did not amount to the fatal mistake. At the police station, he saw his chance. His battering had created a sort of third face, common to both women. He was risking nothing. If his misidentification failed, he could plead an honest mistake. If it succeeded, the trail would inevitably be confused—as it was confused.

"He had the problem of getting rid of the corpse of Betsy, waiting in the garage until he returned from Rubington. It is dangerous to park a car with a corpse in it. A constable may remember the man who walked away from the car. There was, in fact, a constable on point duty at the end of this road, who kept Kynsard anchored until seven in the morning.

"Then he remembered that Gibbern was being hanged at eight. From about a quarter to eight onwards there would be a crowd round the prison, into which he could melt. To give it a maniacal twist—as Gibbern did—he removed the clothing. That was how he became aware of the existence of that scar. Then, of course——"

"Stop, please!" cried Mrs. Tremman. The sense of proportion was coming back. "I think I'm beginning to feel rather ill."

"You need not feel ill on my account!" rasped Kynsard. "The inspector alluded to his facts. The one and only fact he has is that you and I made a mistake in identifying Barbara. He begins by *guessing* that I murdered Barbara. He *constructs* the whole preposterous pantomime with the Chrysler. He *deduces* that therefore I murdered Betsy Trotwood."

Mrs. Tremman seemed to pay no attention. Power of resistance had left her. She spoke to Turley.

"Inspector, if it was not poor Barbara— "

"It was Trotwood," said Turley. "The corpse had a clip of three false teeth. Your daughter had none. Trotwood had the teeth fitted by Mrs. Kynsard's dentist."

"If it was not poor Barbara, where is she?"

"The Chrysler makes that clear enough, Mrs. Tremman. The alibi was too clever. He allowed himself only five to ten minutes in which to dispose of the corpse. From which it's a simple inference that he must have hidden the body between here and Rubington."

"A brilliant mosaic!" exclaimed Kynsard. "A logical sequence without a single flaw—and equally without a single fact!"

Turley bent down and opened his bag. From it he took a house-dress, a pair of shabby, gaping house-shoes, and a wooden mallet.

"In the only possible place on that road—the bombed-out cider factory," he said. "Can you identify those garments, Mrs. Tremman? That's all we'll ask you to identify tonight."

A CATALOGUE OF
SELECTED DOVER BOOKS
IN ALL FIELDS OF INTEREST

A CATALOGUE OF SELECTED DOVER
BOOKS IN ALL FIELDS OF INTEREST

RACKHAM'S COLOR ILLUSTRATIONS FOR WAGNER'S RING. Rackham's finest mature work—all 64 full-color watercolors in a faithful and lush interpretation of the *Ring*. Full-sized plates on coated stock of the paintings used by opera companies for authentic staging of Wagner. Captions aid in following complete Ring cycle. Introduction. 64 illustrations plus vignettes. 72pp. 8⅝ x 11¼. 23779-6 Pa. $6.00

CONTEMPORARY POLISH POSTERS IN FULL COLOR, edited by Joseph Czestochowski. 46 full-color examples of brilliant school of Polish graphic design, selected from world's first museum (near Warsaw) dedicated to poster art. Posters on circuses, films, plays, concerts all show cosmopolitan influences, free imagination. Introduction. 48pp. 9⅜ x 12¼. 23780-X Pa. $6.00

GRAPHIC WORKS OF EDVARD MUNCH, Edvard Munch. 90 haunting, evocative prints by first major Expressionist artist and one of the greatest graphic artists of his time: *The Scream, Anxiety, Death Chamber, The Kiss, Madonna,* etc. Introduction by Alfred Werner. 90pp. 9 x 12. 23765-6 Pa. $5.00

THE GOLDEN AGE OF THE POSTER, Hayward and Blanche Cirker. 70 extraordinary posters in full colors, from Maitres de l'Affiche, Mucha, Lautrec, Bradley, Cheret, Beardsley, many others. Total of 78pp. 9⅜ x 12¼. 22753-7 Pa. $5.95

THE NOTEBOOKS OF LEONARDO DA VINCI, edited by J. P. Richter. Extracts from manuscripts reveal great genius; on painting, sculpture, anatomy, sciences, geography, etc. Both Italian and English. 186 ms. pages reproduced, plus 500 additional drawings, including studies for *Last Supper*, Sforza monument, etc. 860pp. 7⅞ x 10¾. (Available in U.S. only) 22572-0, 22573-9 Pa., Two-vol. set $15.90

THE CODEX NUTTALL, as first edited by Zelia Nuttall. Only inexpensive edition, in full color, of a pre-Columbian Mexican (Mixtec) book. 88 color plates show kings, gods, heroes, temples, sacrifices. New explanatory, historical introduction by Arthur G. Miller. 96pp. 11⅜ x 8½. (Available in U.S. only) 23168-2 Pa. $7.95

UNE SEMAINE DE BONTÉ, A SURREALISTIC NOVEL IN COLLAGE, Max Ernst. Masterpiece created out of 19th-century periodical illustrations, explores worlds of terror and surprise. Some consider this Ernst's greatest work. 208pp. 8⅛ x 11. 23252-2 Pa. $6.00

DRAWINGS OF WILLIAM BLAKE, William Blake. 92 plates from Book of Job, *Divine Comedy, Paradise Lost,* visionary heads, mythological figures, Laocoon, etc. Selection, introduction, commentary by Sir Geoffrey Keynes. 178pp. 8⅛ x 11. 22303-5 Pa. $4.00

ENGRAVINGS OF HOGARTH, William Hogarth. 101 of Hogarth's greatest works: *Rake's Progress, Harlot's Progress, Illustrations for Hudibras, Before and After, Beer Street and Gin Lane,* many more. Full commentary. 256pp. 11 x 13¾. 22479-1 Pa. $12.95

DAUMIER: 120 GREAT LITHOGRAPHS, Honore Daumier. Wide-ranging collection of lithographs by the greatest caricaturist of the 19th century. Concentrates on eternally popular series on lawyers, on married life, on liberated women, etc. Selection, introduction, and notes on plates by Charles F. Ramus. Total of 158pp. 9⅜ x 12¼. 23512-2 Pa. $6.00

DRAWINGS OF MUCHA, Alphonse Maria Mucha. Work reveals draftsman of highest caliber: studies for famous posters and paintings, renderings for book illustrations and ads, etc. 70 works, 9 in color; including 6 items not drawings. Introduction. List of illustrations. 72pp. 9⅜ x 12¼. (Available in U.S. only) 23672-2 Pa. $4.00

GIOVANNI BATTISTA PIRANESI: DRAWINGS IN THE PIERPONT MORGAN LIBRARY, Giovanni Battista Piranesi. For first time ever all of Morgan Library's collection, world's largest. 167 illustrations of rare Piranesi drawings—archeological, architectural, decorative and visionary. Essay, detailed list of drawings, chronology, captions. Edited by Felice Stampfle. 144pp. 9⅜ x 12¼. 23714-1 Pa. $7.50

NEW YORK ETCHINGS (1905-1949), John Sloan. All of important American artist's N.Y. life etchings. 67 works include some of his best art; also lively historical record—Greenwich Village, tenement scenes. Edited by Sloan's widow. Introduction and captions. 79pp. 8⅜ x 11¼. 23651-X Pa. $4.00

CHINESE PAINTING AND CALLIGRAPHY: A PICTORIAL SURVEY, Wan-go Weng. 69 fine examples from John M. Crawford's matchless private collection: landscapes, birds, flowers, human figures, etc., plus calligraphy. Every basic form included: hanging scrolls, handscrolls, album leaves, fans, etc. 109 illustrations. Introduction. Captions. 192pp. 8⅞ x 11¾. 23707-9 Pa. $7.95

DRAWINGS OF REMBRANDT, edited by Seymour Slive. Updated Lippmann, Hofstede de Groot edition, with definitive scholarly apparatus. All portraits, biblical sketches, landscapes, nudes, Oriental figures, classical studies, together with selection of work by followers. 550 illustrations. Total of 630pp. 9⅛ x 12¼. 21485-0, 21486-9 Pa., Two-vol. set $15.00

THE DISASTERS OF WAR, Francisco Goya. 83 etchings record horrors of Napoleonic wars in Spain and war in general. Reprint of 1st edition, plus 3 additional plates. Introduction by Philip Hofer. 97pp. 9⅜ x 8¼. 21872-4 Pa. $4.00

THE EARLY WORK OF AUBREY BEARDSLEY, Aubrey Beardsley. 157 plates, 2 in color: *Manon Lescaut, Madame Bovary, Morte Darthur, Salome,* other. Introduction by H. Marillier. 182pp. 8⅛ x 11. 21816-3 Pa. $4.50

THE LATER WORK OF AUBREY BEARDSLEY, Aubrey Beardsley. Exotic masterpieces of full maturity: *Venus and Tannhauser, Lysistrata, Rape of the Lock, Volpone,* Savoy material, etc. 174 plates, 2 in color. 186pp. 8⅛ x 11. 21817-1 Pa. $5.95

THOMAS NAST'S CHRISTMAS DRAWINGS, Thomas Nast. Almost all Christmas drawings by creator of image of Santa Claus as we know it, and one of America's foremost illustrators and political cartoonists. 66 illustrations. 3 illustrations in color on covers. 96pp. 8⅜ x 11¼. 23660-9 Pa. $3.50

THE DORÉ ILLUSTRATIONS FOR DANTE'S DIVINE COMEDY, Gustave Doré. All 135 plates from Inferno, Purgatory, Paradise; fantastic tortures, infernal landscapes, celestial wonders. Each plate with appropriate (translated) verses. 141pp. 9 x 12. 23231-X Pa. $4.50

DORÉ'S ILLUSTRATIONS FOR RABELAIS, Gustave Doré. 252 striking illustrations of *Gargantua and Pantagruel* books by foremost 19th-century illustrator. Including 60 plates, 192 delightful smaller illustrations. 153pp. 9 x 12. 23656-0 Pa. $5.00

LONDON: A PILGRIMAGE, Gustave Doré, Blanchard Jerrold. Squalor, riches, misery, beauty of mid-Victorian metropolis; 55 wonderful plates, 125 other illustrations, full social, cultural text by Jerrold. 191pp. of text. 9⅜ x 12¼. 22306-X Pa. $7.00

THE RIME OF THE ANCIENT MARINER, Gustave Doré, S. T. Coleridge. Dore's finest work, 34 plates capture moods, subtleties of poem. Full text. Introduction by Millicent Rose. 77pp. 9¼ x 12. 22305-1 Pa. $3.50

THE DORE BIBLE ILLUSTRATIONS, Gustave Doré. All wonderful, detailed plates: Adam and Eve, Flood, Babylon, Life of Jesus, etc. Brief King James text with each plate. Introduction by Millicent Rose. 241 plates. 241pp. 9 x 12. 23004-X Pa. $6.00

THE COMPLETE ENGRAVINGS, ETCHINGS AND DRYPOINTS OF ALBRECHT DURER. "Knight, Death and Devil"; "Melencolia," and more—all Dürer's known works in all three media, including 6 works formerly attributed to him. 120 plates. 235pp. 8⅜ x 11¼. 22851-7 Pa. $6.50

MECHANICK EXERCISES ON THE WHOLE ART OF PRINTING, Joseph Moxon. First complete book (1683-4) ever written about typography, a compendium of everything known about printing at the latter part of 17th century. Reprint of 2nd (1962) Oxford Univ. Press edition. 74 illustrations. Total of 550pp. 6⅛ x 9¼. 23617-X Pa. $7.95

CATALOGUE OF DOVER BOOKS

THE COMPLETE WOODCUTS OF ALBRECHT DURER, edited by Dr. W. Kurth. 346 in all: "Old Testament," "St. Jerome," "Passion," "Life of Virgin," Apocalypse," many others. Introduction by Campbell Dodgson. 285pp. 8½ x 12¼.   21097-9 Pa. $7.50

DRAWINGS OF ALBRECHT DURER, edited by Heinrich Wolfflin. 81 plates show development from youth to full style. Many favorites; many new, Introduction by Alfred Werner. 96pp. 8⅛ x 11. 22352-3 Pa. $5.00

THE HUMAN FIGURE, Albrecht Dürer. Experiments in various techniques—stereometric, progressive proportional, and others. Also life studies that rank among finest ever done. Complete reprinting of *Dresden Sketchbook.* 170 plates. 355pp. 8⅜ x 11¼.   21042-1 Pa. $7.95

OF THE JUST SHAPING OF LETTERS, Albrecht Dürer. Renaissance artist explains design of Roman majuscules by geometry, also Gothic lower and capitals. Grolier Club edition. 43pp. 7⅞ x 10¾   21306-4 Pa. $3.00

TEN BOOKS ON ARCHITECTURE, Vitruvius. The most important book ever written on architecture. Early Roman aesthetics, technology, classical orders, site selection, all other aspects. Stands behind everything since. Morgan translation. 331pp. 5⅜ x 8½.   20645-9 Pa. $4.50

THE FOUR BOOKS OF ARCHITECTURE, Andrea Palladio. 10th-century classic responsible for Palladian movement and style. Covers classical architectural remains, Renaissance revivals, classical orders, etc. 1738 Ware English edition. Introduction by A. Placzek. 216 plates. 110pp. of text. 9½ x 12¾.   21308-0 Pa. $10.00

HORIZONS, Norman Bel Geddes. Great industrialist stage designer, "father of streamlining," on application of aesthetics to transportation, amusement, architecture, etc. 1932 prophetic account; function, theory, specific projects. 222 illustrations. 312pp. 7⅞ x 10¾.   23514-9 Pa. $6.95

FRANK LLOYD WRIGHT'S FALLINGWATER, Donald Hoffmann. Full, illustrated story of conception and building of Wright's masterwork at Bear Run, Pa. 100 photographs of site, construction, and details of completed structure. 112pp. 9¼ x 10.   23671-4 Pa. $5.50

THE ELEMENTS OF DRAWING, John Ruskin. Timeless classic by great Viltorian; starts with basic ideas, works through more difficult. Many practical exercises. 48 illustrations. Introduction by Lawrence Campbell. 228pp. 5⅜ x 8½.   22730-8 Pa. $3.75

GIST OF ART, John Sloan. Greatest modern American teacher, Art Students League, offers innumerable hints, instructions, guided comments to help you in painting. Not a formal course. 46 illustrations. Introduction by Helen Sloan. 200pp. 5⅜ x 8½.   23435-5 Pa. $4.00

THE ANATOMY OF THE HORSE, George Stubbs. Often considered the great masterpiece of animal anatomy. Full reproduction of 1766 edition, plus prospectus; original text and modernized text. 36 plates. Introduction by Eleanor Garvey. 121pp. 11 x 14¾. 23402-9 Pa. $6.00

BRIDGMAN'S LIFE DRAWING, George B. Bridgman. More than 500 illustrative drawings and text teach you to abstract the body into its major masses, use light and shade, proportion; as well as specific areas of anatomy, of which Bridgman is master. 192pp. 6½ x 9¼. (Available in U.S. only) 22710-3 Pa. $3.50

ART NOUVEAU DESIGNS IN COLOR, Alphonse Mucha, Maurice Verneuil, Georges Auriol. Full-color reproduction of *Combinaisons ornementales* (c. 1900) by Art Nouveau masters. Floral, animal, geometric, interlacings, swashes—borders, frames, spots—all incredibly beautiful. 60 plates, hundreds of designs. 9⅜ x 8-1/16. 22885-1 Pa. $4.00

FULL-COLOR FLORAL DESIGNS IN THE ART NOUVEAU STYLE, E. A. Seguy. 166 motifs, on 40 plates, from *Les fleurs et leurs applications decoratives* (1902): borders, circular designs, repeats, allovers, "spots." All in authentic Art Nouveau colors. 48pp. 9⅜ x 12¼. 23439-8 Pa. $5.00

A DIDEROT PICTORIAL ENCYCLOPEDIA OF TRADES AND IN-DUSTRY, edited by Charles C. Gillispie. 485 most interesting plates from the great French Encyclopedia of the 18th century show hundreds of working figures, artifacts, process, land and cityscapes; glassmaking, paper-making, metal extraction, construction, weaving, making furniture, clothing, wigs, dozens of other activities. Plates fully explained. 920pp. 9 x 12. 22284-5, 22285-3 Clothbd., Two-vol. set $40.00

HANDBOOK OF EARLY ADVERTISING ART, Clarence P. Hornung. Largest collection of copyright-free early and antique advertising art ever compiled. Over 6,000 illustrations, from Franklin's time to the 1890's for special effects, novelty. Valuable source, almost inexhaustible.
Pictorial Volume. Agriculture, the zodiac, animals, autos, birds, Christmas, fire engines, flowers, trees, musical instruments, ships, games and sports, much more. Arranged by subject matter and use. 237 plates. 288pp. 9 x 12. 20122-8 Clothbd. $14.50

Typographical Volume. Roman and Gothic faces ranging from 10 point to 300 point, "Barnum," German and Old English faces, script, logotypes, scrolls and flourishes, 1115 ornamental initials, 67 complete alphabets, more. 310 plates. 320pp. 9 x 12. 20123-6 Clothbd. $15.00

CALLIGRAPHY (CALLIGRAPHIA LATINA), J. G. Schwandner. High point of 18th-century ornamental calligraphy. Very ornate initials, scrolls, borders, cherubs, birds, lettered examples. 172pp. 9 x 13. 20475-8 Pa. $7.00

ART FORMS IN NATURE, Ernst Haeckel. Multitude of strangely beautiful natural forms: Radiolaria, Foraminifera, jellyfishes, fungi, turtles, bats, etc. All 100 plates of the 19th-century evolutionist's *Kunstformen der Natur* (1904). 100pp. 9⅜ x 12¼. 22987-4 Pa. $5.00

CHILDREN: A PICTORIAL ARCHIVE FROM NINETEENTH-CENTURY SOURCES, edited by Carol Belanger Grafton. 242 rare, copyright-free wood engravings for artists and designers. Widest such selection available. All illustrations in line. 119pp. 8⅜ x 11¼.
23694-3 Pa. $4.00

WOMEN: A PICTORIAL ARCHIVE FROM NINETEENTH-CENTURY SOURCES, edited by Jim Harter. 391 copyright-free wood engravings for artists and designers selected from rare periodicals. Most extensive such collection available. All illustrations in line. 128pp. 9 x 12.
23703-6 Pa. $4.50

ARABIC ART IN COLOR, Prisse d'Avennes. From the greatest ornamentalists of all time—50 plates in color, rarely seen outside the Near East, rich in suggestion and stimulus. Includes 4 plates on covers. 46pp. 9⅜ x 12¼. 23658-7 Pa. $6.00

AUTHENTIC ALGERIAN CARPET DESIGNS AND MOTIFS, edited by June Beveridge. Algerian carpets are world famous. Dozens of geometrical motifs are charted on grids, color-coded, for weavers, needleworkers, craftsmen, designers. 53 illustrations plus 4 in color. 48pp. 8¼ x 11. (Available in U.S. only) 23650-1 Pa. $1.75

DICTIONARY OF AMERICAN PORTRAITS, edited by Hayward and Blanche Cirker. 4000 important Americans, earliest times to 1905, mostly in clear line. Politicians, writers, soldiers, scientists, inventors, industrialists, Indians, Blacks, women, outlaws, etc. Identificatory information. 756pp. 9¼ x 12¾. 21823-6 Clothbd. $40.00

HOW THE OTHER HALF LIVES, Jacob A. Riis. Journalistic record of filth, degradation, upward drive in New York immigrant slums, shops, around 1900. New edition includes 100 original Riis photos, monuments of early photography. 233pp. 10 x 7⅞. 22012-5 Pa. $7.00

NEW YORK IN THE THIRTIES, Berenice Abbott. Noted photographer's fascinating study of city shows new buildings that have become famous and old sights that have disappeared forever. Insightful commentary. 97 photographs. 97pp. 11⅜ x 10. 22967-X Pa. $5.00

MEN AT WORK, Lewis W. Hine. Famous photographic studies of construction workers, railroad men, factory workers and coal miners. New supplement of 18 photos on Empire State building construction. New introduction by Jonathan L. Doherty. Total of 69 photos. 63pp. 8 x 10¾.
23475-4 Pa. $3.00

THE DEPRESSION YEARS AS PHOTOGRAPHED BY ARTHUR ROTH-STEIN, Arthur Rothstein. First collection devoted entirely to the work of outstanding 1930s photographer: famous dust storm photo, ragged children, unemployed, etc. 120 photographs. Captions. 119pp. 9¼ x 10¾.
23590-4 Pa. $5.00

CAMERA WORK: A PICTORIAL GUIDE, Alfred Stieglitz. All 559 illustrations and plates from the most important periodical in the history of art photography, Camera Work (1903-17). Presented four to a page, reduced in size but still clear, in strict chronological order, with complete captions. Three indexes. Glossary. Bibliography. 176pp. 8⅜ x 11¼.
23591-2 Pa. $6.95

ALVIN LANGDON COBURN, PHOTOGRAPHER, Alvin L. Coburn. Revealing autobiography by one of greatest photographers of 20th century gives insider's version of Photo-Secession, plus comments on his own work. 77 photographs by Coburn. Edited by Helmut and Alison Gernsheim. 160pp. 8⅛ x 11.
23685-4 Pa. $6.00

NEW YORK IN THE FORTIES, Andreas Feininger. 162 brilliant photographs by the well-known photographer, formerly with Life magazine, show commuters, shoppers, Times Square at night, Harlem nightclub, Lower East Side, etc. Introduction and full captions by John von Hartz. 181pp. 9¼ x 10¾.
23585-8 Pa. $6.95

GREAT NEWS PHOTOS AND THE STORIES BEHIND THEM, John Faber. Dramatic volume of 140 great news photos, 1855 through 1976, and revealing stories behind them, with both historical and technical information. Hindenburg disaster, shooting of Oswald, nomination of Jimmy Carter, etc. 160pp. 8¼ x 11.
23667-6 Pa. $5.00

THE ART OF THE CINEMATOGRAPHER, Leonard Maltin. Survey of American cinematography history and anecdotal interviews with 5 masters—Arthur Miller, Hal Mohr, Hal Rosson, Lucien Ballard, and Conrad Hall. Very large selection of behind-the-scenes production photos. 105 photographs. Filmographies. Index. Originally Behind the Camera. 144pp. 8¼ x 11.
23686-2 Pa. $5.00

DESIGNS FOR THE THREE-CORNERED HAT (LE TRICORNE), Pablo Picasso. 32 fabulously rare drawings—including 31 color illustrations of costumes and accessories—for 1919 production of famous ballet. Edited by Parmenia Migel, who has written new introduction. 48pp. 9⅜ x 12¼. (Available in U.S. only)
23709-5 Pa. $5.00

NOTES OF A FILM DIRECTOR, Sergei Eisenstein. Greatest Russian filmmaker explains montage, making of Alexander Nevsky, aesthetics; comments on self, associates, great rivals (Chaplin), similar material. 78 illustrations. 240pp. 5⅜ x 8½.
22392-2 Pa. $4.50

HOLLYWOOD GLAMOUR PORTRAITS, edited by John Kobal. 145 photos capture the stars from 1926-49, the high point in portrait photography. Gable, Harlow, Bogart, Bacall, Hedy Lamarr, Marlene Dietrich, Robert Montgomery, Marlon Brando, Veronica Lake; 94 stars in all. Full background on photographers, technical aspects, much more. Total of 160pp. 8⅜ x 11¼.   23352-9 Pa. $6.00

THE NEW YORK STAGE: FAMOUS PRODUCTIONS IN PHOTO-GRAPHS, edited by Stanley Appelbaum. 148 photographs from Museum of City of New York show 142 plays, 1883-1939. Peter Pan, The Front Page, Dead End, Our Town, O'Neill, hundreds of actors and actresses, etc. Full indexes. 154pp. 9½ x 10.   23241-7 Pa. $6.00

DIALOGUES CONCERNING TWO NEW SCIENCES, Galileo Galilei. Encompassing 30 years of experiment and thought, these dialogues deal with geometric demonstrations of fracture of solid bodies, cohesion, leverage, speed of light and sound, pendulums, falling bodies, accelerated motion, etc. 300pp. 5⅜ x 8½.   60099-8 Pa. $4.00

THE GREAT OPERA STARS IN HISTORIC PHOTOGRAPHS, edited by James Camner. 343 portraits from the 1850s to the 1940s: Tamburini, Mario, Caliapin, Jeritza, Melchior, Melba, Patti, Pinza, Schipa, Caruso, Farrar, Steber, Gobbi, and many more—270 performers in all. Index. 199pp. 8⅜ x 11¼.   23575-0 Pa. $7.50

J. S. BACH, Albert Schweitzer. Great full-length study of Bach, life, background to music, music, by foremost modern scholar. Ernest Newman translation. 650 musical examples. Total of 928pp. 5⅜ x 8½. (Available in U.S. only)   21631-4, 21632-2 Pa., Two-vol. set $11.00

COMPLETE PIANO SONATAS, Ludwig van Beethoven. All sonatas in the fine Schenker edition, with fingering, analytical material. One of best modern editions. Total of 615pp. 9 x 12. (Available in U.S. only)
23134-8, 23135-6 Pa., Two-vol. set $15.50

KEYBOARD MUSIC, J. S. Bach. Bach-Gesellschaft edition. For harpsichord, piano, other keyboard instruments. English Suites, French Suites, Six Partitas, Goldberg Variations, Two-Part Inventions, Three-Part Sinfonias. 312pp. 8⅛ x 11. (Available in U.S. only)   22360-4 Pa. $6.95

FOUR SYMPHONIES IN FULL SCORE, Franz Schubert. Schubert's four most popular symphonies: No. 4 in C Minor ("Tragic"); No. 5 in B-flat Major; No. 8 in B Minor ("Unfinished"); No. 9 in C Major ("Great"). Breitkopf & Hartel edition. Study score. 261pp. 9⅜ x 12¼.
23681-1 Pa. $6.50

THE AUTHENTIC GILBERT & SULLIVAN SONGBOOK, W. S. Gilbert, A. S. Sullivan. Largest selection available; 92 songs, uncut, original keys, in piano rendering approved by Sullivan. Favorites and lesser-known fine numbers. Edited with plot synopses by James Spero. 3 illustrations. 399pp. 9 x 12.   23482-7 Pa. $9.95

PRINCIPLES OF ORCHESTRATION, Nikolay Rimsky-Korsakov. Great classical orchestrator provides fundamentals of tonal resonance, progression of parts, voice and orchestra, tutti effects, much else in major document. 330pp. of musical excerpts. 489pp. 6½ x 9¼. 21266-1 Pa. $7.50

TRISTAN UND ISOLDE, Richard Wagner. Full orchestral score with complete instrumentation. Do not confuse with piano reduction. Commentary by Felix Mottl, great Wagnerian conductor and scholar. Study score. 655pp. 8⅛ x 11. 22915-7 Pa. $13.95

REQUIEM IN FULL SCORE, Giuseppe Verdi. Immensely popular with choral groups and music lovers. Republication of edition published by C. F. Peters, Leipzig, n. d. German frontmaker in English translation. Glossary. Text in Latin. Study score. 204pp. 9⅜ x 12¼.
23682-X Pa. $6.00

COMPLETE CHAMBER MUSIC FOR STRINGS, Felix Mendelssohn. All of Mendelssohn's chamber music: Octet, 2 Quintets, 6 Quartets, and Four Pieces for String Quartet. (Nothing with piano is included). Complete works edition (1874-7). Study score. 283 pp. 9⅜ x 12¼.
23679-X Pa. $7.50

POPULAR SONGS OF NINETEENTH-CENTURY AMERICA, edited by Richard Jackson. 64 most important songs: "Old Oaken Bucket," "Arkansas Traveler," "Yellow Rose of Texas," etc. Authentic original sheet music, full introduction and commentaries. 290pp. 9 x 12. 23270-0 Pa. $7.95

COLLECTED PIANO WORKS, Scott Joplin. Edited by Vera Brodsky Lawrence. Practically all of Joplin's piano works—rags, two-steps, marches, waltzes, etc., 51 works in all. Extensive introduction by Rudi Blesh. Total of 345pp. 9 x 12. 23106-2 Pa. $14.95

BASIC PRINCIPLES OF CLASSICAL BALLET, Agrippina Vaganova. Great Russian theoretician, teacher explains methods for teaching classical ballet; incorporates best from French, Italian, Russian schools. 118 illustrations. 175pp. 5⅜ x 8½. 22036-2 Pa. $2.50

CHINESE CHARACTERS, L. Wieger. Rich analysis of 2300 characters according to traditional systems into primitives. Historical-semantic analysis to phonetics (Classical Mandarin) and radicals. 820pp. 6⅛ x 9¼.
21321-8 Pa. $10.00

EGYPTIAN LANGUAGE: EASY LESSONS IN EGYPTIAN HIERO-GLYPHICS, E. A. Wallis Budge. Foremost Egyptologist offers Egyptian grammar, explanation of hieroglyphics, many reading texts, dictionary of symbols. 246pp. 5 x 7½. (Available in U.S. only)
21394-3 Clothbd. $7.50

AN ETYMOLOGICAL DICTIONARY OF MODERN ENGLISH, Ernest Weekley. Richest, fullest work, by foremost British lexicographer. Detailed word histories. Inexhaustible. Do not confuse this with *Concise Etymological Dictionary*, which is abridged. Total of 856pp. 6½ x 9¼.
21873-2, 21874-0 Pa., Two-vol. set $12.00

CATALOGUE OF DOVER BOOKS

A MAYA GRAMMAR, Alfred M. Tozzer. Practical, useful English-language grammar by the Harvard anthropologist who was one of the three greatest American scholars in the area of Maya culture. Phonetics, grammatical processes, syntax, more. 301pp. 5⅜ x 8½.   23465-7 Pa. $4.00

THE JOURNAL OF HENRY D. THOREAU, edited by Bradford Torrey, F. H. Allen. Complete reprinting of 14 volumes, 1837-61, over two million words; the sourcebooks for *Walden*, etc. Definitive. All original sketches, plus 75 photographs. Introduction by Walter Harding. Total of 1804pp. 8½ x 12¼.   20312-3, 20313-1 Clothbd., Two-vol. set $70.00

CLASSIC GHOST STORIES, Charles Dickens and others. 18 wonderful stories you've wanted to reread: "The Monkey's Paw," "The House and the Brain," "The Upper Berth," "The Signalman," "Dracula's Guest," "The Tapestried Chamber," etc. Dickens, Scott, Mary Shelley, Stoker, etc. 330pp. 5⅜ x 8½.   20735-8 Pa. $4.50

SEVEN SCIENCE FICTION NOVELS, H. G. Wells. Full novels. *First Men in the Moon, Island of Dr. Moreau, War of the Worlds, Food of the Gods, Invisible Man, Time Machine, In the Days of the Comet.* A basic science-fiction library. 1015pp. 5⅜ x 8½. (Available in U.S. only)
20264-X Clothbd. $8.95

ARMADALE, Wilkie Collins. Third great mystery novel by the author of *The Woman in White* and *The Moonstone*. Ingeniously plotted narrative shows an exceptional command of character, incident and mood. Original magazine version with 40 illustrations. 597pp. 5⅜ x 8½.
23429-0 Pa. $6.00

MASTERS OF MYSTERY, H. Douglas Thomson. The first book in English (1931) devoted to history and aesthetics of detective story. Poe, Doyle, LeFanu, Dickens, many others, up to 1930. New introduction and notes by E. F. Bleiler. 288pp. 5⅜ x 8½. (Available in U.S. only)
23606-4 Pa. $4.00

FLATLAND, E. A. Abbott. Science-fiction classic explores life of 2-D being in 3-D world. Read also as introduction to thought about hyperspace. Introduction by Banesh Hoffmann. 16 illustrations. 103pp. 5⅜ x 8½.
20001-9 Pa. $2.00

THREE SUPERNATURAL NOVELS OF THE VICTORIAN PERIOD, edited, with an introduction, by E. F. Bleiler. Reprinted complete and unabridged, three great classics of the supernatural: *The Haunted Hotel* by Wilkie Collins, *The Haunted House at Latchford* by Mrs. J. H. Riddell, and *The Lost Stradivarius* by J. Meade Falkner. 325pp. 5⅜ x 8½.
22571-2 Pa. $4.00

AYESHA: THE RETURN OF "SHE," H. Rider Haggard. Virtuoso sequel featuring the great mythic creation, Ayesha, in an adventure that is fully as good as the first book, *She*. Original magazine version, with 47 original illustrations by Maurice Greiffenhagen. 189pp. 6½ x 9¼.
23649-8 Pa. $3.50

UNCLE SILAS, J. Sheridan LeFanu. Victorian Gothic mystery novel, considered by many best of period, even better than Collins or Dickens. Wonderful psychological terror. Introduction by Frederick Shroyer. 436pp. 5⅜ x 8½.   21715-9 Pa. $6.00

JURGEN, James Branch Cabell. The great erotic fantasy of the 1920's that delighted thousands, shocked thousands more. Full final text, Lane edition with 13 plates by Frank Pape. 346pp. 5⅜ x 8½.
23507-6 Pa. $4.50

THE CLAVERINGS, Anthony Trollope. Major novel, chronicling aspects of British Victorian society, personalities. Reprint of Cornhill serialization, 16 plates by M. Edwards; first reprint of full text. Introduction by Norman Donaldson. 412pp. 5⅜ x 8½.   23464-9 Pa. $5.00

KEPT IN THE DARK, Anthony Trollope. Unusual short novel about Victorian morality and abnormal psychology by the great English author. Probably the first American publication. Frontispiece by Sir John Millais. 92pp. 6½ x 9¼.   23609-9 Pa. $2.50

RALPH THE HEIR, Anthony Trollope. Forgotten tale of illegitimacy, inheritance. Master novel of Trollope's later years. Victorian country estates, clubs, Parliament, fox hunting, world of fully realized characters. Reprint of 1871 edition. 12 illustrations by F. A. Faser. 434pp. of text. 5⅜ x 8½.   23642-0 Pa. $5.00

YEKL and THE IMPORTED BRIDEGROOM AND OTHER STORIES OF THE NEW YORK GHETTO, Abraham Cahan. Film *Hester Street* based on *Yekl* (1896). Novel, other stories among first about Jewish immigrants of N.Y.'s East Side. Highly praised by W. D. Howells—Cahan "a new star of realism." New introduction by Bernard G. Richards. 240pp. 5⅜ x 8½.   22427-9 Pa. $3.50

THE HIGH PLACE, James Branch Cabell. Great fantasy writer's enchanting comedy of disenchantment set in 18th-century France. Considered by some critics to be even better than his famous *Jurgen*. 10 illustrations and numerous vignettes by noted fantasy artist Frank C. Pape. 320pp. 5⅜ x 8½.   23670-6 Pa. $4.00

ALICE'S ADVENTURES UNDER GROUND, Lewis Carroll. Facsimile of ms. Carroll gave Alice Liddell in 1864. Different in many ways from final Alice. Handlettered, illustrated by Carroll. Introduction by Martin Gardner. 128pp. 5⅜ x 8½.   21482-6 Pa. $2.50

FAVORITE ANDREW LANG FAIRY TALE BOOKS IN MANY COLORS, Andrew Lang. The four Lang favorites in a boxed set—the complete *Red*, *Green*, *Yellow* and *Blue* Fairy Books. 164 stories; 439 illustrations by Lancelot Speed, Henry Ford and G. P. Jacomb Hood. Total of about 1500pp. 5⅜ x 8½.   23407-X Boxed set, Pa. $15.95

HOUSEHOLD STORIES BY THE BROTHERS GRIMM. All the great Grimm stories: "Rumpelstiltskin," "Snow White," "Hansel and Gretel," etc., with 114 illustrations by Walter Crane. 269pp. 5⅜ x 8½.
21080-4 Pa. $3.50

SLEEPING BEAUTY, illustrated by Arthur Rackham. Perhaps the fullest, most delightful version ever, told by C. S. Evans. Rackham's best work. 49 illustrations. 110pp. 7⅞ x 10¾. 22756-1 Pa. $2.50

AMERICAN FAIRY TALES, L. Frank Baum. Young cowboy lassoes Father Time; dummy in Mr. Floman's department store window comes to life; and 10 other fairy tales. 41 illustrations by N. P. Hall, Harry Kennedy, Ike Morgan, and Ralph Gardner. 209pp. 5⅜ x 8½. 23643-9 Pa. $3.00

THE WONDERFUL WIZARD OF OZ, L. Frank Baum. Facsimile in full color of America's finest children's classic. Introduction by Martin Gardner. 143 illustrations by W. W. Denslow. 267pp. 5⅜ x 8½.
20691-2 Pa. $3.50

THE TALE OF PETER RABBIT, Beatrix Potter. The inimitable Peter's terrifying adventure in Mr. McGregor's garden, with all 27 wonderful, full-color Potter illustrations. 55pp. 4¼ x 5½. (Available in U.S. only)
22827-4 Pa. $1.25

THE STORY OF KING ARTHUR AND HIS KNIGHTS, Howard Pyle. Finest children's version of life of King Arthur. 48 illustrations by Pyle. 131pp. 6⅛ x 9¼. 21445-1 Pa. $4.95

CARUSO'S CARICATURES, Enrico Caruso. Great tenor's remarkable caricatures of self, fellow musicians, composers, others. Toscanini, Puccini, Farrar, etc. Impish, cutting, insightful. 473 illustrations. Preface by M. Sisca. 217pp. 8⅜ x 11¼. 23528-9 Pa. $6.95

PERSONAL NARRATIVE OF A PILGRIMAGE TO ALMADINAH AND MECCAH, Richard Burton. Great travel classic by remarkably colorful personality. Burton, disguised as a Moroccan, visited sacred shrines of Islam, narrowly escaping death. Wonderful observations of Islamic life, customs, personalities. 47 illustrations. Total of 959pp. 5⅜ x 8½.
21217-3, 21218-1 Pa., Two-vol. set $12.00

INCIDENTS OF TRAVEL IN YUCATAN, John L. Stephens. Classic (1843) exploration of jungles of Yucatan, looking for evidences of Maya civilization. Travel adventures, Mexican and Indian culture, etc. Total of 669pp. 5⅜ x 8½. 20926-1, 20927-X Pa., Two-vol. set $7.90

AMERICAN LITERARY AUTOGRAPHS FROM WASHINGTON IRVING TO HENRY JAMES, Herbert Cahoon, et al. Letters, poems, manuscripts of Hawthorne, Thoreau, Twain, Alcott, Whitman, 67 other prominent American authors. Reproductions, full transcripts and commentary. Plus checklist of all American Literary Autographs in The Pierpont Morgan Library. Printed on exceptionally high-quality paper. 136 illustrations. 212pp. 9⅛ x 12¼. 23548-3 Pa. $12.50

AN AUTOBIOGRAPHY, Margaret Sanger. Exciting personal account of hard-fought battle for woman's right to birth control, against prejudice, church, law. Foremost feminist document. 504pp. 5⅜ x 8½.
20470-7 Pa. $5.50

MY BONDAGE AND MY FREEDOM, Frederick Douglass. Born as a slave, Douglass became outspoken force in antislavery movement. The best of Douglass's autobiographies. Graphic description of slave life. Introduction by P. Foner. 464pp. 5⅜ x 8½. 22457-0 Pa. $5.50

LIVING MY LIFE, Emma Goldman. Candid, no holds barred account by foremost American anarchist: her own life, anarchist movement, famous contemporaries, ideas and their impact. Struggles and confrontations in America, plus deportation to U.S.S.R. Shocking inside account of persecution of anarchists under Lenin. 13 plates. Total of 944pp. 5⅜ x 8½.
22543-7, 22544-5 Pa., Two-vol. set $12.00

LETTERS AND NOTES ON THE MANNERS, CUSTOMS AND CONDITIONS OF THE NORTH AMERICAN INDIANS, George Catlin. Classic account of life among Plains Indians: ceremonies, hunt, warfare, etc. Dover edition reproduces for first time all original paintings. 312 plates. 572pp. of text. 6⅛ x 9¼. 22118-0, 22119-9 Pa.. Two-vol. set $12.00

THE MAYA AND THEIR NEIGHBORS, edited by Clarence L. Hay, others. Synoptic view of Maya civilization in broadest sense, together with Northern, Southern neighbors. Integrates much background, valuable detail not elsewhere. Prepared by greatest scholars: Kroeber, Morley, Thompson, Spinden, Vaillant, many others. Sometimes called Tozzer Memorial Volume. 60 illustrations, linguistic map. 634pp. 5⅜ x 8½.
23510-6 Pa. $10.00

HANDBOOK OF THE INDIANS OF CALIFORNIA, A. L. Kroeber. Foremost American anthropologist offers complete ethnographic study of each group. Monumental classic. 459 illustrations, maps. 995pp. 5⅜ x 8½.
23368-5 Pa. $13.00

SHAKTI AND SHAKTA, Arthur Avalon. First book to give clear, cohesive analysis of Shakta doctrine, Shakta ritual and Kundalini Shakti (yoga). Important work by one of world's foremost students of Shaktic and Tantric thought. 732pp. 5⅜ x 8½. (Available in U.S. only)
23645-5 Pa. $7.95

AN INTRODUCTION TO THE STUDY OF THE MAYA HIEROGLYPHS, Syvanus Griswold Morley. Classic study by one of the truly great figures in hieroglyph research. Still the best introduction for the student for reading Maya hieroglyphs. New introduction by J. Eric S. Thompson. 117 illustrations. 284pp. 5⅜ x 8½. 23108-9 Pa. $4.00

A STUDY OF MAYA ART, Herbert J. Spinden. Landmark classic interprets Maya symbolism, estimates styles, covers ceramics, architecture, murals, stone carvings as artforms. Still a basic book in area. New introduction by J. Eric Thompson. Over 750 illustrations. 341pp. 8⅜ x 11¼.
21235-1 Pa. $6.95

CATALOGUE OF DOVER BOOKS

GEOMETRY, RELATIVITY AND THE FOURTH DIMENSION, Rudolf Rucker. Exposition of fourth dimension, means of visualization, concepts of relativity as Flatland characters continue adventures. Popular, easily followed yet accurate, profound. 141 illustrations. 133pp. 5⅜ x 8½.
23400-2 Pa. $2.75

THE ORIGIN OF LIFE, A. I. Oparin. Modern classic in biochemistry, the first rigorous examination of possible evolution of life from nitrocarbon compounds. Non-technical, easily followed. Total of 295pp. 5⅜ x 8½.
60213-3 Pa. $4.00

PLANETS, STARS AND GALAXIES, A. E. Fanning. Comprehensive introductory survey: the sun, solar system, stars, galaxies, universe, cosmology; quasars, radio stars, etc. 24pp. of photographs. 189pp. 5⅜ x 8½. (Available in U.S. only)
21680-2 Pa. $3.75

THE THIRTEEN BOOKS OF EUCLID'S ELEMENTS, translated with introduction and commentary by Sir Thomas L. Heath. Definitive edition. Textual and linguistic notes, mathematical analysis, 2500 years of critical commentary. Do not confuse with abridged school editions. Total of 1414pp. 5⅜ x 8½.   60088-2, 60089-0, 60090-4 Pa., Three-vol. set $18.50

Prices subject to change without notice.

Available at your book dealer or write for free catalogue to Dept. GI, Dover Publications, Inc., 180 Varick St., N.Y., N.Y. 10014. Dover publishes more than 175 books each year on science, elementary and advanced mathematics, biology, music, art, literary history, social sciences and other areas.